TRUE
PATRIOTS

RUSSELL FRALICH

TRUE PATRIOTS

DUNDURN
TORONTO

Publisher: Scott Fraser | Acquiring editor: Rachel Spence | Editor: Dominic Farrell
Cover designer: Laura Boyle
Cover image: shutterstock.com/Andrey Yurlov
Printer: Webcom, a division of Marquis Book Printing Inc.

Library and Archives Canada Cataloguing in Publication

Title: True patriots / Russell Fralich.
Names: Fralich, Russell, 1964- author.
Identifiers: Canadiana (print) 20190160675 | Canadiana (ebook) 20190160683 | ISBN 9781459745704 (softcover) | ISBN 9781459745711 (PDF) | ISBN 9781459745728 (EPUB)
Classification: LCC PS8611.R325 T78 2020 | DDC C813/.6—dc23

We acknowledge the support of the Canada Council for the Arts and the Ontario Arts Council for our publishing program. We also acknowledge the financial support of the Government of Ontario, through the Ontario Book Publishing Tax Credit and Ontario Creates, and the Government of Canada.

Care has been taken to trace the ownership of copyright material used in this book. The author and the publisher welcome any information enabling them to rectify any references or credits in subsequent editions.

The publisher is not responsible for websites or their content unless they are owned by the publisher.

Printed and bound in Canada.

VISIT US AT

 dundurn.com | @dundurnpress | dundurnpress | 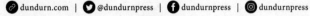 dundurnpress

Dundurn
3 Church Street, Suite 500
Toronto, Ontario, Canada
M5E 1M2

For my long-lost sister, Kristina

Big things have small beginnings.
  — Mr. Dryden in *Lawrence of Arabia*

What you don't know (is) far more relevant
than what you do know.
  — Nassim Taleb, *The Black Swan: The*
   Impact of the Highly Improbable

ONE

"TARGET THEIR BRIDGE."

Claire gave the order. She could feel the gaze of her crew. Would she deliberately kill? She'd been captain for barely two months. Too junior. Not tested. And a woman.

Only minutes earlier, she had watched endless waves pound a small fishing boat, the spray and incessant snow rendering it invisible at times, despite the blazing cone of light from the helicopter above. Off the coast of Nova Scotia, the winter nor'easter that had paralyzed New England with two feet of powder retained enough of its fury to imperil any ocean vessel.

A kilometre away, the CH-149 Cormorant, shaking violently a few wave heights above the turbulent ocean, was trying to keep its searchlight fixed on the ship that bucked between mountains of water.

"It's the MV *Atlantic Mariner*. Out of Boston," the pilot said over the radio.

Claire squeezed the microphone dangling from the ceiling. "Captain O'Brien, do you see anyone on board?"

A moment of white noise and then, "There must be. Will advise."

The sailor manning the radio on the bridge of the coastal patrol vessel HMCS *Kingston*, Petty Officer Second Class Sullivan, turned to Claire. "Maritime Command said that the vessel never acknowledged radio contact, ma'am."

"They never asked for any help." Lieutenant Wiseman, executive officer and second-in-command, brushed past in the tight space, as Claire sat in the captain's chair.

"Doesn't matter, XO." *Something's not right*, Claire thought.

"There's no transponder signal," Sullivan said.

"We're not going anywhere." *My first rescue.*

"It must have drifted."

Wiseman nodded. "And it looks like a lobster boat anyway."

"Isn't lobster season here in the spring?" Sullivan kept his gaze on the radio's lights and buttons.

"Agreed." Claire leaned forward in thought. "There's something weird about this. We keep trying."

"They shouldn't be out in this storm, ma'am," said Sullivan. "How could they not have seen it coming?"

O'Brien's voice crackled on the radio: "No one sighted. Do you want us to continue?"

Claire framed the distressed vessel in her binoculars for a moment, lowered them, then pointed to Wiseman. "Distance to target?"

"Weather's interfering with radar accuracy."

"Best guess."

"Three thousand metres and closing, ma'am." She noticed a new spike of stress in Wiseman's voice.

Claire raised her binoculars, flicked some loose strands of hair out of the way, and continued looking at the tiny shaft of light blinking between shifting mounds of black water. *My first chance to do something good.* She'd wait it out. She grabbed the microphone again and squeezed the button. "O'Brien, this is the *Kingston*. Hold position. Continue the search. Advise when low on fuel."

"Acknowledged." A moment later, the pilot's voice returned with a new edge. "There's someone down there."

Claire saw it, too. A single dark figure emerged from the bridge of the helpless vessel. The helo narrowed the spotlight until the person stood like an actor alone on a stage. The man — he walked like a man even at this distance — took a few steps and held what appeared to be a short pole.

Wiseman turned to her. "Vessel at two degrees starboard, ma'am. Range, one kilometre." A change in the familiar background rustle told her that the six-person bridge crew had moved into a higher state of readiness.

She saw the fishing boat suddenly spring to life, with running lights bright. The boat swung toward the *Kingston*, appearing as a small supernova against the black of the frothing sea.

This was not a normal reaction. "XO, report," she said.

Wiseman watched the radar display for a moment. "Target approaching. Ten knots and accelerating."

Don't they want to be rescued? "Collision course?"

Wiseman turned to face her. "Roger, ma'am."

Was the boat deliberately trying to collide with the *Kingston*? They were supposed to be on a rescue mission. None of the threat simulations during her training at CFB Esquimalt had ever foreseen this situation. She remembered what her instructor had said: *When in doubt …*

"Sound action stations," she ordered.

A perceptible pause told her they were wondering if she was serious. Then the XO acknowledged her command. "Roger, ma'am. Sounding action stations." Most of the crew was older than her thirty-one years, and she wasn't sure how they would react to a new and untested officer in what might become a crisis.

The looping klaxon blared on the bridge and throughout the ship.

"Ship-to-ship." She pointed to Sullivan.

"Ready, ma'am."

She gripped the microphone: "*Atlantic Mariner*. This is the captain of the HMCS *Kingston*. We are here to assist you. Acknowledge."

Only static crackled on the speaker.

"Repeat message every thirty seconds."

"Aye aye, ma'am." Sullivan scribbled the message on a small pad.

She didn't have much discretion as the captain of a coastal patrol vessel. She needed permission from her superiors back in Halifax to use the Bofors 40-mm cannon that could annihilate the boat in one shot. With a long chain of command that went up to the minister of defence, she was unlikely to get it within a day. Until then, she could use the M2 0.50-calibre machine gun mounted to the starboard side of the bridge.

She had a single machine gun to defend the ship.

But was the fishing boat a threat? Its action was strange and unexpected, but she wasn't sure if it posed a danger or if there was some other, more innocent explanation. Maybe the boat's crew was merely trying to get closer to aid in their rescue.

Any threat situation had to meet three criteria. First, there was intent. The boat hadn't threatened anyone. It seemed to ignore the helicopter with the blazing light.

"Let's see if that ship is deliberately trying to ram us. Steer one three five."

The helmsman repeated her command and swung the wheel.

She grabbed on to the overhead handle as the ship veered dramatically to the right, still pitched by wave after wave. She watched the fishing boat's reaction.

"Midships," she said. The light from the *Atlantic Mariner* dimmed for a moment, then quickly brightened again.

"Target is following our move, ma'am," said the petty officer on the bridge, scanning the fishing boat from the bow.

So that's intent, Claire thought. *Or do they just want to get rescued? Why didn't they acknowledge our hail or the helicopter hovering above them?*

Her indecision felt familiar: Should she pursue a law degree and satisfy her parents' ambitions, or join the navy?

Simple. Keep it simple. Stick with the three criteria, she told herself.

The second criterion was proximity.

"Distance?" she called.

"Six hundred metres. Closing at thirty knots," said the navigator. A quick mental calculation and she estimated that the boat would penetrate the ship's three-hundred-metre safety perimeter in less than twenty seconds. Then she would consider it a mortal threat.

Seconds to decide.

O'Brien returned on the radio. "There's something else, *Kingston* ..."

She watched the man and saw the pole shift until it pointed directly at the helicopter.

"RPG! RPG!" O'Brien's voice sounded more angry than scared.

A flash from the ship ahead.

The rocket-propelled grenade ripped past the chopper as it banked sharply to the right, dipped, and accelerated away.

"Confirm RPG," Claire said into the microphone, suddenly oblivious to the klaxon blaring in the bridge.

Captain O'Brien answered in short bursts over the radio. "RPG. Confirmed. Taking evasive action." She could see the helicopter veer away from the boat at an extreme angle.

"Did they just fire at the helo?" said Claire to no one in particular, standing in disbelief.

Wiseman looked at the tactical screen in front of him. "They missed, ma'am. The helo is leaving at high speed. Recommend we do the same."

She hopped back into the captain's chair and glowered at the XO. The MV *Atlantic Mariner* now satisfied the third criterion: capability. They had a weapon that was a threat to the ship and her crew. One RPG could do serious damage to the bridge or the engines, or blast a hole below the waterline, potentially sinking the ship.

"Close up, M2," she ordered. It was the only weapon she could command in the time that she had. You couldn't stop the boat with the gun, but you could stop her crew. "Target their bridge. Now."

She stared into the XO's eyes until he repeated the command.

The sailor hesitated for a second before answering "Aye aye, ma'am" over the commlink. She could feel the gaze of the other crew on the bridge. Their unease about her qualifications as captain weighed on her like a physical force. *Too young. Too inexperienced. Too female.*

She fought her drifting doubts. "Ship-to-ship," she said to Sullivan.

He flicked a switch on the radio console. "Ready, ma'am."

She yanked the microphone: "*Atlantic Mariner*, this is the Canadian warship HMCS *Kingston*. We are trying to assist you. You have fired on our helicopter without known reason. Do not approach this ship. Stop your engines, cease fire, and acknowledge, or we will fire upon you."

She stood up again. "Range and speed," she said with a distinctly more serious tone: one she knew the crew would notice.

"Four hundred metres. Thirty knots."

She squeezed the mike in her hand. "I say again. Stop your engines and acknowledge or we will fire upon you."

Only a few seconds before it got too close.

"Three hundred metres."

The boat had just entered her exclusion zone.

"Any change?"

Wiseman said, "No, ma'am. Collision course. Recommend —"

"M2." She heard herself gulp over the noise of the bridge. "Open fire."

The gun coughed with a low thumping *rat-tat-tat-tat* as bullets knifed through the bridge of the little boat only a couple of soccer fields away. Claire could see tracers streak to the boat and splinter the bridge. The man holding the RPG was nowhere to be seen. Sparks leapt skyward, and the boat stopped dead in the water, limping lifelessly on the swells.

"Cease fire, M2." The gun stopped immediately. "Full stop." The engines went silent.

The fishing boat was now a fiery, smoky pyre. The Cormorant returned to the scene like a cautious cat. Under the gaze of its spotlight, the boat listed to its port side, sliding into the waves. In less than a minute, it was gone. Leaving only a faint grey cloud, it sank beneath the waves, along with its crew and any evidence that would explain their odd reaction to the rescue.

She glanced at the two sailors who manned the machine gun outside the bridge. They looked stressed. They had killed someone, probably for the first time in their lives. She had to reassure them.

They had defended their ship and crew. They hadn't hesitated to obey her order, even if she wasn't yet a captain that everyone trusted and respected. She called to them over the commlink, "Good shooting."

Her hands trembled holding the microphone. She wiped sweat and salt from her forehead with her sleeve. A chill shivered through her body. She had killed someone. She tried to mask how she really felt with a thin smile. The bridge crew turned toward her. There was shock in their expressions.

She took a deep breath.

She had more than passed her first test as captain. Maybe her parents would now acknowledge her career choice with at least a twinge of pride. But fatigue tugged at her, threatening to drag her down deep like the mysterious boat. The crew was waiting for her to say something more.

She raised the microphone. Her hand was still shaking. She rammed out each word before the shock sucked her voice away. "Well. Done. Everybody." Another breath. Scowled at the XO. "The vessel we encountered presented a direct and immediate threat to the ship, and you dealt with it with professionalism."

"Ma'am." Sullivan pulled off his headphones. "How do we know there isn't another one out there?"

TWO

ONE HAND THRUST INTO THE AIR. His eyes, attuned to any movement in the classroom, locked on it, propelled by an instinctive response from his brain. Forty students sat arrayed across three levels of amphitheatre seats. In a second, a forest of hands sprouted throughout the room.

He pointed at the first hand and read the name card on the desk in front of her. "Yes, Alexa."

The forest vanished and a tall brunette came into focus: early thirties, dressed in a grey jacket over a white blouse, brown hair loose over her shoulders. She seemed suddenly aware that all eyes were trained on her. "They shouldn't do it alone? They won't be able to afford the investment cost. An alliance is better."

Another hand rose high, this time on the right side of the tiered classroom, along the final bank of chairs, near the far corner. The man wore his dark suit, black tie, and white shirt like a comfortable shoe. He was one of the few older students. Daniel read from his name card. "You don't agree, Philip?"

"They have to do it alone. No choice. Can't partner with a competitor. It would be business suicide." Hands now folded on his table, and with a straightened back, he looked at ease as he spoke. Someone who was used to being listened to.

Daniel was waiting for the next hand to be raised when he noticed that all student eyes turn to his right, toward someone entering the classroom. The door swung open and clanged against the wall. Lloyd marched in and made a beeline for Daniel. "Call for you."

The first words you've spoken to me in weeks? And you interrupt me now?

"Can't it wait?" He couldn't just stop. He had ten minutes left to wrap up the MBA class.

"The caller says it's urgent. Tried calling you several times. Said your cellphone was off."

Daniel flicked his head toward the class. "I'm busy."

"Said it's urgent. Won't take no for an answer. I put them on hold."

There was only one person he wanted to hear from. Vanessa hadn't answered his calls since Friday. His regular visit with Emily was planned for tomorrow night. He was worried. He turned to face the class and saw anticipation in the students' body language. They were tense, unsure about what he was going to do, but curious, too.

"We'll finish our summary on competitive tactics in business next week."

* ✳ *

He rushed to his office in the adjacent building and one floor up with Lloyd trailing far behind.

He unlocked his office door, flung it wide, grabbed the receiver, and held it close, trembling in anticipation. "Vanessa?"

There was a pause on the other end. "Hello, professor. My name is Patrick. Patrick Forrestal. And I need your help."

Is this a joke?

THREE

DANIEL BURST THROUGH the double doors of the Westin Nova Scotian and marched past the elevator, slinging his bag over his shoulder while holding the latest *Report on Business* magazine. An earnest face with glowing white teeth smiled from the magazine's cover along with the person's name printed in huge type: *Patrick Forrestal*. No identification was really needed, though. Everyone in the business world knew him as the multi-millionaire saviour of a dozen wildly successful companies, former Ernst & Young Entrepreneur of the Year, and a much-sought-after company board member.

Daniel couldn't believe his luck in getting a meeting with him.

Forrestal was a national business celebrity. Daniel was a middle-aged assistant professor, essentially a junior professor-in-training at a small university at the far edge of the country. A call from Forrestal would make any faculty member jump. He could call any of the big-league schools — Harvard, Chicago, the London School of Economics — and they would drool at the chance to be close to his magic touch.

But Forrestal wanted to speak with *him*.

In a daze of incredulity, Daniel had only grasped snippets during the phone call the day before: "I need your help, professor ... I've heard much about you ... You come highly recommended." Then a pause. "I need your expertise in a venture I'm considering."

"What sort of venture?" Daniel had asked.

"I prefer talking face-to-face. I'll be in town tomorrow. Would you be able to meet me at ten at the Westin? Room 1415. We can talk then."

Following the call, Daniel replaced the telephone handset, stood, walked to his door, and stuck his head into the hallway. A slab of light leaked from Lloyd's office two doors down. Lloyd was the senior professor in the department and had hardly spoken to Daniel since he joined two months ago. Daniel took the few steps down the hall to peer into the office. The bald but still handsome sixty-year-old was reading something on his computer screen. His smile dissolved when he saw Daniel.

"Next time, answer your own damn phone." He didn't beckon Daniel to sit in one of the two empty chairs in his office.

Daniel said nothing and remained standing in the hallway.

Lloyd clicked and closed the mail window on his screen. "Why the fuck would Patrick Forrestal call you?"

Daniel visibly jumped at the open hostility in the voice. "I don't know."

"Was this arranged by the dean, too?"

Daniel's appointment to the department was unorthodox. Instead of going through the usual process, he was hired directly by the university president and the business school dean. Daniel would never tell Lloyd why this happened, but the timing was right, and the dean had made him an offer he couldn't refuse. His marriage was over. It was time to leave Montreal. And the more distance he put between himself and his former professions, the better.

In many ways, Daniel didn't fit the typical junior professor profile: he was a decade and a half older than a newly minted Ph.D. graduate; he had at least a decade of international business experience; had lived in three countries and worked in a dozen others. Not the staid and stable background of a typical academic. Daniel's top-down appointment and odd background irked many, but it bothered none more than Professor Lloyd Fanshawe, the *éminence grise* of the department. Daniel wondered if Lloyd interpreted Daniel's hiring as a sign of his own impending decline, a direct threat to his alpha male status. Getting a call from Forrestal would thrust Daniel's reputation in the department into the stratosphere. Forrestal's rock-star status might brush off on him. Lloyd would not be pleased.

"Of course not," Daniel said.

"What did he want?"

Daniel paused. "I don't really know. He wants to talk about some sort of venture."

"Here?"

"He didn't say. He wants to meet me tomorrow."

Lloyd returned his gaze to his computer screen. "Don't fuck it up."

Asshole.

* ✳ *

Daniel had spent the night assembling a profile. Who was Patrick Forrestal, The Legend? Founder of the Fireweed Corporation, based in Toronto. The website was slick, with a logo of a purple flower that he didn't recognize. He read a short quote in italics in the lower right corner: *Like the hardy plant that sprouts after a forest fire, Fireweed Corporation helps carefully selected companies prosper in the face of adversity.* He was worth at least half a billion dollars according to *Business Week*. Investors loved and hated him. They loved his unbroken string of guaranteed dividends over a decade; they hated his unavailability for meetings. He never met face-to-face. Until now.

After three hours of shallow sleep, Daniel had darted to the hotel. Now, he paced in front of the elevator, taking a few moments to gather his thoughts and concentrate on the questions he would ask the shining star of modern Canadian business. A new beginning for Daniel was at stake. A clean break from his shame.

The door dinged and opened, and a sharply dressed woman, wavy blond hair, late twenties with a deep brown tan, darted away, keen to avoid eye contact, perhaps worried about unwanted male attention in a confined space, or because she was focused on a meeting that she had clearly dressed for. He couldn't tell.

He stepped into the empty elevator and pressed the button for the fourteenth floor. The door closed, enveloping him in an old Arcade Fire hit whining from the tinny speakers. He turned, adjusted his tie, and was surprised by what he saw in the wall mirror. Yes, the lines on his face had etched away some of his youth. But the mirror still reflected an image — somewhat attenuated perhaps — of what he had once been. He had most of his blond hair, and he could see only the faintest beginning of a middle-aged paunch. The glasses still looked good, though. And he still had what Vanessa called "that jazz crooner look" in his dark suit and thin black tie. In spite of trying to pulverize any last aftershock of the old life, maybe it was still there — lurking, waiting.

The doors spread open to reveal a busy corridor. Daniel was surprised, not expecting to see anyone. He hugged the wall as he passed other guests. Two Asian couples searched for their rooms, keys in hand, one man fumbling with two enormous pink bags. He thought he heard a crisp Beijing accent in their muted conversation. He could hear children talking in 1404 and a television blaring in the room next to it. An older man in a hotel uniform emerged from 1410, pleading with someone unseen in the room. *Yes, on behalf of the hotel management, he would personally resolve their complaint.*

Daniel refocused his thoughts and continued walking until he stood in front of room 1415, where a "Do Not Disturb" sign dangled from the door handle. Another adjustment of his tie. Watch beeped exactly ten o'clock. Breath check. He slid his right palm along his trousers to remove the accumulated sweat.

Two quick, polite knocks. That should be enough.

He heard only the muffled drone of music from within the room.

Whoom. Whoom. This time he hit the door with the side of his fist. The sound echoed along the now empty corridor.

He waited for the door to open.

"Mr. Forrestal?"

His previous careers had forced him to develop a Teutonic punctuality and attention to detail when necessary. He was at the right place at the right time. He was sure. He fished out his cellphone. The hotel receptionist he called had no response from within the room. The phone inside squawked at least ten times.

Maybe Forrestal had forgotten about the meeting.

And left the radio on?

He returned to the lobby, which buzzed with the random sounds of a dozen conversations. The attendant at hotel reception suggested looking for Forrestal in the lobby or bar. That fruitless search took less than two minutes. Another five passed before the hotel manager appeared from a door behind the reception desk with a professional smile glued to his face and the crossed keys of Les Clefs d'Or glittering on his lapels. Daniel recognized him as the man in uniform he had seen earlier.

He tried to look panic-stricken. "Mr. Forrestal. In 1415. He's not answering."

The manager kept his gaze on his computer screen. "Did you knock on his door?"

"He didn't answer."

"You can leave a message."

"He might be passed out. Or worse."

The manager flicked a glance at Daniel. "What do you mean?"

"His heart pills. He forgot them. He's not young anymore."

Two minutes later, he stood in the elevator with the manager on his way back to the fourteenth floor.

The door opened. They stepped out as a thirty-something man approached from the far end of the corridor. Daniel noted that the man was wearing a sharp black suit, a turtleneck, and a black toque, and he was holding a silver briefcase in his right hand. *Odd attire*, Daniel thought, but then refocused his mind on his present task. The man brushed past, seemingly lost in a song that played only in his head. He hummed a tune that Daniel thought he recognized but couldn't quite place. He walked into the open elevator and stared at the mirrored wall before pressing a button with his free hand. The door hissed closed.

Less than a minute later, Daniel stood in front of the door to room 1415 as the manager inserted his master key, opened the door, and froze.

Daniel scowled as he inhaled a familiar odour, saw the mess around the body on the floor, and heard George Harrison singing about floors that needed sweeping from the bedside iPod dock.

FOUR

IN SEVEN DAYS, I will be a hero to millions. People will praise my name along with other giants of Confederation: Macdonald, Diefenbaker, and even Harper. They built the nation. I will build a new one. A better one.

The tour bus droned northward along Highway 2 from Cardston, where the premier had just given a speech. Ahead, Fort MacLeod's roads spread out like an X-ray. A spindly rib cage of dusty brown roads, tastefully decorated houses, and small strip malls, all set against the plains rising toward the distant snow-covered Rocky Mountains. In the dim horizontal light of a cloudy winter noon, the town looked like it had chain-smoked since adolescence.

Today's media event was planned in front of the Fort, the Museum of the North-West Mounted Police. The premier would speak for fifteen minutes. *The backdrop will work well*, Garth thought. The NWMP, the precursor to the Royal Canadian Mounted Police, brought law and order to the Prairies. They helped transform and civilize the West. Now it was time for the next phase.

Minutes after the bus stopped, Garth sat in front of the camera and began to sweat under the blazing lights. He adjusted his microphone. *Nice way to cap off a good day campaigning. With a friendly network, one that sympathizes with our cause. With a few soft-ball questions, this will make me look like a leader*, he thought.

The reporter, a woman with short blond curls and a dark red dress, strode in and introduced herself. He didn't catch her name. She was stunning. Early thirties. A trim figure that said "no kids." Lean legs of a mountain biker, a smooth graceful neck, and a cute button nose. He would ask her out after the interview. He smiled while she adjusted her earphone and nudged her chair ahead. The red light on the camera flicked on.

"This is CTV News, and I am speaking with Garth Haynes, manager of the pro independence campaign and former executive director of the Alberta Independence Movement. Welcome, Mr. Haynes, and thank you for joining us at such a critical time in the campaign."

"It's a pleasure to be here."

"With the vote now only five days away, how are you feeling about the latest polls that put you at only forty-seven percent of the popular vote? At the start of the campaign, the premier was quite confident of victory. But clearly your support has softened."

This was not the friendly question he expected. Garth forced a smile. "We feel it's important to talk to the right people. Our support has consolidated. Albertans see the advantages that independence offers."

"But don't some see this as a desperate attempt to capitalize on a short-term bump in support due to the Supreme Court ruling?"

What kind of question is that? "There's nothing desperate or short-term at all about our efforts. Our message is merely the natural continuation of a movement that's taken decades to prepare. It all started with the CCF, then Social Credit, the Reform Party, and the simple cry of "The West Wants In." Of course there's been progress with the Conservatives in power for many years. And now it's the East that wants in. We see a chance to improve Confederation for all Canadians. To make it fairer for everyone."

"So for Albertans, 'fairer' means a separate country?"

His shock at the surprisingly aggressive questioning was beginning to dissipate, replaced with a bubbling anger, like acid in his throat. "We see a historic opportunity to correct some remaining imperfections in the Confederation arrangement. To make it better."

She looked at him. "You mean better especially for the West —"

"We do pay the bills."

"So it's all about money? You have oil. The other provinces don't?"

"Look, it's not our fault that Canadian identity has distilled down to this, um, dichotomy."

"East versus West?"

He held his breath in frustration. She was just trying to bait him into saying something stupid. He slowed his speech to give a fraction of a second extra before he spoke, plenty of time for his brain to double-check each word. "Quebec called the shots before, but no one cares about them anymore."

She glanced at her notes. "So you don't consider them a founding nation of the country?"

Garth wondered if the reporter had been switched with one from the CBC. He expected such a question from the Socialists, but not from more impartial, free-market media.

"Of course they are."

"But they just don't matter anymore?"

He leaned forward. Then, as he realized that the shadows thrown by the lights would make him appear more sinister, he leaned back again. "Quebec's voice has diminished as a result of the new reality of the country. They represent a smaller fraction of the population. They've shrivelled to a whiny rump of Separatists, but their culture of eternal persecution remains."

"Isn't culture important?"

Another ambush question. The acid moved higher up his throat. "All that weird music, European statist attitude, and Cirque du Soleil flamboyance? Yes, they produced Céline Dion, but for every successful cultural export, Quebeckers have also churned out countless oddball artists reminiscing about a past that never existed."

"You must admit, though, that they're distinct. Isn't independence also about preserving Albertan culture? Aren't there parallels with Quebec's argument in your campaign message?"

"Canada has never oppressed them." The words were coming out faster now. He was losing control, sentence by sentence. "Canada has never tried to suffocate them or threaten their French language. But Quebeckers still complain." He could feel his face redden, his eyes shooting daggers at her. "Westerners are creative, hopeful, energetic, entrepreneurial, and caring. Once, Easterners had hope, too, but they spoiled their chance with Liberal elite politics, squandering their manufacturing dominance. And now they're mostly a smouldering pile of Socialists intent on confiscating the West's bounty as their own." He took a big gulp of air.

"So what does your party offer Albertans and Canadians?"

"Our movement is about the will of the people, the silent majority, and the control of our own destiny." He glared at her with steely eyes.

"Wasn't that the slogan used in the Quiet Revolution back in the sixties? *Maîtres chez nous*?"

Garth relaxed his cheeks, but he knew his eyes still betrayed his anger at the ambush. "We all want the same thing: to be left alone to do our own thing. Who could argue with that?"

"How about the other provinces that don't necessarily share in the Alberta oil bounty? Wasn't it oil that triggered your latest scaremongering about declaring an independent country?"

"Not scaremongering. Telling people the facts. It was the Montana Pipeline. Ottawa is still blocking it."

She leaned closer. "Doesn't Ottawa have that right? Isn't international trade under the federal government's control?"

"We negotiated with our southern neighbour to send oil their way. To have better access to the U.S. market after the failure of Keystone XL. It was a great deal for Albertans. And Ottawa killed it."

"The Americans cancelled Keystone, I believe."

He admitted to himself that she was well briefed, but he couldn't stray from the official message at such a late stage in the campaign. "The Northern Gateway Pipeline was put on hold — it's probably going to be cancelled — by Ottawa. The Energy East Pipeline never got off the ground, and Ottawa has delayed the Mackenzie Valley Pipeline in the Northwest Territories for decades. We're stuck on three sides. We only have one option left. Go south."

"You took your argument about provincial rights to the Supreme Court last year. And you lost. Many pundits predicted this outcome."

"Premier Brewster knew the Supreme Court would rule in Ottawa's favour. So now we take our argument directly to the people."

"As a former member of the Prime Minister's Office, couldn't you have persuaded the prime minister to see Alberta's viewpoint?"

"I chose to leave the Prime Minister's Office at that time."

"Weren't you fired for publicly supporting the independence platform?"

How does she know that? Everyone agreed to keep the details confidential. "I decided to work for something I believed in."

"Sources inside the Prime Minister's Office say that you were given an ultimatum by the PM. Either support him or support the referendum."

Bitch. "No comment."

She shifted in her chair as she leafed through her notes then turned her gaze on him. "Let's return, then, to what an independent Alberta would offer."

"Our policy is really quite simple."

"Not according to the latest polls. Voters are unclear about your true intentions."

Garth put on a well-practised smile. *Time to put her in her place.* He wasn't one of the good ol' Brownshirt boys that populated the movement. He had an education, he was a rational thinker, and he had thought long and hard about how to argue for the cause. He had put together new facts to respond to the mounting criticism in the hostile, pro-Liberal media. He was sure the premier would approve.

Now it was time to reveal his sound bites that would overwhelm any opposition. "Number one, 'Canada' is really Ontario and Quebec. Together, with half of the country's population, their political power is unbeatable. They will always stop any real attempt to improve Confederation.

"Number two. The Montana Pipeline, when completed, will create fifteen thousand jobs and seven billion in wealth, with another two billion per year in transport fees directly paid into the province's coffers.

"Finally, number three. Alberta, as an independent nation, would be the thirty-fifth largest Western economy, slightly bigger than Finland's. If Finland can do it, so can we."

She looked at the camera operator behind him. "Unfortunately, that's all the time we have for now. The premier is about to speak. Thank you for speaking with us, Mr. Haynes."

That's it? No response from her? He felt robbed. "Not a problem."

Garth stood up and ripped off his microphone. He thought about the wasted personal opportunity with the reporter.

His iPhone began playing the *Hockey Night in Canada* theme song, which signalled a call from someone on a short and select list of contacts. He pulled it from his pocket and read the screen. Area code 208. Idaho.

"What?" he barked, holding the phone to his ear.

The call could be intercepted. He wanted no trail of evidence leading back to him if his plan failed. The loony left-wingers were listening for anything to use against him and the campaign. His special team used only the prepaid phones he had purchased. They used fake names. They used a short list of code words. And he used two phones, one for official campaign duties, and the other, clearly marked with a strip of blue tape, for unofficial business. That second phone would be smashed after the campaign was over.

"It's me. Larch."

Suddenly, Garth was no longer angry about the condescending tone of the interview. He felt serenity, hope, and sadness at the same time. He could anticipate the gravity of the news he was about to hear. He had waited so long for this moment. He hoped for some personal peace. But something gnawed at him that he couldn't recognize or acknowledge. He paused. "So?"

"Mission complete."

Garth let out a long, slow, tired breath. He stared at the distant podium where the premier had begun to speak.

Garth took a moment, trying to imagine the final, satisfying scene. "I'll need confirmation before payment."

"Of course. Check the local news sites in a few hours."

"Payment will be delivered then."

Silence lingered at both ends.

"Anything else?"

"There's a problem."

Garth said nothing.

"Potential witnesses," continued Larch.

"And what are you doing about it?"

"I'm tracking them down."

"Will this be a problem?"

There was a slight pause, a few seconds of static. "No."

"You betcha. Call when you're done." Garth pressed *end* and put his phone in his pocket with his other secrets, leaving only one thought echoing in his mind: *In seven days, I will be a hero to millions.*

FIVE

DANIEL STARED LONGER than was probably polite at the silvery shield lying on the thin wooden table. "MacKinnon," it read. The police detective leaned forward in his chair on the opposite side to continue what he had promised would be a friendly chat. "And you had no prior relationship with Mr. Forrestal before this meeting?"

Daniel tore his gaze from the shiny symbol of local authority. Power and authority were certainly what the Halifax Regional Police headquarters had put him in mind of when he had approached the building a half hour earlier. From the outside, it resembled a gigantic strongbox. But it was unclear whether the architects wanted to keep the criminals from escaping or keep the community from seeing what occurred deep in its bowels. He scanned the concrete walls of the office, seeing a framed degree hanging on a tilt and a faded family picture of the detective, flashing a confident smile, beside an athletic wife wrapping her arms around two teenaged sons.

He focused on the detective's gruff face. "He only called me yesterday and asked to meet to discuss a business venture."

"What sort of venture?" MacKinnon removed his glasses and placed them on the table.

"He never told me."

"Any guesses?" He twiddled his pen.

"Something local, I suppose."

MacKinnon consulted his notes. "And what relationship exists between Mr. Forrestal and Halifax?"

"Nothing that I know about. He's a big fish."

"What do you mean?"

"Important and prominent, I mean. He invests in Toronto, London, Tokyo — New York, too. Big cities. I wouldn't have thought Halifax was big enough for him."

Forrestal would have found Halifax positively quaint, Daniel thought. Certainly an odd choice. It was a city some had accused of never quite living up to its potential. A military fortress that never fired a shot in anger. A major source of Allied military power in the First World War that was virtually obliterated when two ships collided in its harbour. Although once a commercial and financial boom town when Canada was a young country, it had long ago abdicated its crown to more dynamic cities farther west.

"But he contacted you," MacKinnon pressed.

"I guess there was something here he was interested in."

"Any ideas?"

"Most of his high-profile investments are — were — in real estate. He would always beat the market."

"How did he do that?"

"Most analysts credited his unique mix of properties in his portfolios."

"How did that work?"

"It's all about risk balancing. If one property goes down in price, provided your portfolio is broad enough, there's probably another one increasing in price somewhere."

MacKinnon scribbled furiously then stopped. "Did he have investments beyond real estate?"

"Yes. He had the banks, of course, and some blue-chip stocks, companies that traditionally do well. And he also invested in high-growth high-technology companies. Computers. Telecommunications. Internet. That sort of thing. Those were the ones that made headlines. But those were a while ago."

"Would you say investments are your expertise, Professor Ritter?"

"Sort of."

"Care to elaborate?"

"I used to be a business consultant. If a company wanted to expand its business in foreign countries, they called me in to advise."

"What kind of advice did you give?"

Daniel waited two seconds longer than an innocent response would take. "I helped them assess the worth and the risks of the proposed country and target company."

"How did you do that?"

"By getting to know the country and the people involved."

"So it's reasonable that Mr. Forrestal would seek your expertise?"

"Well, yes, assuming he wanted to buy a foreign company. But he could have asked any one of my colleagues or my professional competitors. They would be much more knowledgeable about the local opportunities. I only moved here at the end of last year."

"I'm interested in why he chose you."

"I don't know why he chose me." Daniel regretted his answer as soon as he said it. Repeating a question was a sure sign someone was on the defensive or looking for time to construct a plausible lie. He was sure that's what MacKinnon was thinking.

MacKinnon stared at the floor for a few seconds then returned his gaze to Daniel. "You said that you've never done business with him before. How would he have known about you?"

"From TV perhaps. I have a weekly show on CBC about local business news."

MacKinnon nodded slowly. "Yes, I remember seeing you on the news. Do you ever talk about businesses in Montreal on your show?"

"Not that I can recall."

"And did you ever mention him or any of his businesses?"

Daniel shook his head.

MacKinnon scribbled more notes and then returned to look at Daniel. "And what did you do before you became an expert business consultant?"

Daniel had only a second to continue the smooth rhythm of the conversation. "I had many different jobs. I worked in a restaurant. I was a teacher. Tour guide, too, for a while."

MacKinnon leaned closer. "And you left it all to return to school? Is that right?"

"It seemed like the right thing to do at the time."

"And now you're a professor. A teacher."

"Scholar, yes."

MacKinnon scribbled something on his pad then pulled from his pocket a clear Ziploc evidence bag containing a wallet-sized photograph. He slapped it onto the table in front of Daniel. White lines were slashed across the image at random angles where the photo had been digitally reassembled after having been ripped up into tiny pieces. The image was only three-quarters complete; there was a big bite out of the top left corner. It showed a man, a woman, and a boy standing together in front of an amusement park. Walt Disney World in Orlando, Daniel guessed. The top of the man's face was missing. From its faded, orange-brown tinge, he guessed it had probably been taken with a cheap camera in the 1970s or 1980s.

"Let's change the subject. We found this picture at the crime scene. We couldn't find all of the pieces. Do you recognize any of these people?" MacKinnon pushed the photo forward. The man and the woman posed stiffly; the boy and the woman stood together on the right side of the image, and the man, standing apart on the left, held a briefcase and stared seriously into the camera. All looked a bit nervous. Nobody smiled.

Daniel knew that his immediate reaction was being judged. It's what he would have done. "No, can't say that I do."

Why would a kid look sad at Walt Disney World? While the picture had faded, the tension on the faces of the three subjects was clear. Daniel guessed that maybe the parents' relationship was on the rocks, and the trip was perhaps a last-ditch attempt to save a doomed marriage.

Perhaps the son was desperately trying to keep them together, but his fatalism was clear in his expression.

"Who are they?"

"Are you sure you don't recognize anyone?" asked MacKinnon.

"Is one of them Mr. Forrestal?"

"This photograph was found near the body."

Daniel looked closer. The torn photo made recognizing the man difficult. Maybe there was a faint resemblance between the man in the picture and Forrestal, although he'd only ever seen his picture online. Trying to meet him in person hadn't helped.

"Is that him?" He pointed to the man. He looked young, strong, tall. Different than the recent photos he'd seen of Forrestal.

MacKinnon said, "Do you know the woman and the boy?"

Daniel wondered whether Forrestal was killed because of what he did to the boy or what he did to the woman. He looked again but found nothing else familiar. He shook his head.

MacKinnon scribbled more notes and switched off the recorder.

Daniel was only partly content. Yes, he had stick-handled most of MacKinnon's questions, answering clearly without revealing too much. But he had also felt surprising pressure from a skilled interrogator. He smiled.

"You get the answers you were looking for?"

MacKinnon said nothing for a moment. "Perhaps, but I'm more interested in what you're not telling me, professor."

Shit.

SIX

TWO MEN WATCHED the port gate from their white cube van on Avenue Pierre-Dupuy, across from the cubist architectural curiosity of Habitat 67. With the engine off, the February cold started to seep through the cracks until they could see their breath. The driver rolled his window down now that there was no real difference in temperature inside and out.

"So?" Zeke said and then puffed after a brief bright glow lit the tip of his cigarette.

"We'll wait another fifteen minutes." Each syllable condensed into a small cloud. Gus leaned his elbow through the open window and stared toward the gate. He was tired of talking. It was better if only the bare essentials were said after the last screw-up.

"I just wanted a fuckin' Big Mac." Zeke couldn't shut up.

"The Papa Burger not good enough for you, kid?"

"I like the special sauce."

"You know, it's just mayonnaise and stuff. Nothing special about it."

"The cop didn't spot us."

"You don't know that."

"But we were almost at the drive-thru —"

"That would have boxed us in. No escape if they made us."

"They were just going in to get a coffee or something."

"You don't take chances with the cops, kid."

Zeke looked at his boots. He tried and failed to say nothing for a moment. He smiled faintly. "Then we'll call it in?"

Gus sighed, weary of life and its complications. He had longed for a simpler life when he joined the Alberta Independence Movement, punching out of a career dead end in the army. You did what you were told, you got rewarded. Money. Girls. A car. Even a house. What he liked most, of course, was power. He soon discovered, however, that with power came complications. At first, he tried to will away his problems using his new-found power to get others to clean up his messes. But he learned something only a more experienced person would know: Even the boss has a boss. And Gus's voracious appetite for young prostitutes resulted in one emaciated redhead dying in a dank, plywood-walled motel outside Red Deer. Even the other white power affiliates noticed. The leader sent two enforcers. They used two-by-fours to express his disapproval. They took his girls and his house away. He knew what they would take away next. He had followed the rules since, and he was following them now.

Call when the package arrives. Call if the package does not arrive. Do not open the package.

"Yes, we'll call it in," he said.

Zeke's face twisted into what normally would be called a smile for the first time since they had parked. "Then can we get a Big Mac?"

Gus looked at the younger man sitting in the passenger seat. It was like gazing at himself a decade ago. Zeke was looking for purpose, wanting to make a difference to their noble cause. And keen to follow orders, with the expectation that someday it would be his orders that others would follow. Then he saw himself in the rear-view mirror. Only half of his face showed. He still looked handsome for a thirty-five-year-old. Brown eyes, hair neatly shaved. A bit of stubble hardened his face, the effect he wanted. He kept in shape and he could still bench press three hundred pounds. But he knew his days of high status within AIM were numbered. In a few years he would be unable to stand up to the young pups like Zeke.

"Fuck, sure," he said.

Across the street, a steel fence held a scuffed sign: "*Port de Montréal. Entrée Interdite.*" The sight of another French sign made Gus spit through the van's open window. The spit froze before it hit the ground. Why couldn't Quebec speak English like everyone else? Passing the border from Ontario, the sudden change of language complicated navigating in ways that his handler had forgotten or chose not to mention. He got that *Sud* meant *South*, and *Nord*, *North*. But he would have saved at least an hour in gridlock if he had understood *Voies fermées* on the Trans-Canada coming into the city.

He accepted that this assignment, which had taken him and a junior member from their homes north of

Calgary to the far east of the country, was but another test of his loyalty. He was one of the older members of the group, and his loyalty was occasionally questioned. Maybe he was just too old to stay with the group. Maybe he was having thoughts of going out on his own. Better to keep him busy and far away, the leadership probably concluded.

So he and the new recruit were waiting for a shipment three thousand kilometres from home, surrounded by those goddamned frog signs that he barely understood. Like being in a foreign country. He knew biker gangs at the top of the unwritten hierarchy, several notches above AIM, controlled the Montreal port. It made smuggling a bit easier than trying to move across a guarded land border. But he didn't know what lurked in the container they waited for. Only that it was in several large boxes, was very heavy, required a cube van to transport back, and had to be at the chapter house outside of Airdrie by Sunday afternoon at four.

He sighed as he scanned the scene on the other side of the port fence once again. Beyond the sign stood row upon row of stacked rectangular metal boxes. Long black, brown, and white ones, each with mysterious contents that someone valued. A lone forklift puttered between the rows, searching for the right container to bring down.

"Do you see it?" said Zeke.

"No. We're looking for a quarter container. A small one that fits in the van. Delivered to the gate."

Gus pulled his cellphone from his front pocket and dialed. He waited until it rang twice and a familiar voice answered, "Yes?"

"No package. Should have been here an hour ago."

The line was quiet.

"What do we do?"

Gus waited a few more seconds for an answer. "Get out of there. I'll call with instructions."

"Okay." He ended the call and glanced ahead, then at the rear-view mirror. The road was empty of traffic in both directions. "We're done."

He twisted the ignition key and the van sputtered back to life, lights weakly highlighting the empty road ahead. He drove back into the city, just another commuter about to get stuck in pre-lunch traffic. Gus turned right to access the Bonaventure Expressway. With a sickening metal-on-metal screech, the van spun right, popped its hood, and banged to a stop. Steam gushed from somewhere in the engine. A grey sedan had slammed into Gus's door. Stunned, Gus didn't react, but Zeke did. He jumped out of the passenger door, pulled out his pistol, and walked calmly to the car. Gus just watched. It was something he would have done ten years ago, acting without thinking about the consequences. To show they weren't intimidated. He leaned over, opened the glove compartment, and removed the rental agreement as he heard three loud pops, glass shattering, and a muffled scream from inside the car.

Idiot.

SEVEN

"WHAT?" GARTH BARKED into his blue-striped iPhone as he watched the news coverage of the premier's fiery speech at the NWMP headquarters in Fort MacLeod. It was a good speech, with plenty of sound bites that had been included in the newscast and in the major political pundit blogs. People would take them more seriously now. He gazed out the bus window as the southern out-skirts of Calgary whizzed by in horizontal brushstrokes of light and dark.

"It's Oak," said the voice.

Garth perked up. This would be good news. Oak was the master fixer, specially hired from the U.S. Ten years working for the RightWay political action com-mittee, the powerful Conservative political dealmaker, the one who got W. his second term by bringing in the disenfranchised Christian vote. His work on the last two Republican congressional campaigns made him the perfect man for the job. He was a master at logistics.

He knew how to get things done. He had come highly recommended.

"And?" There was a long pause.

"There's a problem."

Garth stared blankly as the world outside flashed by. This part of his plan had to work. There could be no margin for error. He had paid top dollar. Jesus, now he had *two* problems.

"What happened?" Garth's breath almost cut out.

"The operation for the second shipment was not successful."

Garth paused and considered the consequences. How many facets of his plan relied on the packages being at the right place at the right time? He had to think fast.

"Tell me exactly what happened."

"We don't exactly know. There are … complications."

"The importance of the package cannot be overstated. What options are there to recover it?" He was careful not to mention the contents by name. He had warned his team that their phone calls could be monitored, given the prime minister's displeasure at his participation in the referendum. True, they had been responsible for the triumphant return of the Conservative Party to political power after years in the Liberal wilderness. But the PM could inform the solicitor general, who would call the superintendent of the RCMP and the directors of the two spy agencies, CSIS and CSEC, and voila, monitored conversations. Everyone on his special projects team had a code name. He wanted something generic, something that didn't have any special meaning, something that wouldn't attract attention. He recalled that one of his excited, overeducated campaign workers with a degree in English literature said the name *Garth* meant something like "a person who lives in an orchard" in Middle English. He thought it was an odd thing to say, but it was also memorable. So he picked tree names for his team members.

"What happened?"

"The first shipment crossed the border on schedule early this morning. The third shipment crossed the border two hours later without incident. They will both be in Airdrie by the end of the day. But the second shipment was intercepted. It left as scheduled but it never arrived in Montreal."

Garth sighed in frustration. "I knew that shipping it that way was too complicated. You should have sent it across the border at Coutts. It's the most direct route."

"As we discussed, security at all land borders is tighter than normal. It's because of your referendum. Homeland Security has drones flying over any potential transfer point along the border. The best way to get such a large shipment across the border is to divide it into smaller pieces. The smaller deliveries are on track."

"I'll call you back in five minutes." Garth ended the call then texted Ash: Confirm arrival of two shipments.

He waited a long minute before his phone pinged. Shipment #1 arrived ten minutes ago. Unloading now. Confirmed. Shipment #3 crossed border. Confirmed. Ash.

Then he called back Oak, who picked up after one ring and said, "The first one arrived a few minutes ago."

"I know. What about the big stuff?"

"As I said, it was intercepted. I've lost contact with the courier. I assume it's lost."

Garth didn't say anything.

Oak continued, "I can get another one on site in two days."

Garth thought about how the missing equipment would complicate other parts of his plan. "How much will it cost?" The original shipment had cost over ten million dollars, money easily raised earlier in the campaign. However, with only four days until the vote, donations had peaked and there were now fewer potential sources of revenue.

"On this short notice, I can get a half shipment for six. I'll break it up into two deliveries."

It was extortion. But he had few options. Timing was key. Everything had to be in place by the morning after the referendum. He had to ensure that this shipment got through.

With a sigh that was surely audible to Oak, Garth said, "Tell them I'll transfer the money to the same account by end of business today New York time. You know what I want."

"Done."

"No more screw-ups."

Garth hung up and focused his thoughts. The source would never bail out, nor would the shipment be sold to someone else once it had been committed to him. He knew these people. They had strong recommendations from the RightWay organization contact and impeccable Conservative connections, both to the Republican Party and the National Rifle Association. They had supplied what they called "special political operations" for several congressional elections. They always delivered. He had called yesterday to confirm that the third, and largest, shipment had left Boston early in the morning.

He had no reason to doubt them. There were twelve shipments in all, scattered across a range of sea and land border crossings, sent from several distribution points: Detroit, New York, Chicago, Boston, Seattle, and Helena, Montana. The suppliers wouldn't be paid their final installment until all shipments arrived.

All had gone well … until now. What happened? And how was he going to get the most important shipment by Sunday? He was running out of time.

His fear amplified. What was there to be scared of? He was down to only one focus in his life. No more distractions. *It will be easier after people join us*, he told himself, *after I'm a hero. To millions.*

EIGHT

FINDING THE SECOND WITNESS was almost as easy as finding the first. There were only two people Larch worried about. They had both seen him as they walked out of the hotel elevator. One was clearly the hotel manager, judging from the uniform. The other was most likely the ten o'clock appointment. He had all but made it to the stairs beside the elevator when the men appeared. Forrestal had not said whom he was supposed to meet. So Larch had searched for any clue and found a day planner.

Larch took a cab to his hotel near a cluster of factory outlet stores in Dartmouth. It provided the greatest number of escape-route options, with access to two highways and a direct path to the airport. His room faced a side alley where no prying eyes could see. He shut the door and emptied his briefcase. Forrestal's day planner tumbled onto the thin mattress. The pages had all of the necessary details. He thought it ironic that the scion of Canadian high-technology start-ups would record his appointments by hand.

Larch flipped through the pages until he saw what he was looking for.

Tuesday. 10 a.m. D. Ritter. Connaught Land.

It was too easy.

Now he had the identities of his two targets. And more than two days to complete the job. More than enough time.

NINE

DETECTIVE MATT MACKINNON returned to his office after an absence of fifteen minutes according to Daniel's watch. He handed Daniel a glass of water and switched the recorder back on as he approached the table. "I've spoken with the inspector. We have some new information. So I'd like to ask you a few more questions." He didn't sit. Instead he began to orbit the table, hands clasped behind his back.

"So you found the body only minutes after he was killed?"

Daniel sucked back the water. "I had an appointment to meet him in his hotel room. He asked me to come."

"So you just left whatever you were doing to come meet with him?"

"Of course. I already told you. He's a big fish."

"He arranged for you to come, then?"

"Yes. He told me to meet him in his room at the Westin." He held the empty glass, trying to will more water down his throat. The detective was a skilled interrogator, using the subtle, tangential questions Daniel had learned to use, too. He turned to look directly at the officer. "I didn't kill him, if that's what you're thinking."

"I didn't say that you did. However, I find the sequence of events to be … intriguing." MacKinnon twisted his chair so that its back faced the table. He straddled the chair and leaned forward.

Daniel put the empty glass on the table and recounted again how he had received the phone call from Forrestal, gone to the hotel in the morning, knocked on the door, and fetched the hotel manager.

"Arriving so soon after the death, perhaps you saw the killer."

"Perhaps."

"You went to the room earlier?"

Daniel didn't like where this was going. The detective was asking the same question in different ways, in reverse chronological order, forcing Daniel to answer quickly. It was a good way to see if he was lying. *Am I a suspect?* "The door was locked and no one answered."

"It was about the same time as he was killed."

"I didn't hang around. I went downstairs to get the manager."

MacKinnon paused. "We're reviewing footage from the security cameras. We'll wait for confirmation of your story."

Daniel crossed his arms, expecting a new questioning track.

"Let's begin another train of thought. Who was with you?" MacKinnon didn't disappoint.

"No one. It was only me."

"What did you see in the hallway before you arrived at Mr. Forrestal's door?"

Daniel paused. "It was surprisingly busy."

"Why do you say that?"

"Hotel corridors are usually empty. When I arrived, it was full of people. There was a young couple. A woman. She was young and very pretty. She …"

Daniel's attention was caught by a man in a dark suit beckoning through the door window. MacKinnon turned and drooped his shoulders. He opened the door then mumbled something that Daniel couldn't quite make out. But the response was clear.

"Suspected smugglers. Your case. First coordination meeting in two days."

Daniel saw MacKinnon nod, a nod empty of interest. He waved his colleague away, closed the door, and resumed his seat, reactivating his professional interview face.

"Keep going."

"Uh, there was a man. The hotel manager. He was talking to someone in another room. He was quite loud. That's it."

"The preliminary report says you were accompanied by the hotel manager. The same person?"

"Yes. He came with me the second time I went to the door."

"Did you see anyone then?"

Daniel tried to recall until an image materialized in his mind. "Yes, there was a man with a briefcase —"

MacKinnon leaned closer. "Tell me about him."

"The man?"

"Was he the only one you saw leaving with some sort of bag or container?"

Daniel replayed the scene in his mind. Chinese couple arriving. Man leaving, but with no bag. A young woman leaving. Did she have a bag? He couldn't remember. A man leaving with a briefcase. "Yes, I believe so, but there may not be much to tell."

"Tell me anyway. Describe him."

"Sort of average. Well dressed." Daniel searched his memory. He stilled his mind until the image and sounds and scents came into focus, a skill with which he was quite out of practice. "He was in a good mood."

MacKinnon stopped writing and looked directly at Daniel. "Why do you say that?"

"It's nothing really. He was humming a song."

"What song was it?" He was scribbling again.

"I don't know. One by the Beatles? The one Eric Clapton does. With the guitar solo."

MacKinnon pulled out an iPod from an evidence bag, fiddled with the menu wheel, slapped it on the table, and pressed *play*. After only a few bars of "While My Guitar Gently Weeps," Daniel nodded.

"That's it. That's the song."

MacKinnon cut the music, shoved the iPod back into the bag, and held it in his hand. "This is Mr. Forrestal's iPod. The song was playing when the forensic team found the body."

"So what does this all mean?" said Daniel.

"You tell me. We didn't find the murder weapon in the room. Or in any room on the fourteenth floor."

"So the killer must have taken the weapon with him." Daniel relaxed a little.

"That's what I think."

"The weapon, what was it?"

"A pistol. Something small."

Something that could be carried under a folded newspaper or in a briefcase.

"So you see, Professor Ritter, you can help us after all. You can identify Mr. Forrestal's murderer."

"That's good, then."

"Yes, but the murderer probably knows this, too."

TEN

CTV NEWS SAID THE CROWD exceeded twenty thousand. The Calgary Saddledome was bursting at the seams for one of the final rallies of the campaign. But the premier paced the green room, usually reserved for Keith Urban or other musicians waiting to go on stage, with his arms crossed, staring at the floor while Garth stood in silence. Premier Brewster stopped and turned to face his employee.

"What the fuck have you been up to, Garth?"

"We're —"

Brewster jabbed his finger at Garth. "We're fuckin' five points behind, and you seem to have lost focus. We're here to win. But we're not winning right now. Your job is to make sure that we win while I prepare the post-referendum details."

"We will win."

"Don't bullshit me. You've been sloppy."

"Who says?"

"I just watched it. The interview on TV. You adlibbed, didn't you?"

"It was an ambush."

"Of course, you moron. I know how this game is played. I've been doing this for years. You fell into an easy trap. You just fuckin' wanted to antagonize them." He paced in a circle once, twice, then he stopped, turned to face Garth, and pointed his finger at him. "We're bleeding support because of your bozo eruption." He ran a hand through his hair as he looked at the ceiling in frustration. "Jesus. Finland?"

"Law number three —"

"You just make this crap up, don't you? The way you said it made it sound like we want to create our own country."

"We do."

"No, we don't. We'll do it if we have to, but it's definitely not our first choice."

Garth froze. He hadn't expected the premier to deny their quest for nationhood. They had dreamed about it together for a decade. He hadn't hesitated when Brewster phoned him for help. He'd gladly resigned from the Prime Minister's Office to take a place by his side. But now he saw something new and disturbing on the premier's face. It looked like hesitation. "Of course we do. You're not getting squeamish now? So close to victory?"

"I know what I'm doing, Garth. Alberta as an independent country is a moronic idea. We're landlocked and no one's on our side. B.C. and the territories hate us, Saskatchewan can't do much to help, and Montana doesn't give a damn what happens. Get real. What we need is bargaining strength against the Feds. But now you have the media saying we want to separate. Like we're another fuckin' Parti Québécois. Davison was right. He warned me about hiring you. He told me of your work in his PMO. Your fringe group is sloppy. And you're a bit of a whiner, too."

"Our AIM brothers got the job done."

Brewster stretched his back. "Not this time. We won't whine our way out of Confederation. I've got a full house of supporters out there." He pointed toward the stage below in the centre of the arena. "I don't want your goose-stepping goons scaring people away. We're down to the wire, and I think you're drifting off-message."

"I've made the message clearer."

"Stick to *my* message. I'm the only one who gets to improvise. Not you. I pay you to manage expectations, not create new ones because you're pissed off."

Garth's shock morphed into an anger he could barely control. The premier's attitude was insulting, and Garth was realizing the premier's true problem: he was beginning to lose his nerve now that pressure was increasing and the poll numbers no longer predicted a big win. Garth grimaced as he remembered his strategic plan. At least a new and independent Alberta would be ready to defend itself. And, if necessary, he would have the power base to take command when the premier displayed weakness.

Brewster said, "You do know what we'll do when we win?"

"I want a country. I expect to be well rewarded for my service."

"You'll get your fucking Cabinet post."

"I want to be minister of defence."

"Yeah, yeah, but we have more trouble ahead between now and your new job title."

"I've made contingency plans. No problem."

"Yes, a problem. First, we have to negotiate with the Americans. Otherwise, they'll just roll over us. Our oil will help guarantee that they have enough for at least a generation, even if there are problems with the Saudis or Iran or Venezuela. We could become their fifty-first state. I'll become governor. We'll have two senators and a dozen or so congressmen. But do you know what will happen if we lose this referendum?"

"You'll still be premier. Still in power."

"No, I won't. I'll be powerless. Embarrassed. I'll join a long list of political rejects. Losers. I'll become just a curious historical footnote. I'll be ridiculed by schoolchildren for generations of Canadian history classes." Brewster leaned closer. "I guarantee that it will be far worse for you. This is not going to happen. We are not going to lose. And definitely not because of you getting careless in front of the media. I want a five-point shift in our favour by Saturday night."

Garth shook with brittle tension.

"How do you plan to fix it?" Brewster pressed closer until he was almost nose to nose with Garth.

Garth smelled the stench of steak and stale beer from the premier's mouth, but he didn't flinch, didn't say a word. He knew the question was rhetorical.

"I'll tell you. Time to play hardball. Our message has become compromised. You compromised it. We need to focus the voters' attention on the other side. I want negative headlines about the No side. I want something spectacular. I want it far away from here. And I want it clear that the No side is behind it. Got it?"

Brewster didn't wait for Garth to acknowledge his demand. He spun around with extra flair, as if he sported a long black cape, and left, leaving the door ajar.

Garth nodded slowly to himself. Now he knew what he should be scared of. He had his focus back. He saw new headlines materialize in his mind, and he knew what to do. He grabbed his cellphone and punched in Ash's number. It was time for Plan B.

ELEVEN

IN THE MOMENTS SINCE Zeke shot the driver of the car that had crashed into their van, Gus hadn't spoken. An accident maybe, but Zeke had overreacted. Their job was to remain unseen, and in three short shots, Zeke had blown their anonymity. There would be witnesses for sure. Gus slammed the van into gear and sped away, the van's automatic transmission wheezing at the surprising demand for maximum acceleration. Zeke was also quiet. Perhaps he now realized the gravity of what he had done, but Gus wasn't convinced.

"We have to dump the van," Gus said.

Zeke didn't react.

"We have to find another one. Keep an eye out."

They tucked into a side street from Sainte-Catherine, went under the Jacques Cartier Bridge, and continued eastward toward Hochelaga-Maisonneuve. In the early evening, traffic was heavy. They passed countless parked cars but no vans.

Gus's cellphone buzzed. He pulled it out from his jacket. "Yes?"

"It's me." Ash. The boss. "Get your butts moving. You'll pick up the next shipment in New Brunswick. It's on its way right now. You've got to be there in twelve hours."

"Where?"

"I'll send you a location. It's on the Bay of Fundy. It's remote and quiet. You won't have any problems. What have you got?"

"A cube van."

"Big enough. Don't bring attention to yourself. Got it?"

"Where are we taking the shipment? The same place as before?"

"I'll tell you later."

Zeke grunted, "There's one."

A lone unmarked white van, similar in size to theirs, sat on the far side of the street. Gus turned onto the first cross street and parked their vehicle. He wiped the steering wheel, dashboard, and door handles with a grimy towel from behind his seat. He shoved the rental agreement in his jacket pocket, hopped out, and walked to the empty van. He glared at Zeke; it was his turn to redeem himself. Zeke understood and sauntered over to the passenger's side window, shielded the view with his hand, pulled out a slim jim, and in a few seconds had unlocked the door. Gus was impressed with the well-rehearsed smoothness of his action.

Zeke crawled into the van, leaned over, and unlocked the driver's door. Gus slipped into the driver's seat and pulled the ignition wires as he had done countless times before. He rubbed his hands to warm up, and in less than a minute the van sputtered to life. He shifted the gear to *drive*, looked over his left shoulder, then ahead, and drove east. Deeper into the mysterious plan. Deeper into this foreign land.

TWELVE

CLAIRE HAD STOOD AT ATTENTION for too long and was beginning to feel woozy. Her body still buzzed with the adrenalin rush of the failed rescue the day before. She struggled to bottle her energy, squirming, wanting to move.

She replayed in her head her encounter with the fishing boat, questioning every decision. Sending the helicopter from CFB Greenwood was just normal search-and-rescue procedure. The *Kingston*, steaming at high speed toward the boat, was also standard protocol. But it was more chance than part of any plan that all three vessels met at the same place at the same time.

It was only her third time as captain, solo, without a more senior officer on board to watch her every move. Captain Hall reassured her that he was developing confidence in her as an officer. He said he wanted her to build up time in command with a few routine shore patrols. *One step at a time.* The coming storm provided an opportunity to see what she would do in adverse conditions. But not too adverse. The patrol wouldn't stray more than a dozen kilometres offshore.

Three hours into the patrol, the message arrived. A fishing boat not responding. A search-and-rescue helicopter was dispatched from CFB Greenwood, a scenario she had practised dozens of times. All other ships were either on duty elsewhere or in dock for maintenance. Finally, a chance to show the brass and her parents what she was capable of. Of course, she wasn't supposed to kill the crew and sink the boat.

The captain scribbled something in a notebook on his desk. He had summoned her as soon as she returned the *Kingston* to port in Halifax. Claire allowed herself a small smile: *Only two months into my first command, and already I have combat experience. Maybe he wants to give me feedback, maybe even give me a commendation.* She loved her career, in spite of the disappointment on her parents' faces when she had announced her decision to ditch a dead end job, and the matching boyfriend, and join the navy. This feeling, this trembling feeling, of using the power given to her to do good — this was why she had joined. *I made a difference yesterday.*

Her smile dissolved as she thought about the person she had killed. She had taken a life. Maybe two. Maybe more. The man could have had a family. A child, a wife waiting, rocking on the veranda at sunset, not yet knowing the terrible news. Maybe there was someone else on board, too.

She had taken at least one life. Had she made a difference? She didn't know. Her thoughts collided.

She had to stare straight ahead, so she couldn't quite make out what the captain was writing, even with her peripheral vision. He was making her wait, flaunting his authority. He stopped writing, put his pen down. He aimed his eyes at her.

"Yes, sir?" Claire said.

"Marcoux, what happened out there?"

She held her mouth open for a second. "It's all there, in my report from this morning."

"Yes, a precise chronological list of events." He rummaged across his desk until he held a short, stapled stack of papers. He read from the last page. "That ended in the sinking of the boat and the death of at least one person."

"They threatened the ship." She looked at the floor and then toward Hall. "I didn't have a choice."

"Border Services says it was narcotics smuggling." He fished out another short report from his table and held it in the other hand.

"They seemed very well armed for smuggling dope, sir."

"More likely Ecstasy. Pseudoephedrine. Very popular at parties. Very profitable. That's Border Services' take on this." He tossed both reports onto his desk.

"But we'll never know, will we?"

The captain leaned back in his chair and laced his hands behind his head. His movement drew her attention to his bulging arms, angular chin, intense eyes, and thinning head of tightly cropped black hair speckled with grey. He was quite fit for someone twenty years older than her. Overall, a very handsome man, Claire thought. He reminded her of Denzel Washington in his prime.

"No, we'll never know. Unless someone salvages the wreckage," Hall said.

"It's under hundreds of metres of water. Salvage seems unlikely, sir."

"Depends on what the cargo is."

"Yes."

"What do *you* believe, Lieutenant Commander?"

"I'm not sure. If they were smuggling drugs they could have just thrown it overboard. We'd have had no evidence against them."

Hall didn't say anything.

"Sir, that boat shouldn't have been where we found it. There were at least two people on board. At least one RPG. And it was from Boston. I don't think it was drugs."

"Then what?"

"I don't know, sir. Something worth keeping. Something … more serious."

He scowled. "We'll see. Coast Guard, FBI, CBSA, and RCMP are on alert …" He looked down, eyes averted for the first time since he'd started talking, and took a deep breath.

"Sir?" Claire felt a bead of sweat form on her right temple. Hall looked more upset than she had ever seen. She didn't know how to respond.

"Lieutenant Commander, I need to understand something." His eyes, suddenly burning, were locked on hers. "How do you feel about taking a life in the line of duty?"

She took a moment, gathering her thoughts. "I don't know exactly, sir. It happened so fast."

His eyes burned into hers. "I need to know." He leaned forward and slammed his hands on the desk. "Now."

She noticed that he hadn't asked her to stand at ease. She was still frozen at attention. "I did what I thought was best to defend my ship." As soon as she said it, she regretted it. Sounded like an official bureaucratic statement. Like someone trying to cover their ass. "Sir …"

"You need time to process this."

"I don't need time, sir. I know how I feel."

"No, you don't. I expect a lot from my captains. You know that I think you're an exemplary officer and I've supported your career." He startled her as he stood up.

Her heart skipped a beat. She sucked in air in a short, sharp gasp.

"But taking a life is a major event for any military member. I have questions about what happened out there. Your mission was to assess and rescue if necessary. You seem to have changed the mission."

She didn't know how to respond. Her brain produced three simultaneous answers, producing gridlock in her mind. She forced one out. "Never, sir. The mission changed when they fired at the helo. They were about to fire at us, too. I was defending the ship."

"Yes, that is *your* story. But I've heard another one." He pulled a single piece of paper, half-filled with text, from his desk. "I received a report from Maritime Command. It includes an email from one of your crew."

One of my crew? Who?

"The crew member says that you didn't even try to de-escalate the situation. Barely tried to talk to them. Never tried to arrest them. You just fired. Shot to kill."

Who was it? Who would stab me in the back?

Claire wondered if he disapproved because she failed to rescue the crew or because he hadn't been there to sink the ship himself.

"Sir, have you ever taken a life in your career?"

He looked hard at her. "Never. I can't help you deal with this."

Captain Hall returned to stand behind the desk, putting physical distance between them. "You've put me in an uncomfortable position. Maybe I promoted you too fast. I have to consider the behaviour of all of my ship captains. This is no longer just about you. I have others to consider as well. What kind of precedent does this set? By condoning your actions this morning, am I setting a new standard of aggressive action for the other captains to follow?"

He looked down at the open folder on the table for a moment. "Do you know who asked me these questions? The commodore of the Atlantic Fleet. And he was on the phone with his boss. This goes all the way to the CDS."

Claire couldn't believe it. *The chief of defence staff, the top general in the military, is interested in me?*

Hall took a breath and continued, "I've been ordered to clean this up before it turns into another scandal for the navy. We've had too many of these recently. Remember the officer who passed Five Eyes information to the Russians a few years back? The drunk and disorderly behaviour during a port visit in Virginia? The *Protecteur* being towed to Hawaii after an engine fire? The commodore wants no more problems."

"I have my duties on the *Kingston*. We have patrol duty again tomorrow at seventeen hundred."

Hall shook his head. "Not anymore. Pending a formal review, you are relieved of command."

She only heard the final few words. *Relieved of command.*

Captain Hall shifted his gaze to the email in his hand. He set it on his table and looked again at Claire. "There will be a preliminary investigation with Maritime Command. You will be contacted shortly."

Claire couldn't move. Her career was crashing down in slow motion. Short of a court martial, being deprived of command was the worst-case scenario. *How did things get so bad?* She had walked into the captain's office full of satisfaction, energy, a sense of personal fulfillment. Now, she was walking out shamed and directionless, her parents' fingers pointing. *Psychologically unreliable.*

"Can I get back to my crew?" she said.

"I have ordered them to stand down pending further notice."

"But —"

"No contact with your crew. That's an order. Take some time off. We'll contact you."

She looked right at him, not at the point on the wall straight ahead. She pleaded with her eyes but he was having none of it. *I know I did the right thing out there. I thought you were on my side. Why are you punishing me?*

He waved her off. "Dismissed."

THIRTEEN

GARTH RATTLED IN HIS SEAT as the campaign bus rolled over another snow-covered pothole on Highway 2. The other workers were busy on their phones, their faces tinged blue from the glow. He flipped on his laptop and navigated to the CBC, Global, and CTV websites. Forrestal was the top story of the day. A headline blared: "Business Icon Found Dead in Hotel." There was a picture of the smiling businessman taken from his company's website, followed by a short article. Police confirmed foul play. They were investigating and seeking the public's help to solve the crime. A contact number concluded the piece.

He felt a stupid tear emerge from his right eye, but it was not enough to stop him from opening another browser tab, selecting his offshore bank website, typing in a twenty-six-digit code, and transferring five thousand U.S. dollars to a numbered account in the Cayman Islands, the same one he had sent five thousand to a few weeks earlier. He then sent ten thousand to a new account and forwarded a confirmation message to Birch's email address, as agreed.

Larch had kept his promise. Garth now had his revenge, his ultimate victory, over the man whose selfish actions had traumatized him for decades. But something was wrong. When playing this scene in his mind, over those many years, Garth thought in the end he might, for some obscure reason, feel sad. He didn't. At first he felt the relief that he expected. But it soon faded, replaced by something else, something surprising, something that had been lurking under the surface and only now came into view. Something he hadn't felt since he was a child.

He was scared.

FOURTEEN

DANIEL RITTER'S SMILING FACE filled the screen of the smartphone. Larch had loaded the image from Ritter's official university page. He didn't find much information about the company mentioned in Forrestal's diary, except that Connaught Land was based in the city of Dartmouth, the troubled cousin of Halifax, according to the news headlines. There was only one *D. Ritter* in any phone listing. A Google search quickly identified him as a business professor.

The picture provided the final confirmation. Mr. Ritter was indeed the man he had passed in the hallway. No doubt.

Larch realized how closely he'd missed being caught. He had been told to complete his assignment before the 10 a.m. meeting. Opening the door and fooling the security system had been easy. The target had been standing alone, shoulders hunched in grief over a photograph torn into pieces, and then turned to face him, surprised at Larch's sudden presence by the door. Larch had had his few minutes with his target, enough to do his duty. Only a few moments separated a successful mission from a spectacular failure. Perhaps it would have been cleaner to have killed both of the men from the elevator at the time. He wouldn't now be forced to track them down. But any trail of evidence tying his work to his client would be unprofessional, and his reputation could suffer a fatal blow.

But there was still time to clean it up. Provided the hotel manager and Ritter did not survive Saturday night, he would be able to complete a successful mission, preserve his reputation, and retrieve the final half of his payment.

He pocketed the cellphone, slung his backpack over his shoulder, grabbed his suitcase, checked out of the hotel room, descended into the parking garage, jumped into his rental SUV, and joined the anonymous traffic in the gathering gloom outside.

Less than two kilometres away, in the police station just beyond the western end of the Macdonald Bridge, Daniel was sick of looking at mug shots. Hundreds had already flashed by on MacKinnon's computer screen. None of the faces were smiling. This was understandable, since the photos were taken after arrests. He recognized a former high-school classmate, who had been voted most likely to succeed. Many of the faces betrayed a sense of resignation at being caught. But none of them resembled the man he saw for a second or two in the hallway. He worried that his image of the man was receding, growing fuzzier by the hour. Would he still recognize him in another day?

Detective MacKinnon returned, bringing a laptop computer and a doughnut-sized Tim Hortons bag. He closed the door behind him and handed the bag to Daniel. "Sorry about the delay. We should be done soon. I really appreciate your help."

Daniel opened the bag and popped two Timbits in his mouth one after the other. "I haven't found him," he said between mouthfuls.

"Maybe we have." MacKinnon sat down in the chair across from Daniel and opened the computer. He began to type. "The security camera covering the fourteenth floor was damaged, but we have footage from the hotel lobby."

Daniel pushed away from the screen. His aluminum chair screeched a short distance along the floor. The sound echoed in the concrete room. "Let's have a look."

MacKinnon swung the computer around so Daniel could see the screen and its frozen image of him and the hotel manager walking quickly to the elevator. "According to forensics, Forrestal is already dead at this point. And here you are, on your way to see him. Running the coverage backward, we find several people in the lobby. I'd like you to look at them and tell me if you recognize anyone."

He rotated the computer around and typed then spun it back to face Daniel. The screen showed a woman in a black dress walking along the corridor from the elevator. The pretty one. The one who came out of the elevator as he entered. Daniel shook his head. The next picture, a hotel employee with room service food on a tray, and anonymous guests milling about the lobby.

Daniel didn't recognize any of them either. The pictures continued for a few minutes until he saw himself and the hotel manager walk away from the camera, toward the elevator. Then the video showed a man in a black suit and black turtleneck, holding a silver briefcase, approaching the camera then moving directly underneath, and most likely out the main entrance and onto the street.

"That's him." Daniel pointed emphatically.

MacKinnon stood and walked over to stand beside Daniel. He nodded at the jittery picture. "You recognize him?"

"Yes. He's the one I saw in the hallway just as we approached Forrestal's room."

"Why so sure?"

"He was humming that song." Daniel was pleased.

MacKinnon studied the face and smiled. "So now we know what he looks like."

FIFTEEN

DANIEL HAD TO SHIELD HIS EYES from the dying late-February sun as he emerged from the front door of the Halifax Regional Police Headquarters on Gottingen Street. It had been a stressful few hours. MacKinnon was a skilled interrogator, forcing Daniel to reveal more than he had anticipated by asking rapid fire questions without giving enough time to construct answers. Daniel's real thoughts had begun to leak through. MacKinnon was clever.

MacKinnon didn't want him to stray too far in case he had more questions. He promised to call Daniel if anything new developed.

The sky was painted blue to orange to red near the western horizon. Snow began to fall and bitter gusts of wind cut through his coat, even with his collar tucked up. His apartment in the South End was seven blocks away. He flagged down a passing cab.

In the rear seat, as the taxi lurched around potholes, he pulled out his cellphone and dialed. *Pick up the phone, pick up the phone*, he pleaded, but he heard her voice message again, in her neutral, businesslike voice, as if speaking to a colleague. After the beep, he said, "Please call me. I haven't heard from you. I'll be on the six o'clock flight tomorrow, as usual. It's been a crazy few days here. I'll tell you all about it when I see you and Emily at the airport. Tell Emily I love her."

Why isn't she answering my calls? The police interview had lasted longer than he had anticipated, but he still had plenty of time to get a good night's sleep back at the apartment, wake up early, throw some clothes into his carry-on bag, get a quick present for Emily, and catch his regular flight back to Montreal. Every two weeks, he got to spend time with his daughter. Part of the court settlement. But worry crept in. He had no way of knowing what his ex-wife was up to.

The cab jerked to a halt. He paid the fare and strode into the apartment lobby. A short elevator ride to the fourth floor took him to his apartment. It was supposed to have been a temporary place, until he decided his next step as a single man and an estranged father. All he had left was Emily, and only for two days at a time.

Halifax was his clean start, a personal-life reboot, and a chance to redefine himself away from the trauma of his former careers and the guilt of a failed marriage.

He grabbed the lonely beer in the fridge. He opened his laptop on the coffee table and confirmed his seat on the Air Canada flight to Montreal leaving in twenty-four hours. On Travelocity, he got a room at the Novotel downtown, a short taxi ride from his former home. He couldn't stay there. Vanessa had her own life now. He just wanted to see Emily.

With that settled, he tried to make a mental summary of what he knew. Forrestal's murder was a professional job. Daniel and the police knew what the murderer looked like. The police were on the hunt. But they were baffled as to the motive. Who would want the star Canadian entrepreneur dead? Sure, not all business deals succeeded. He must have had enemies, but it was unthinkable that anyone would want to kill him. Forrestal had made one spectacular deal after another for years. Daniel couldn't recall any failures. Everything the man touched turned to gold. And what did Forrestal want to talk about? Did he have a deal in mind? Why did he want to talk to a junior no-name professor? If he wanted advice, he should have sought out someone more experienced, like Lloyd, or someone still in the business. There were plenty of others. *Does he know about my prior career?*

He pulled out his cellphone and dialed. There was a way to find at least one answer.

After three rings, a flat voice said, "Fanshawe."

"It's me, Daniel."

There was a long pause before Lloyd said, "Did you fuck it up?"

"What?"

"You didn't like the deal?"

"What deal? There was no deal."

Lloyd paused for a second before continuing. "So what did he want?"

"He never said."

"You did piss him off. I knew it."

"No, he's dead."

Daniel could hear accelerated breathing at the other end of the call.

"Did you hear me?" Daniel said.

"You killed him?"

"Are you nuts? Of course I didn't. He was dead before I got to meet him. Police say he was murdered."

Lloyd stumbled with his words. "What happened?"

"I don't know. When I got there he was already dead."

"How do you know he was murdered?"

"Oh, it was pretty obvious. He was shot. In the head. Looked like an execution. It was pretty disgusting."

"I can't believe it. Everybody loved Patrick. I can't believe it."

He called him Patrick. "Me neither."

"Who killed him?"

"Don't know. I just spent hours being interviewed by the police."

"And they let you go?"

"Of course. I didn't do it."

"So who did? Was it robbery?"

"I don't think so. It was a professional hit."

"Christ."

"You have any idea who did it?"

Lloyd paused. "Not a clue. He was always a winner. All the way."

"Well, somebody was pissed off —" The line went dead.

Lloyd is still an asshole, Daniel thought, *but his reaction was interesting.* He shut off his phone, placed it on the night table beside his bed, and stared out his window. Lloyd said everyone liked Forrestal, that he was always a winner. *He knows Forrestal personally.*

Maybe there was one loser out there.

The sun had dipped below the horizon, and darkness started to blanket the city. The falling snow was heavier now, covering the city's secrets, wrapping everything in white with a tinge of jaundice under the sodium streetlights. Daniel felt dizzy, disoriented, as if floating through space, each snowflake a star, travelling faster than light through the vacuum of space.

Another storm was coming. He didn't know what form it would take, but he sensed that the strands of fate that tied him to a dead entrepreneur would soon throw him into another dangerous situation. A killer was out there somewhere and the skills that Daniel had tried to deaden might have to resurface. His old life might be starting to ooze back.

SIXTEEN

CURLED UP IN THE ROCKING CHAIR in her apartment, Claire stared at the clock on the wall, following each tick of the second hand. She wasn't used to having time on her hands. With nothing to do but wait, her thoughts spun downward into the abyss that she never wanted to acknowledge, that she always tried to hide away. The harder she pushed them back, the clearer the memories flooded in.

"*Maman*, I'm home." Home was a brownstone three-bedroom condo in Outremont, the tony neighbourhood on the north side of Mont-Royal, where upper-class francophones, the political elite, lived out their oversized dreams. She hopped up the steps, opened the door, and saw her mother tapping away at her laptop on the kitchen table.

Late-afternoon sunlight streamed through the kitchen window, lighting up her mother's face. A cool summer breeze teased the white curtains.

Her mother turned as Claire walked through the vestibule. "*Salut, ma chérie.*" She smiled.

"*Salut, maman,*" Claire said from rote.

"I sold two paintings today."

"*À qui?*"

"A collector in Geneva. Can you come with me to deliver the paintings? We could pick up the cheque together. Then we can go shopping in Paris. Just like old times. Mother and daughter."

Her mother ran an art consulting company from her kitchen. With a long list of clients in Europe, the U.S., and Asia, she offered portfolios of high-quality Canadian art. Not Group of Seven or Riopelle, but lesser-known artists with big potential to increase in value.

"*Maman*, I've got plans of my own." Claire dropped her backpack full of unloved textbooks and pulled out a letter. "I've been accepted."

Her mother held her arms out. "Wonderful! Université de Montréal? I'm so happy that law school finally accepted you."

Claire frowned. "*Non, maman.* I'm not going to be a lawyer. I want to do something interesting. For me."

"I thought we'd already settled this." She crossed her arms. "So what is it then, sociology, history?"

Claire pouted. "*Oui.* History. I love it." She thought her mother, at least, would understand, but it had been a losing battle the last few months.

"What can you do with a history degree? Work at Starbucks? No one will pay you to study the history of paintings."

"It's my life, my choice. I'm not here to make up for what you and *papa* regret in your own lives."

Her mother recoiled at the ferocity of the statement. She turned and stared out the window. The light through the window blinds painted horizontal bars on her face. "Such a waste."

"I want to know how we can make things better."

Mother looked at the floor. "You know what he'll say."

Her father arrived after six, looking ragged after another day in Quebec's pre-eminent high-tech company. He was a senior manager of a major aircraft project, but she didn't know many details about what he did there. All she saw was her father aging rapidly, trying in vain to compartmentalize the stress of the office and prevent it from infecting the family.

He set his briefcase down and hung his coat on the hook by the front door. Claire gave him a hug that was more worry than warmth. "*Papa*, when are you going to stop working there? It's killing you."

"Don't start that again."

"I wish you would get another job."

"It's not that easy at my age. With the salary and the bonus, we can afford our trips and your brother's hockey camps."

Her *maudit* brother, Patrick, and his *maudit* unattainable dream of making it as a professional hockey player. He just wasn't that good. She could see he would never make the NHL. Why couldn't her parents? Their blindness was shocking.

She thought her father was important, with a big job, a big title, and lots of responsibility. He got it because he worked hard. That was his message to his children. Maybe he had fought for the job, but now it seemed to consume him, and he appeared more powerless than before, accepting his fate without a fight. She vowed never to be like that.

She thrust her letter in his face.

He read it in silence. "After all that we've done for you, *ma petite*?" He sighed.

"*Papa*, it's my decision."

He looked at her with sad eyes. "But law school would be good for you. You're studious. Your marks are good. You're strong-willed. It's a career. Don't throw it away with a history degree." Another sigh. "What do you get with that?"

"I don't know. That's why I'm going to university. To find out."

"I'll tell you what you get. Unemployment."

"You think I won't learn anything useful?"

"Name one person with a history degree who did anything useful."

"Lester Pearson, prime minister of Canada. One of the greats, you said once."

"You serious?"

"I checked on Wikipedia. I knew you were going to ask."

"So, you are going to Ontario then?"

"Yes. Guelph."

Her father shook his head and wheezed as he sat in his regular chair at the far end of the kitchen table. "You should stay here, with your people."

She threw him a look of disgust. "Our people?"

"I've worked with *les Anglos* for many years. They will never accept you."

The stress of his sagging career was clear in his droopy face and hunched shoulders. She would never be like him.

Back in her apartment, her white uniform tunic lay across her sofa like a flat corpse. Dressed in a ratty T-shirt with a coffee stain that countless washings failed to clean and grey track pants, her hair uncombed, Claire stayed in her one-bedroom apartment and ignored the spectacular view of Halifax Harbour. She chipped away at her tub of Häagen-Dazs chocolate-chip ice cream while some talk show blared from the TV. She didn't want to hear her parents say, "I told you so."

There was no one else she could talk to. She hadn't spoken to her navy friends in the months since she had been promoted to captain of the *Kingston*. There hadn't been time. The captain's chair had called to her, as if it had been waiting for a long time. During her first tour of duty as an ensign, she stood in awe at the chair where only the captain could sit.

Seven years in the navy wasn't a long time to wait for a first command. She had moved swiftly up the ranks. She passed several classmates from basic officer training. A few of the men did not accept that a woman could be a better officer than they could. She knew that they, or someone who sympathized with their plight, had passed around rumours about her supposed lack of virtue. About the *real* reason she had risen so fast. About who in the chain of command she had slept with. And how well she kept her liaisons secret.

If a man were subject to such a rumour, he'd gain "cred," but it wasn't the case with her. She could hear it in the way some of the junior sailors addressed her as "ma'am" on her last posting as the executive officer of another patrol vessel. With a snicker. With a leer that seeped from the raunchy scene they pictured in their heads.

She had long given up trying to correct the record with her fellow sailors. Her protests met with deadened eyes and raised shoulders. Some of her superior officers got a bit too close when discussing orders. One suggested taking shore leave together. Another told her to smile more.

She was trapped. There was little she could do. Complaining to her commanding officer would only get her a reputation as a difficult officer to work with and would damage her chances at promotion. She would have to bottle up her frustration, while the perpetrators interpreted silence as a de facto acceptance of their behaviour. She focused on her career and tried to be the best officer she could be. *It will be worth it in the end*, she told herself in the lonely nights with only the drone of the engines and indifferent bleeps of the navigation console for company.

The first time she sat in the chair on the *Kingston* — her first command — an electric shock surged through her body. She had come home. This was where she belonged, surrounded by *her* crew. Ready to do what was right, helping those in need. To use the lethal power of her ship to enforce good over evil.

For the first time, she felt complete. Becoming captain vindicated her earlier decisions that had crushed her parents' expectations. They wanted an honourable professional, a son-in-law, and grandchildren; she gave them an odd career choice, one where women stood a good chance of being sexually assaulted, had to endure long periods of absence and as a result had little likelihood of finding a serious boyfriend. Sure, there had been plenty of offers, but each was tainted by chain-of-command issues. The offers had come from her superior officers or from someone she supervised. None could be accepted.

These problems faded as Claire considered again her current position. Someone on the *Kingston* was trying to sabotage her career by making false allegations about her conduct directly to her boss. Even her new-found power wasn't enough to shield her from harassment.

And Captain Hall had taken away what mattered most to her.

She stared at the phone that wasn't ringing and thought about her future — once sunny and warm, now clouding over, threatened by an imminent gale that was beginning to shred her self-confidence, leaving only a pile of self-doubt.

SEVENTEEN

DANIEL JOLTED OUT OF A DEEP SLEEP. The clock on the night table glowed four something. In the darkness, he heard only his own startled breathing and the buzz of the fridge from the kitchen. He grasped at fragments of his dream. Before Emily. The beginning. Ten years ago. A steaming June afternoon.

He remembered being exhausted that day, struggling to focus as he stuffed the final papers into his briefcase and thought about his flight to Tokyo. He had worked two long years at Duhamel, McWhirter & Lin, supporting complex business negotiations between Canadian manufacturers, their Chinese production companies, and the Chinese government. In spite of his best professional efforts, for every entrepreneur who had succeeded at negotiating low-cost manufacturing of their products in this country, ten others had failed, whimpering all the way home, with their corporate tails between their legs.

His office occupied the southwest corner on the thirty-fifth floor of a spanking new tower a few blocks east of the high-end Wangfujing shopping district in Beijing. As with most things there, it looked good on the outside, but he never quite trusted the workmanship. He expected to arrive one morning to see the office reduced to a pile of rubble.

On the very few days when pollution didn't smear the air with grey and a taste like death and dust, he could see a vast swath of the giant metropolis at his feet. It gave him a sense of power, a feeling of control over his destiny — even in this country, bursting with the energy of a billion people.

He had second thoughts about grabbing the bottle of Glenmorangie. The twenty-five-year-old single malt was a present from Jean-Philippe, his unofficial second employer at the Canadian embassy: thanks for a job well done. His job there as trade attaché wasn't complete fiction; he did indeed deal with trade issues between companies.

He decided he had earned the bottle, so he snatched it. As he turned away from the floor-to-ceiling window, he saw his whole life squeezed into four cardboard boxes stacked in the corner near the door. Each had a sticker with the company logo, his name, and his new address at company headquarters in Montreal. His overseas tour of duty, a requirement of all mid-level executives, was over; it was time to come back home for his pick of more senior assignments.

Wang Jie, his department's secretary, leaned his head into the open doorway. He was always dressed in the best Italian suits despite a local Chinese salary. "Taxi here, Da-ni-er."

Daniel said, "Xie xie," patted the top box to reassure it that they would soon see each other again, placed the bottle in his briefcase, and picked it up.

He shook hands with everyone in his group on his way out. Everyone smiled. He thought they liked working with each other. They had appreciated his speech at a local restaurant a few hours earlier. He had spoken of friendship and cultural ties. He had even tried his hand at a few lame *xiangsheng* Smothers Brothers–style puns in Mandarin with one of the local vice-presidents who had the right sense of humour. They laughed on cue at the requisite punchlines and tossed scattered compliments afterward about how much his Chinese had improved in his two years in Beijing. He was proud of his progress with such a challenging language. But, as he listened to his colleagues, he stepped outside himself for just a moment, watched his performance, and wondered if he was just playing a part in a play that someone else had written.

A gleaming black Mercedes SL sedan with tinted windows and, thank God, air conditioning waited in front of the main doors to the office tower. His name was written in Chinese characters on a small card, held by a driver dressed in an immaculate dark suit and tie. He nodded to the driver, who opened the door. He slid in and looked forward to shutting out China for an hour or so. He fell asleep instantly.

He awoke with a start as the door opened to reveal the human maelstrom that was the Beijing airport. He thanked the driver, got out with his briefcase, and grabbed his carry-on bag.

His platinum points card allowed him to short-circuit the check-in and security clearance process. His feet were resting on a footstool in the Japan Airlines business lounge less than thirty minutes after exiting the taxi.

With a glass of California Merlot in hand, he wondered what he was returning home to. Montreal was the last place he wanted to be. No one would greet him at the airport. Acquaintances had drifted away because he hadn't had the energy to maintain contact. He had somehow fine-tuned the ability to corrode any relationship over the years. There was no one left in the city he could call a friend. He would go to his assigned hotel. The company would help him find an apartment or a house. Maybe a house in Westmount. But he would be less conspicuous with a small apartment in NDG, Montreal West, or the West Island.

But something *was* pulling him back, unseen but powerful, like a gravitational force, drawing him into the orbit of something he didn't understand.

It wasn't family. He had no wife, no children, no family to speak of. The trauma of the shocking loss of his parents lingered. At first, he hungered to exact revenge on the scammer, the trusted financial planner who stole his parents' life savings. The police said it was an accident on Autoroute 15. Fresh snow. Dim evening light. Driving too fast. But Daniel knew better. They had had enough humiliation. Decided to check out. Together. Rage burned like acid. He had stood alone, abandoned, and helpless.

Fate soon bounded his life on two sides. He initially trusted the judicial system to punish the so-called financial expert. After an interminable process, the guilty was sentenced to five years. Now Daniel knew the value of his parents' lives. There was nothing he could do. He didn't want to be around when the criminal was released. A future of happy memories vanished in one terrible night. He vowed to find a way to leave the city. With no siblings to share mourning, he had refocused his grief into an unassailable personal drive. He was sure that it was the intense pressure of his later careers that interfered with any attempt at forming lasting relationships with women.

So why am I returning to Montreal?

It wasn't his age. Thirty-five wasn't too old. He sensed that there was much yet to be done before he reached the apogee of his career. He was one of the younger vice-presidents of the company, and his career seemed assured now that he had finished his tour in the Far East, with results that even the CEO had called "spectacular." He had been promised his choice of plum assignments. But surprisingly, the thought left him feeling empty. Something that he had chased throughout his career was right in front of him, and with his colleagues egging him on, encouraging but jealous, he thought about pushing it all away. His path seemed to lie elsewhere, like a star, distant, bright, but not ready to reveal what lay beyond its glare.

Why am I going back?

Maybe it was a desire to simplify his life. He had worked two careers simultaneously, and that effort had taken its toll. Not satisfied with helping Canadian companies succeed in the world's soon-to-be number one market, within three months of arriving in China he had taken on another position. He had accepted an invitation to attend a soirée at the Canadian embassy. There, he had met Jean-Philippe, an attaché who shared stories of tempestuous Montreal weather, crumbling infrastructure, sparkling culture, and city corruption. At the end of the evening, the attaché had made an interesting proposal.

In the airport lounge, the screen above the row of wine, whisky, and brandy bottles flashed the upcoming departures. Flight JL 22 to Tokyo Haneda was now delayed two hours. He was stuck. Normally, he would spend the time in the business lounge, putting the finishing touches on a presentation, double-checking financial figures to present on behalf of the Canadian client, or calling to confirm restaurant reservations necessary to seal a deal. But this trip existed only to move him twelve time zones back home. With a special stop just for him. He would spend two days at his favourite *onsen* spa just outside the ski resort of Hakuba: to relax, get a massage, and celebrate the conclusion of his tenure in Asia.

Even being this tired and having nothing official to occupy his time, his brain craved some problem to work on, some target to follow, and he had little experience with shutting off. He scanned the lounge for something, anything, of interest. CCTV, the official Chinese state broadcaster, blared from one wall-sized television, while NHK from Japan and BBC were on the others. The room filled up fast with middle-aged men, outfitted in identical dark suit + white shirt + tie combinations, drinking glasses of their favourite booze, talking on their phones, or reading newspapers. Available seats disappeared fast. The one to his left was soon occupied by a woman, something rare in this neck of the business woods.

She was a tall, wavy-haired brunette. But with his wine glass now empty, he didn't notice how the glow from the TVs lit up her eyes, emphasized her smooth cheekbones, or showed how pretty she was. He also forgot how he excelled at incomplete relationships.

"Hi." He tried English first.

She responded immediately. "Hi."

Now what?

"My name is Daniel."

She seemed to be debating whether or not to tell him her real name. "Vanessa."

"Hi, Vanessa. Are you coming or going?"

She looked puzzled. "Excuse me?"

"Are you coming back home or going away from home?"

"Back home." With the few words she had spoken, he had detected an Aussie accent, or something related.

"Where's that?"

The answer must have been complex. She paused before she answered. "Sydney. I live there now. But home is Auckland."

"And what kind of work do you do?" Seemed like a good question to ask a single Kiwi *wahine* in a Japan Airlines business lounge.

"I'm in advertising. I'm a manager for a marketing company."

He said nothing more, to see if she would want to continue the conversation. He didn't have to wait long. "And you?"

"I am, or I was, a business consultant here in Beijing."

"You were? What happened? Nothing bad I trust."

"No. My assignment here is complete, and I'm on my way back home. Two years in this country is enough."

"I can't even imagine. I've only been here for two weeks and I'm overwhelmed. Where's home?"

"Canada. And what brought you to China?"

"I had meetings in Beijing. Tried to get a contract to market Maotai in Australia."

"Were you successful?"

"Sort of. Got one contract signed, but the second one will require another trip in a month or so. It's so far to go. I don't know how many more of these trips I have in me."

His tiredness evaporated, replaced by adrenalin, urgency, and a complete focus on her. Her eyes that sparkled like miniature galaxies.

"Are you on the flight to Haneda, too?"

She flashed a smile. "Yes. I'm taking the flight out of Narita to Sydney tomorrow night."

They would have never crossed paths if the flight hadn't been delayed. For a moment, Daniel ignored his training, soaked deep in science and rationality, and believed in fate; this had not been a chance meeting, but had been somehow preordained. They sat twelve rows apart on the short flight to Tokyo and met again at the baggage claim where she heaved a large, pink, indestructible-looking bag from the carousel.

They had drinks and dinner at the hotel restaurant.

Dinner became room service in her room the morning after.

* ✳ *

Vanessa didn't learn about Daniel's second vocation until just before the wedding. She didn't react well. In retrospect, Daniel wondered if it was a harbinger of the rocky relationship to come.

"You're a spy?" she said, eyes wide in shock.

He tried to calm her, sensing the betrayal in her voice. "Not a spy. I helped out from time to time. I just told some people at the embassy about what I was doing at work."

"And did your work include Chinese companies?"

"Of course. I collected information that could pose a commercial or security threat to my country."

"Does that include me?" She pointed at herself for emphasis.

He looked at the floor for a second before returning his gaze to her. "I did have to report that I wanted to marry you."

"You *asked* their permission?" Now her hands were high in the air.

"It sounds worse when you say it like that. You're not Canadian. You're a foreign national. They didn't like that."

"So they won't let you marry me? Is that what this conversation is about? *Two days* before our wedding?"

"I took them out of the discussion." He held her shoulders with his hands, staring directly into her eyes. "I quit."

She paused before responding, the tension gone. "You can leave, just like that?"

"I had a short-term contract. I didn't want to do it anymore. I was tired of the training. The boot camp. The paranoia. The terrible choices." He held her tight. "It prevents you from forming close relationships."

* ✳ *

Three months after their first encounter, they married. They held a bare bones ceremony in the Church of the Good Shepherd on Lake Tekapo, New Zealand. As the sun peeked through the windows of the church, her father couldn't hold back his tears, while her mother sat stoically, chanting about the need to start a family close to home. Naturally, his side of the church was empty.

She was the best transaction he'd ever completed. She gave him new purpose. He took a leave of absence from the firm so he and Vanessa could spend their first year together in Australia. Their time became a whirring kaleidoscope of adventures: tramping in the Outback, lounging on various beaches on the weekends. He even tried Vegemite. Prolonged separation from the constant red-line pace of the consulting and intelligence worlds forced him to question his earlier choices. He had more money than he knew what to do with, but work had left him with a hollow feeling inside, questioning why he was doing it at all. Now his life had a reason. He would build a life with Vanessa.

Returning to school was her idea. He convinced her to try out the sub-Arctic climate of Canada's main party city. It worked well for the first few years. She quickly found a marketing job with Cossette, working with some of their American clients. But the sunny lifestyle grew stormy after Emily was born on a crisp March afternoon. After graduating with his doctorate in business administration, Daniel found work on the East Coast as a junior professor. But Vanessa was through with an unstable expat life. She had other plans, and divorce soon followed. Daniel moved without them, leaving the only family he had left in Montreal. He returned every other weekend, but raising an infant alone in a foreign city was too much for Vanessa. Daniel's irregular visits to the apartment triggered more fights with her, leaving Emily crying at the far end of the hallway.

Now, in his Halifax apartment, with starlight dimly shining through his bedroom window, he sat at the edge of his bed, remembering the last, precious Technicolor image of his dissolving family. As he wondered what they were doing now, Daniel let a tear trickle down his cheek. He was down to a family of one for the second time.

EIGHTEEN

LARCH BELIEVED HE WAS a cautious man. He thought this trait had allowed him to live much longer than his professional colleagues. "Leave no trace" wasn't just a good motto; it was environmentally friendly, too. He returned his rental car, took a cab to the Delta Barrington Hotel downtown, and registered with an official-looking British passport under the name Mitchell Gant.

His faint English accent impressed the tall, dark-haired beauty at check-in. She smiled and he smiled back, careful not to indulge in any flirtation. He didn't want to be remembered by anyone. The receptionist was certainly attractive, but he wasn't there to pursue women. It would be unprofessional. And Sandrine would not be pleased. At least until he bought her some guilt jewellery at the duty-free on the way back home.

A small envelope was waiting for him at check-in. He tucked it into his jacket pocket and strode to the elevator. After examining his room, he looked out the window at a view of the harbour; Dartmouth was barely visible in the fog. He had packed enough clothes for three days, plenty of time for his new assignment. He thought he might even be done tonight, depending on his luck.

Time to check for any updates on his assignment. He opened the envelope. It contained only a SIM card. He took out his Samsung smartphone and swapped his SIM card with the new one, snapping the case closed. With his phone in hand, he walked back to reception and asked the clerk for the nearest internet café. She was a bit puzzled, since the hotel offered free Wi-Fi, but she pointed to a café in the mall next to the hotel. He thanked her with his best imitation of Prince William (or Basil Fawlty, he couldn't be sure).

The problem with hotel internet was that he had to identify himself. He had to give his name and room number. Anonymity was more assured if he used the internet in the café next door in the Historic Properties Mall. He nursed a small coffee and logged in to the open Wi-Fi and checked a Gmail account with a long, seemingly haphazard combination of letters and numbers. Yes, three draft mails had been written less than an hour ago.

The first email was short. 12:00. Ash.

The second one said Meet today. Birch.

The third email had no subject. It contained only an address and a time.

NINETEEN

THE SLANTED LIGHT of another frosty morning streamed through the floor-to-ceiling windows. Larch felt a weak heat on his face. He waited in a café across the street from a small condo on Barrington Street, in the heart of downtown Halifax, and only a few blocks from the Westin. Commuters rushed along the sidewalk, leaving moments of conversations in discrete puffs rising in the air. The target should have arrived by now. He checked his watch for the umpteenth time.

And there he was. Across the street, opening the door of the condo entrance. Larch waited a few moments. The light flicked on in a condo on the second floor. The one he expected. He knew the target lived alone.

It was time to move. He stood up, parked his empty coffee mug in the grey plastic tub, strode out the door, and crossed the street busy with passing cars. The lock on the outer door was easy to pick, no more than ten seconds. He shifted, so he looked like he was fumbling for his key. In the morning rush, he was sure no one would notice him.

The elevator dinged and the doors slid open to reveal a short hallway, a small mirror on the opposite wall, and doors to two condo units. Light seeped from under the door on the left.

Larch knocked five times in a broken rhythm so the sound would jump out from any background noise of the city. He heard footsteps from the other side of the door. The handle turned, and the door opened to reveal a middle-aged, balding man in a wrinkled white shirt and black slacks. There were dark circles under his eyes, evidence of a long, uninterrupted shift at the hotel.

"Yes?" His expression was one of unfamiliarity, surprise, or maybe disdain.

Larch didn't give him any time to react. He pushed the man aside, stepped into the room, and closed the door behind him.

"What are you doing? You can't just barge in," the man said.

Larch put a finger of his left hand to his own lips, ordering the man to be quiet, while his right hand fumbled in his jacket pocket.

"You don't know me, Mr. Carignan, but we need to have a chat."

"How do you know my name?"

"Please sit down." Larch pulled out his Beretta and pointed it at the man. He motioned to the chair behind him. Mr. Carignan sat compliantly, while his face betrayed the shock of finding himself in such an incomprehensible situation.

Larch grabbed a short, black cylinder from his other pocket. He began to screw it onto the muzzle of his pistol while he walked to the only window in the living room and checked over his shoulder for any sign that he'd been followed.

"You're the hotel manager at the Westin, are you not?" A police car crawled southward in the morning traffic.

"How do you know that?"

The cruiser moved down the street and then out of range. Satisfied that he could detect no suspicious movement along Barrington Street, he turned to face his target.

"Yesterday, you saw a dead body at your hotel."

"Who told you that?"

"There was another man with you."

"What do you mean?"

"The man who was in the elevator with you."

"You mean poor Mr. …?" Carignan's expression went blank for a moment, and then anger stressed his eyebrows, chin, and cheeks. "Oh, him."

"Tell me about this other man."

"Why do you care?"

"Because I do." He waved the gun.

"He said he was a colleague of Mr. —"

"Forrestal. Go on."

"Yes, Mr. Forrestal. This guy bothered the entire front staff. Very pushy."

"So you just let him in the room?"

"I asked him whether he had a relationship with Mr. Forrestal."

"Did he?"

"Not at first. But then he did admit that he was worried about Mr. Forrestal's health. He wanted to be sure that he had taken his heart pills for the day."

Larch's mouth dropped open. "And you believed it?"

"We have provided Mr. Forrestal with special services before. He had a wide range of, let's say, diverse personal needs."

"So you opened the door, just like that?"

"He thought that Mr. Forrestal had forgotten his pills. I had no reason to doubt him. He seemed to know a lot about him, things even I didn't know."

Larch's eyes narrowed. This professor was no bookworm with limited social skills. He was able to convince the manager of a five-star hotel that he knew about the private medical condition of a very prominent and powerful businessman. The professor deserved further investigation. "And it was you who called the police?"

"Who *are* you?"

Larch raised the pistol, aiming it at the man's chest. "I'm just cleaning up a loose end." He only needed to fire once. He fired three times, picked up the ejected shell casings with his handkerchief, and stuffed them in his jacket pocket. He was a professional, after all.

TWENTY

RESIDUAL IMAGES OF Vanessa and Emily slashed at Daniel's attempts to sleep. His mind generated snapshots of them at the beach: Emily eagerly building a sand castle, Vanessa lying on a towel, head up, watching proudly through sunglasses the artistic talent of their seven-year-old. His mind flashed forward to see the Emily of the future, staring at herself in her bedroom mirror, taking one last, nervous look before meeting her prom date waiting awkwardly downstairs. There she is at eighteen, tall, beautiful, strong, and ambitious — ready to take on university, ready to take on the world. Vanessa putters nearby, making last minute adjustments around Emily's dorm room. She places a small family picture on the windowsill. Mother and daughter. Another picture with Emily and probably a best friend, arm in arm. As the scenes scrolled by, he wondered, stepping outside of himself, where was he? Had he left any trace of himself in her life?

Around seven, he gave up, climbed out of bed, and tried to scrub away the sadness with a shower and shave. He resolved to be part of Emily's life, no matter what separated them. Tonight, he would tell her himself.

Daniel emerged from his apartment building dressed in his professor uniform: a dark grey shirt and black jeans covered by a heavy Gore-Tex coat, with black leather oxfords, and a brown leather backpack swaying from his shoulder. Walking ten minutes to campus, Daniel replayed the security camera image in his mind, trying to note the distinguishing characteristics of the murder suspect, and blocking out images of Emily. The black clothes. He was tall, over six feet. He filled out his coat quite well, suggesting he was in good physical shape. The black toque was odd. Maybe to cover his hair? Or he was bald and self-conscious? The man's face wasn't clear in the image. He tried to recall seeing the man walk to the elevator while humming a tune. He had only had a brief glance, and he hadn't been paying attention. He had been focused on preparing to meet Forrestal. *What did he look like?* A fuzzy image of a man in dark clothes slid along an ill-defined corridor. The dark apparition moved into the elevator. And he had never turned around. Normally, one would turn to face the panel and push the right button. But he hadn't. Of course. It was deliberate. The man hadn't wanted anyone to see his face.

Daniel had a few minutes to freshen up before class. He walked through a crowd of people in the main hallway to the Sobey School of Business building and darted into the busy men's bathroom, pushing through three men on their way out.

Larch followed the second target into a men's bathroom. He stopped in front of the nearest sink, turned the faucet, sprayed some water onto his face, and watched the target enter a stall and close the door. A half-dozen students lingered at the other sinks; another two stood at the urinals. His reflection in the mirror stared back: just another stressed professional who had left the office in a hurry to make his class.

He tried to look forgettable. Some would call him lanky, a bit tall and a bit too thin. It was part of his trade. He lived with considerable stress, far more than the average executive. But he handled it exceptionally well.

He didn't just manage people's lives; he managed their probability of living. His job was to make that probability equal to zero at the right time, and he had already done that twice in the last twenty-four hours.

He specialized in taking a life in a way that was difficult to trace. His targets were not victims, since that implied innocence. No, these people deserved their fates. They were important people but also people who had harmed his clients. He was very discreet, obsessed with leaving no evidence, not even a fingerprint that could be traced. Five years of success had given him a special reputation in his field. And he charged appropriately. Only the very wealthy or well connected could contact him and afford him.

In the mirror, he saw a face that looked older than his thirtysomething years. Long, streaking wrinkles crinkled around his sallow eyes. He still had his black hair, although grey had begun to seep in along the sides. A Toronto Blue

Jays baseball cap and black-framed glasses disguised his face just enough. A SMU sweatshirt, blue jeans, and white sneakers completed the older-student look.

Taking a life was not easy, but he had deadened his empathy with extensive research of the targets to understand why they deserved to die. Also, an expensive taste in rare cognac, the experience of multiple kills, and a comfortable fortune in a Cayman Island numbered account helped him remain indifferent. He had considered buying a small island once but had decided that doing so might attract too much attention. That was the last thing he wanted.

He was getting tired of the lies, though. His girlfriend, thirteen years his junior, waited for him at his beachside house in Mustique to complete his next "road trip." Sandrine knew nothing of his profession, of course. Maybe after a few more assignments, he could think of cutting down on his workload and spending more time with her.

He had seen much of the world in his travels, but hadn't really seen it; he had only really paid attention to his work. Paris had been three passports, an airport, a hotel, one street in the *neuvième arrondissement*, three silenced shots, then a metro ride to the Gare de Lyon, followed by a quick TGV trip to Geneva. Maybe he could take Sandrine to see the Champs-Elysées, the Tour Eiffel, and Les Jardins du Luxembourg. He smiled at the image of the happy tourists, and longed to join them in their ignorance.

His smile dissolved as he returned to the task at hand. He had been sloppy, and if he didn't fix it soon, his reputation would suffer. His client had proved to be a surprise. Referred by the Washington, D.C.–based group he had worked with several times, the client had at first seemed to him to be yet another senior political operative, seeking specialized competence in direct and targeted action. The assignment seemed more to involve something personal, though. This made it different than his other jobs. In any event, the business case for the job was clear-cut. The original target, a coward, had crossed an un-crossable line, and he was deservedly punished. Targets deserved no sympathy, but collateral targets were a different matter. They had done nothing to harm anyone, yet they had to be dealt with — just another contingency. Another unpleasant aspect of being a professional; it just had to be done.

With a few photos and contact information in hand, he only needed one phone call and an hour on the internet to find his new target. Birch had provided the rest. The target had a class beginning at noon. He had waited patiently until the target appeared.

The target emerged from the stall, washed his hands, dried them with a few sharp flicks, and walked toward the exit. Two students remained at the urinals.

Larch kept his gaze lowered to avoid direct eye contact. He reached into his jacket pocket with his right hand and walked up to the target, as two middle-aged men barged through the door and brushed the target aside. Then a herd of younger men, students, sporting T-shirts with the abstract logo of the university, flowed into the bathroom.

It wouldn't be easy now. He couldn't finish the job here. He couldn't do it in the classroom either. He needed to isolate the target so he would have total control of the situation. No surprises. No witnesses. No evidence. He was a patient hunter. He would keep following and his chance would come again.

Daniel returned to his office, gathered his lecture material in a binder, and closed the door behind him as he proceeded to the classroom in the adjoining building. His attention was focused on three questions with no answers. *Why was Forrestal killed? Would the killer know my identity? Would the killer look for me now?*

His cellphone buzzed. The display said HRM Police. It was MacKinnon.

"Yes, Detective?"

"Where are you?"

"On my way to class. On campus."

"Are you alone?"

"Of course."

"Get over here. We need to talk. Now," said MacKinnon.

"What's going on? I've got a class in a few minutes."

"Your life is in danger."

TWENTY-ONE

GARTH HAD FINISHED BARKING his morning orders to the campaign team. The minions returned to their desks to start working on their new assignments. As he snapped shut his binder of notes, his secret cellphone buzzed with an incoming text message.

Check email.

He swiped a few screens and read the email waiting in the draft folder. The message had been updated only minutes earlier.

Confirming instructions. Will create headline event at No campaign demonstration, as ordered. Regular fee. Ash.

He erased the email and replaced it with Approved. Must be complete by dinnertime today.

Time to start disrupting the enemy's campaign. Garth leaned on his desk. He hyperventilated thinking of the successful conclusion of his plan; his vision compressed until only a small, thin tunnel of light remained.

TWENTY-TWO

"ARE YOU FREE?"

The driver nodded. He didn't speak; he just sat like a lump, a large lump, one who after a long career of professional sitting barely squeezed behind the steering wheel. He was over sixty and unshaven, and he stared at Daniel from the rear-view mirror. Apparently, his eyes did all the talking that was necessary.

Daniel ignored the eyes and gave the police station address. The cabbie shifted into drive and accelerated with a jolt. On the radio, an annoying, know-it-all all-news-channel host ranted about politics, immigration, and unemployment in quick succession.

Once they turned onto South Park, the cabbie spoke. "There's something going on ahead. Looks like something big."

"Can't you get around it?"

The driver shook his head. "I don't know if I can get you to the station. That's a big crowd. Where did they all come from?"

Daniel slid the window down and stuck his head into the frosty air. Hundreds of people spilled out from the Public Gardens to occupy the street. A few cops were scattered around and trying to corral the crowd away from Victoria Park and onto Spring Garden Road, but they seemed outnumbered and overwhelmed. Cars were jammed between the crowd ahead and the traffic behind. The cab lurched to a stop at the curb.

Daniel grabbed his backpack and opened the door. "I'll get out here and get another cab on the other side." He paid the fare in cash. The eyes in the mirror did not approve of the modest tip.

Daniel stepped out into the low sunlight and sighed at the swarm of humanity not fifty metres ahead. Drums banging. A cacophony of a hundred simultaneous conversations, each trying to be heard over the others. A bright red sign proclaiming "We love you, Alberta!" caught his eye. Beside it, smaller ones: "Keep my Canada together," and "Vote No!"

Parts of the crowd chanted something with a bunch of vowels that rhymed after a few beats, but Daniel couldn't make out the words. He walked through snow and slush, approaching the crush that flowed between him and his urgent appointment with MacKinnon.

The crowd was still thin where Daniel walked. Where the mass of people surged down Spring Garden, the road seemed impenetrable. But there was plenty of room in front of the café where he stopped. At first, he didn't notice the man to his right, as he was lost in his own thoughts about how he was going to navigate the horde ahead. Then he spotted him. The man was around thirty, at least six foot five. Two hundred pounds of death, wrapped in a leather jacket, black jeans, and black boots. Daniel imagined dense, dark tattoos on both arms, commemorating each kill. He could easily pass for a biker gang member. Yet his arms seemed oddly too short for his frame. A massive amoeba of a man, used to getting his way.

The man threw a rock at the café window, and it shattered, spraying pieces of glass onto the sidewalk. "Mind your own fuckin' business," he said to no one in particular.

Another man approached. "What are you doing?" He was in his late thirties, holding a "We love you Alberta!" sign high on a flimsy stick. His head only reached the shoulders of the first man.

Amoeba Man walked right up to him, pushing his finger into the other man's arm. "Keep your fuckin' nose out of my business." He jumped, ripped the sign from the stick, and stomped it into the ground. "Alberta is for Albertans to decide."

The second man turned around. "Stop. You can't do this." A woman standing nearby, with her own "Vote No!" sign explaining which side she was on, joined the fracas, shouting a surprisingly loud "Hey, fuck off" at Mr. Amoeba.

He didn't take it well. He grabbed the stick from the hands of Small Man, held it high, and glared at the woman, who was not intimidated and glared back at him. The small man hip-checked the massive brute, trying to retrieve his stick, but Amoeba just thwacked him on the head with it.

The woman reacted immediately. "What the fuck are you doing?"

Daniel didn't care about the referendum. He did know that Alberta wanted to secede from Confederation — it was the news headline for the past few weeks — but he no longer took sides. He had his own problems to deal with. On the other hand, the man represented an immediate threat.

Daniel sensed that the aggressor would be within his defensive circle in a few more strides. Daniel could move to the right, off the sidewalk, and into a low pile of dirty snow to allow them to argue unhindered. Tempers were sure to flare. Any fight would be short and would end only with the shorter one getting a broken nose or, worse, splayed unconscious on the road. He kept walking straight ahead. The other man would have to move to his right to avoid the collision with Daniel and his backpack.

The smaller man froze in fear. Daniel sized up the situation in a second. Should he interfere or keep on walking?

TWENTY-THREE

LARCH SCANNED FOR ANYONE who looked out of place in the Uncommon Grounds café. Two baristas, one a young man with a nose ring and a shaved head, the other a redhead in her early twenties with a tattoo on her right arm, scurried between the cash register and the espresso machine. Two jittery customers waited in line, anticipating their shot of caffeine. A young couple occupied a table in the far corner, trying to catch the faint heat of the sun while they studied. He couldn't quite make out the subjects of the textbooks on the table; probably chemistry, or maybe economics. The other dozen or so tables were empty.

He placed his carry-on bag on a chair in front of a table next to the exit, just in case. He joined the line at the cash then placed his order. He returned to his seat, nursed his drink, and never stopped watching the room. He checked his watch and waited.

One latte and a cookie later his phone vibrated.

"Yes?"

He nodded to no one in particular as he listened to a short monologue from Ash. He said, "Well done," before clicking the phone off and slipping it back into his shirt pocket. Ash, a member of his client's group, the Alberta Independence Movement, had flown in a biker gang member to disrupt the demonstration a few blocks down the street. Judging from the whine of a police car, its siren blaring as it streaked past the café, Ash's *agent provocateur* had been successful.

A moment later, an older gentleman opened the door. He looked as if he had money to spare. He was tall, stately looking, slightly overweight, with a balding head trimmed with grey around the edges. He wore the requisite red scarf tied loosely around his neck. As he approached the cash, his eyes darted nervously around. Larch kept his eyes down, nevertheless tracking the man.

The gentleman grabbed a coffee and a copy of the *Coast* tabloid, stood still, and scanned the room. He noticed Larch's carry-on bag and approached his table.

"Larch?"

Larch nodded. "Birch?"

Larch motioned for Birch to take the seat facing him. Birch sat down and placed his coffee on the table.

Larch checked his watch. "What can you tell me about him?"

"Let's get something straight. I don't work for you. You work for him."

"We don't have much time."

"And he's a good friend."

"You were his supervisor, he said."

"That's right. He did an MBA. When I was at the University of Calgary. I'm only doing this because he asked me for a personal favour."

"Now that we have the excuses out of the way, what can you tell me about Mr. Ritter?"

Birch handed him a small piece of paper with writing on it. "Here's his address."

"I know that already."

"Have you talked with him? Did you convince him?"

"Not exactly. I didn't have the opportunity. But I will certainly try again."

"And you'll contact me to confirm that he agrees to our terms?"

Larch nodded slowly. "As soon as he agrees."

"He's smart and stubborn, so you'll have to spell out the benefits for him."

"I don't think that will be a problem. I've convinced many others before."

"So Patrick said. But he's smart. He'll ask a lot of questions."

There was a short silence before Larch said, "How smart?"

"He did some work in the industry before he joined the university."

"What kind of work?"

"Consulting."

"What does consulting work mean?"

"Writing reports."

Larch had just met Birch and already he didn't like him. Birch was condescending, dumbing down his answers, and leaving out useful and important details. "So that's good preparation for being a professor?"

Birch seemed to sneer as he answered. "He's not a professor. He's an assistant professor. More junior."

Larch let it slide. A professional gets the needed information. "What else does he do?"

"How should I know? Oil painting? Bird watching? Macramé? I have no idea."

Birch wasn't telling him anything useful. He would have to scope out the target himself before trying again. "So we're done?"

"I don't want to be involved. That was my deal."

Larch stood up and walked out of the café, leaving the door to slowly squeak shut.

TWENTY-FOUR

DANIEL CLOSED HIS EYES FOR A SECOND, trying to will himself out of the tense situation, as would a little boy, but the threat reappeared as soon as he opened them. He scanned the crowd but saw no police officer. He stopped, still holding his backpack over his left shoulder, and adjusted his glasses. "Excuse me. Can I get through?"

The continent of a man did not release his grip on the stick. He held it low, like a samurai sword. "You a cop?"

"No, just trying to get through."

Small Man checked the top of his head for blood. Mr. Amoeba pivoted to face Daniel. "Then fuck off, old man!"

Another woman popped out from the crowd. "Brian, are you okay?"

Brian was definitely not okay, judging from the blood trickling down from a gash on his head.

"Not your fucking problem," said the man.

"Are you all right?" Daniel spoke to Brian but kept his eyes fixed on the aggressor.

Brian mumbled something, incoherent with shock.

"If there's a problem, I can call the police. They can help." Daniel took out his cellphone. Before he could dial, the aggressor swatted it onto the road.

"Don't need no fuckin' police."

Daniel sensed a crowd gathering, but he kept his focus on the mountain with two feet, two massive hands, and a bad attitude. He seemed to fit a familiar pattern.

"See, I can solve this right now." The man switched his hold of the stick so that it resembled a baseball bat in his right hand and, without warning, swung and cracked Brian's face.

Brian reeled and crumpled onto the ground. The man turned and swung again but missed, as Daniel anticipated the strike and swerved his head slightly to the right. The giant raised the stick high again and slashed downward. Daniel jerked back and dropped his backpack. He felt the breeze as the stick arced past his left ear. The man was fast and knew how to fight.

"Stand still," the man barked.

Daniel took another short step back. Now, the backpack lay between Daniel and the assailant. The man took a step forward. He hadn't noticed the bag. For a second, he was off balance. That's when Daniel struck.

Daniel could not punch hard enough to hurt such a huge person. But he could stop him in ways that didn't require so much force. He aimed for the giant's Adam's apple and jabbed it once with his fingers. Hard. He could hear cartilage creak. The man's eyes bulged, while he grabbed his neck instinctively with his free hand.

But the man soon shook it off. *The guy is tough*, Daniel thought.

Daniel swerved to the man's right, grabbed the wrist still holding the stick, and jammed his leg so it was behind the man's knee. He pulled down on the wrist and twisted backward. The man grimaced and grunted as Daniel used his own weight against him. They slammed onto the sidewalk and snow, and the stick tumbled uselessly to the ground.

But he recovered quickly. He shoved Daniel aside as if he were a small child and sprung up without even using his hands to prop himself up. Like in martial arts movies. He was surprisingly strong.

Daniel used the momentum from the push to roll out of range. He stood up, fists in front, ready for the next assault. The man rushed again, swinging his enormous right hand with a roundhouse punch that Daniel could see coming. He stepped back, then in and to the left. His fist hammered the spot behind the man's rib cage where the kidney should be. That should have caused indescribable pain and immobilized the man. It didn't. He just grimaced and launched a short back-fist flick from his right hand that slammed into Daniel's right temple. Daniel dropped to the pavement and couldn't see for a moment. His vision returned only to see the man kicking the backpack out of the way and advancing to finish the job. The bag sailed in the air and crashed onto one of the steps in front of the pile of broken glass.

Daniel stood up, a bit wobbly, and took another step back and to the right. A crowd started to close in. He was losing manoeuvring room fast. The man advanced, enraged. Daniel, weakened, was now in mortal danger.

It was then that a small, red can clanged the man's head from behind. The tin dropped to the sidewalk and rolled onto the curb beside Daniel's foot. He saw the familiar red Campbell's soup logo.

A momentary silence rippled through the crowd.

The man felt the back of his head and turned to see who had thrown the soup. Daniel could see a woman holding a can of soup in each hand, a canvas grocery bag at her feet. She was a bit shorter than he was, blond hair, wrapped in a dark-coloured parka with the hood down over her shoulders. Even at this distance, her eyes bored holes into the man.

"Hey, doofus," she called.

"Who the fuck are you?"

Daniel stood as the man turned his body to face the can thrower. Daniel went for his knee. The knee is a strong joint when it's moving within its range of motion, but it's weak when pressed from the side. The move didn't require much force, and in his disoriented state, it was all Daniel could do. He gave a short, sharp kick. A loud, sickening crunch confirmed that the joint had broken. The man collapsed onto his back, banging his head on the pavement. Unconscious in a flash. Daniel jumped and grabbed the man's midsection and the stick-wielding arm. The woman advanced and grabbed the other arm. They both stared at each other, panting from the exertion, their breath steaming and mixing in the air.

"Would somebody please call the police?" said Daniel.

The man was out cold, but neither Daniel nor the woman took any chances.

"You're not going to thank me?" she said as she glared at him. Daniel heard smooth French-Canadian curves in her accent.

"For what?"

"Saving your ass, maybe."

"I could handle him."

"From under his boot?"

"I got him now."

"Right. Two morons. Fighting. Over what exactly?"

Daniel glared at her.

They both held firm until the flicker of blue and red appeared from behind, and two police officers emerged from the crowd. He saw a flash. Someone had taken a picture. Others held their phones aloft, recording the scene so they could post it to their Facebook or some other social media page. Daniel imagined the caption: "Heroes Take Down Threatening Hooligan."

He took a deep breath. "I'm Daniel."

There was definitely a hint of a smile behind the tousled hair and the troubled, hurricane eyes that transfixed him. "Claire."

Paramedics arrived soon after. The man regained consciousness, along with his pain and fury. But now his hands were constrained by handcuffs. The police took statements. The crowd corroborated Daniel's story. Claire handed back his backpack.

TWENTY-FIVE

DANIEL'S LEFT FIST THROBBED, his head hurt, gashes covered both arms, and his left leg was numb. The paramedics patched him up. After a prolonged protest at their order to send him to the hospital for further tests, they allowed him to go. Claire didn't have a scratch.

The police detective had interviewed the other witnesses, and now it was Daniel's turn.

"I was on my way to see Detective MacKinnon," said Daniel.

"MacKinnon, right." The detective scribbled notes and mumbled something with a skeptical tone. "What is the nature of your business?"

"It's part of a murder case."

That caught his attention. "Just a minute." He turned away and clicked his radio. Daniel couldn't hear the brief conversation, only saw him nod occasionally. He turned back. "Detective MacKinnon will be here shortly."

Daniel nodded.

The officer faced Claire. "And you are?"

She handed him her military ID. "Claire Marcoux."

Daniel noticed that the detective's look changed from uninterested to surprised, verging on respectful.

"Well, Lieutenant Commander. What's your story?" said the detective.

Daniel was curious, too.

"I was walking home from the Superstore, after my run around the Citadel," she said, hoisting two grocery bags, "and I was surprised to see the crowd. I tried walking around, but it got bigger. So I just walked through it."

"And then you saw Mr. Ritter here?" The officer tilted his head toward Daniel.

Claire looked away for a moment and grinned. "Yes. He seemed to need a bit of help. So I gave him some."

"How, precisely, did you help him?"

She pulled out a can from one of her bags, turning it until she could read the label. "I threw a can of Campbell's soup. Tomato. It was on sale. I threw it at the crazy man to distract him."

"And what is your relationship with the suspect?"

"None. I've never met him before."

"And with Mr. Ritter?"

She paused. "Never met him before either." She looked at him curiously.

Daniel felt a frisson of energy as he returned her gaze.

"Thank you, Lieutenant Commander." The officer fished out a business card and handed it to her. "We may have further questions for you. I've noted your contact details. If you have any questions, please contact me."

"Certainly."

"And please wait here, Mr. Ritter, until the detective arrives. He should be here soon."

"Of course."

"Thank you both for your co-operation." And then he moved on to others waiting in the crowd.

They were suddenly alone. The rally had long ended, and the participants, so eager earlier, had lost focus or interest and had left. Only a few stragglers milled about, some on their way to the bars along Spring Garden or to the boutique stores. A few were finishing interviews with other police detectives. But no one tried talking to Daniel and Claire.

Daniel was the first to speak. "Thank you."

"Was that too hard? You needed my help."

"I thought I had things under control."

"You were going to lose."

She's right. There was something special in her eyes. Something that beckoned him in. Something he hadn't felt since he met Vanessa in the business lounge years ago. His "red alert" warning sign flashed in his mind. *Will she be part of my life's reboot?*

He pulled out a business card and handed it to her. "In case you need my help one day."

Claire tilted her head and scrunched her face a little. "Not likely." She pulled out a pen from her coat, wrote her phone number on the card, and handed it back. "In case you need mine."

Daniel gave her a fresh card and tucked the one with her number on it into his pocket. She nodded and smiled. Since neither of them seemed to know what to say next, she picked up her bags and turned to go.

"Stop. Stay where you are."

Daniel and Claire spun around to see who had issued the command. Two serious-looking men were walking quickly toward them. Daniel recognized the one on the left as MacKinnon.

"Detective MacKinnon. Your message had me startled."

"Daniel, this is Constable Perry."

MacKinnon appeared perplexed at seeing Claire there with Daniel. "And you are?"

"Claire Marcoux." She shook hands with both detectives. "We just met. I helped Mr. Ritter here. Another detective took my statement."

Daniel wanted to spend more time with Claire, and these detectives were interfering with his plan.

"We'll contact you again if we have any further questions, Ms. Marcoux." MacKinnon motioned for her to leave.

Claire smiled at Daniel as she walked past. "See you around maybe."

Daniel watched her leave. When she was out of earshot, he turned to MacKinnon. "So my life's in danger?"

MacKinnon started again. He seemed to be the more senior of the two. "Professor, you mentioned a hotel manager who accompanied you to Mr. Forrestal's room."

"Yes, but I don't recall his name. French, but not Québécois. Maybe Loïc or Thierry."

Perry was blunt. "We know his name. Can you tell us what you remember about him?"

"Not much. He was a bit of a prick. He wouldn't open the door. It took me a long time to convince him."

MacKinnon said, "Did you contact him after the interview with the police?"

"No way. I didn't like him. He didn't like me."

"Did he say anything to you?"

"No. Why don't you ask him yourself?"

Perry looked at MacKinnon for a second and then directly at Daniel. "We'd love to."

MacKinnon added, "But he was found dead two hours ago."

TWENTY-SIX

GARTH DIDN'T KNOW WHAT TO DO about his boss. Brewster was doing his thing on stage, making big promises in exchange for votes. Judging from the noise inside, the crowd clearly supported him. Another good speech that helped to build momentum, according to the plan. A plan that depended on Garth coming through.

His blue-striped iPhone chirped. The number had a 613 area code. Ottawa. Code name: Aspen. Another key part of Garth's plan.

The voice was hoarse. "It's me."

"And?"

"I know why the big shipment didn't arrive."

Garth waited.

"It was intercepted by a navy patrol."

"I thought you said the ship would be protected?"

"It was a total fluke."

There had been too many flukes, Garth thought. "How do you know?"

"I've just seen the damned report."

"I've arranged for two more shipments from the same source. They should be leaving tomorrow. I don't want them touched."

"This better be worth it."

Garth repeated his orders. "I don't want them touched. You make sure that no one messes with them. Got it?"

"I'm not some little shit you can spit on. I've been doing this for thirty years. You promised me my country. You better deliver. I've been waiting a long time for this."

Garth did need him. He was a high-ranking military officer who had arranged the shipment's free passage from Boston. Garth backed off. "You're right. You're right. We're getting close to the big finish here, and this is the time when I need you more than ever. Your country is counting on you."

He heard a faint sigh. "I'll need details of the ships and the routes."

"I'll have them sent directly to you shortly. Remember, this has to work. If we fail, we're both screwed. No country and no future. For you or for me."

TWENTY-SEVEN

BACK AT THE POLICE STATION, Daniel was seated in front of MacKinnon's desk again. He patted his shirt pocket that still held Claire's card, debating whether he should call her up later. But more pressing matters demanded his attention.

He didn't know how to take the news of the hotel manager's sudden death, the only other possible witness to Forrestal's murder. He was an arrogant SOB, but he didn't deserve to die. "What happened?"

"Shot." Perry spoke with no emotion.

"A professional hit," said MacKinnon.

"Like Forrestal?" said Daniel.

MacKinnon nodded. "Apparently. We believe that there may be a threat to your life."

Daniel cleared his suddenly dry throat. "Somebody wants me dead?"

"Looks like it."

"But I haven't done anything."

Perry said, "More of a case of fear of what you saw or heard. Someone doesn't want any witnesses."

"With the manager out of the way, you're the last one," MacKinnon added.

Yesterday, I was just an anonymous person with enough troubles of my own.

"So what now?"

MacKinnon looked right at Daniel. "Constable Perry here will keep an eye on you."

And today I have police protection.

Perry tilted his head in the faintest of nods and added, "We have the video capture and your description of the suspect, although it's not much to go on, frankly. If he's the professional that we think he is, he probably can disguise himself."

"We have a BOLO out on him," said MacKinnon.

Perry said, "But it'll be difficult to find him. Whoever he is, he's good at keeping a low profile."

MacKinnon continued, "Perry will accompany you back home and stay outside for the night. And we'll track your cellphone."

Perry handed him a business card with a cellphone number on it. "If you need anything, just call me. I'll be right outside." Daniel wasted no time in programming it into his own phone.

"Great." Daniel stared at the card in his hand. Would Perry be enough protection from an adversary who seemed more resourceful every day? Would Daniel be forced to deal with it himself?

* ✳ *

Twenty minutes later, they pulled up to Daniel's apartment building on Tower Road. Perry raised his hand, signalling to Daniel to wait in the cruiser. Perry slid out of the car, looked all the way around, slowly scanning, and nodded. Daniel emerged from the cruiser into the flat light of the late afternoon, nervous about being the prey this time. The hotel manager had had no protection, and he was now dead. Perry's presence, or perhaps the pistol at his hip, was only modestly reassuring.

Perry said, "Move fast."

Daniel walked quickly to the door, opened it with his key, then strode into the waiting elevator. On the fourth floor, he and Perry proceeded to the door marked 409. Perry took the key, right hand on his weapon, opened the door, and disappeared into the apartment. A moment later, looking more relaxed, he allowed Daniel in.

"All clear in there. I'll be in the cruiser all night. Don't go out unless you tell me first. Remember, call me first."

Daniel said, "Can I order a pizza? I'm starving."

"Yes, but I'll meet the delivery guy." Perry leaned in a bit. "Whatever you do, don't answer the door unless you know it's me."

"Sure."

"I'm serious. Do not open the door."

TWENTY-EIGHT

LARCH PARKED HIS BLACK CADILLAC SRX across the street from a five-storey apartment building that looked clean and modern, but also like it wanted to proclaim something grander than it was. Gratings in front of each window simulated balconies that the residents no doubt wished they had. The lobby sprouted a waterfall along the right wall, but it wasn't working. Through the ground floor window, a basement gym sat with two un-used treadmills and a set of weights that probably had yet to feel any real sweat.

Surrounded by a gaggle of cloned buildings, it was a modest place to live. Car traffic was light, but the sidewalks were packed with students. A couple in their early twenties walked toward the building. The man was tall, moustached, with dark tousled hair, wearing jeans and a jean jacket, heaving a case of Alexander Keith's. She was a foot shorter, brunette, in a black sweater and black jeans. They giggled as they opened the door and continued to the elevator.

They weren't who he was waiting for.

Larch was a patient hunter. He had already heard the consequences of the first part of his plan from the park a few blocks away, with police converging to deal with trouble at the pro-No rally. His client would be pleased with the headlines sure to appear. His left hand dangled out the window. He held a Marlboro, which leaked a thin stream of smoke. Two empty Coke cans lay sideways at his feet, a scrunched Subway wrapper sat on the empty passenger seat. He looked through a pair of Celestron 7x50 binoculars at the second window from the left on the fourth floor. He didn't react as a solo police car drove by. He knew that Ritter was on his way home from campus. The cellphone sniffer, locked onto Daniel's number, remained silent on the passenger seat; he had made only one call so far today.

Birch had supplied him with a few details about the target's life. But it wasn't much. The absence of info was something that gnawed at Larch. Ritter had been a professor for only a few months, according to Birch. But what did he do before? There was little trace of him. A Google search revealed only that he had worked for a business-consulting firm in Montreal. He found a short newspaper clip that mentioned someone with at least the same first and last name involved in a minor traffic accident. In Hong Kong. What did Mr. Ritter do then? Why hide it?

Larch would have liked to have had answers to these questions, but he didn't need them. What he needed to do was focus on the present, on getting the job done. Now was all that mattered.

He was expecting to see Ritter walk up to the building, since his source had told him that the professor usually walked between his home and the university; however, today his target didn't. He arrived in a police cruiser.

The cop got out first to check out the scene. Then, Ritter appeared and ran a few steps along the far sidewalk, collar up on his winter jacket, and chin tucked in against the cold. He carried a plastic bag in one hand, a dark backpack in the other. The policeman followed closely. A minute later, Larch saw the light flick on inside Ritter's apartment. The cop soon returned to his cruiser and waited there, about thirty metres from the main entrance to the building.

The fact that Ritter now had police protection meant that it was going to be more difficult to deal with him. It was time to tie up this loose end fast.

He slipped out of the car, backpack in hand, and walked directly across the street, a block behind the cruiser. He pivoted on the sidewalk and approached slowly, trying to appear as casual as possible. Two young women walked into the lobby just before him. One of the women, the taller blond one, apologized for not holding the door open for him. He muttered something meant to be unremarkable. He waited until the shorter woman with a black toque pushed 4. He pushed the floor above.

In the awkward silence between floors, one woman's cellphone chirped. She didn't answer it. After he got out on the fifth floor, he took the stairs back to the fourth and slowly opened the door into the hallway. It was empty. He walked along the corridor, noticing which doors had light leaking from under them and which did not.

Light spilled along the floor from room 409. He banged on the door twice. No answer from 409. *He must be in there*, he thought.

Ritter's door didn't open, but then a man appeared behind him, holding a pizza in one hand.

TWENTY-NINE

"AT EASE, CAPTAIN," said the man seated in the leather chair. Commodore John Miller, head of Maritime Fleet Atlantic. Captain Hall remained stiff and upright in front of his boss; he assumed the proper stance by clasping his hands behind his back. Hall did not appreciate being summoned because of the actions of one of his ship commanders. To focus his energy, he mentally reviewed his career: twenty-six years in the navy, a full captain, and responsible for a sizeable part of the Atlantic Fleet, with three thousand under his command. Not bad for a dorky kid from North Preston.

The commodore held a slim report, flapping it in the air as he spoke. "I want to know more about what happened with the *Kingston* out there. Your report says it was a rescue gone bad."

"Yes, sir. She answered a distress call. The vessel fired on the rescue chopper from Greenwood and then threatened the *Kingston*. The *Kingston*'s captain did what she had to do to protect her ship."

"Yes, Captain, that's what I read in your report. But I'm concerned."

"About what?"

"Overreaction. It was her first tour of duty as captain without oversight." He leaned closer. "You promoted her too fast, did you not?"

Hall nodded. "I've relieved her of duty pending a board of inquiry."

"Was she caught by surprise?"

Hall took a moment before answering. "No one, even with experience, would have expected a ship in distress in sea state 7, a full gale, to resist being rescued."

"Sounds like we need some practice out there, Captain."

"Sir?"

"One of your captains sinks a ship instead of rescuing it, and you're not worried about crew effectiveness?"

"The crews are well trained and ready for any contingency."

"I'm glad to hear you say that. I think it's time to see what they can do. I want them all out at sea by tomorrow night, ready to engage in a surprise warfare exercise."

"Where, sir?"

"Grand Banks." Two hundred kilometres off the coast of Newfoundland. "What's available?"

Hall knew his fleet. "Three frigates, sir. The *Ville de Québec*, the *Charlottetown*, and the *Montréal*."

"Any coastal patrol vessels?"

"They're either in the Caribbean on drug interdiction duty with the U.S. Coast Guard or in dry dock for repairs."

"And the *Kingston*?" Miller pressed.

"Off duty, pending the results of the formal review."

"Very well. As soon as the review is complete, I want the *Kingston* to join the exercise."

Hall replied only after a noticeable moment of silence. "Aye aye, sir." It sounded half-hearted.

Miller began to turn away from Hall, then he stopped and faced his subordinate. "You have concerns, Captain?"

"That would leave us with no assets covering the American border."

"Is that a problem?"

"Our southern flank would be exposed. We'd have no ability to support the Coast Guard or Border Services."

"We're not at war. CBSA can cover it. I'm more worried about undertrained ship captains who are caught by surprise and overreact during a crisis situation. Lives could be at stake. I have personally vouched for the fleet to the minister on this."

Hall knew the discussion was over. The commodore wasn't much for chitchat.

Walking back to his office in the adjoining building, something gnawed at Hall. The commodore expressed a valid concern, but Hall wondered about the exposed southern flank. With no navy ships available for rapid deployment, either in Halifax or steaming anywhere near Nova Scotia or New Brunswick, the Canadian Border Services Agency's patrol craft — oversized dinghies really — would be severely stretched to monitor and protect from a wide range of threats from the south. He remembered what CBSA had said earlier: the ship that the *Kingston* sunk likely had been smuggling drugs. The commodore must have faith in the CBSA, otherwise it felt like an open invitation for anyone to come on in.

THIRTY

DANIEL IGNORED THE KNOCK ON THE DOOR. Perry had
told him to. Probably someone with the wrong apartment number. He was hoping it might have been the
pizza guy, but he hadn't arrived yet. And Perry would
have come with him or at least called to say he was on
his way. He left another voice mail for Vanessa, explaining that he would miss his flight back to Montreal.

He heard the muffled conversation in the hallway behind his locked door. *My neighbour Rachel on another
date?* he wondered. But the tone of the conversation
seemed strained. Maybe she hadn't chosen well again.
Maybe he should see how she was doing. She had a bad
record when it came to choosing men: they didn't usually last more than a couple of dates before she tossed
them, or they hit her. It really wasn't his business, and he
was no expert in sustainable relationships.

They had met often in the elevator, and they had developed the relationship one does in the same apartment

building. Friendly, but you didn't want to know too much about the other person. She was pretty, but she wasn't his type — a Pandora's box of trouble, for sure. He sensed that he wasn't her type either. He didn't want to reveal too much anyway.

Maybe a short, simple intervention would help this time.

But Perry had told him not to open the door.

He peered through the peephole in the door and saw a short man with his pizza arguing with another man. No Rachel anywhere. The delivery guy took a step back from the door and knocked. The other man had his back turned, so Daniel couldn't see his face.

He picked up his cellphone and pushed redial. Perry answered.

"Pizza's finally here."

"I'll be there in a minute. Wait until I get there."

"I'll be there in a sec," Daniel said through the door. He hadn't eaten anything substantial since his interrogations with MacKinnon. He peered again through the peephole and saw the other man walk toward the elevator at the far end of the hallway.

Free and clear, Daniel's stomach took over his decision-making process. He creaked open the door until it left just enough room to pass a pizza through, careful to stop the door with his foot. "How much?"

"Twelve bucks."

Daniel reached into his pocket and handed over a twenty. "Keep the change."

"Thanks."

Daniel grabbed the box. Over the delivery guy's shoulder, Daniel saw the other man turn suddenly and walk briskly toward him. The man pulled the pizza guy out of the way, slammed him against the wall, and punched him in the stomach. The pizza guy slumped over, dropped to his knees, whining in agony.

The image of the man in the hotel hallway, humming the tune, suddenly flashed in Daniel's mind. The toque on the head, the black coat.

He was the killer from the hotel.

Not a word was said. The man pulled out a pistol from his right pocket.

Daniel pivoted and pulled back into his room, dropping the pizza on the hallway floor, slamming the door shut, and locking it. He swerved around the bag on the chair, grabbed his coat, and slid open the door to the balcony. The front door shuddered with a loud *whoomp*. And then another. And another, until the bolt gave way under the massive stress of someone kicking the door down.

He rammed open the glass window, hopped over the faux balcony railing, and swung over to the one below, just as he felt a bullet whiz to his right. He heard a ping along the wall of the adjacent building, followed by the sound of gravel hitting the pavement below. Adrenalin drove him forward.

Daniel swung down to the next balcony, and the next, until he slammed onto the gravel of the driveway. He ran to Perry's car waiting outside on the street, but another bullet whizzing by his head forced him toward the back of the building. *Where's Perry?*

He ran to his own car in the crumbling parking lot. The decaying yellow Hyundai hatchback hadn't fared well in its half-dozen or so Atlantic winters, in spite of what the used-car salesman had bragged. The door opened with a creak. The lock didn't work anymore, but then again, there was no point in locking it now. He jammed the key into the ignition and twisted it into life. It complied with a reluctant wheeze from the engine. He jammed the manual stickshift into reverse, and the car screeched back from its parking spot. After a desperate three-point turn in the confined space between parked cars, he squealed onto Tower Road.

Daniel scanned for any pursuing car, but the street was quiet, the snow muffling any sound. A few dark shapes were scattered along both sides of the street. He spun the car left. The back wheels slid on the snow until he corrected the steering and sped the two blocks to the end of the street.

The police cruiser was still there. But there was no sign of Perry. He took another left along South Street.

Where the fuck is Perry? Probably in the elevator on the way up. He shook the questions away and focused on the single priority: to get maximum distance between him and the shooter, no doubt Forrestal's killer. He had to get back to the police station.

Traffic out of the city was bumper to bumper at eight in the evening. The remnants of the party after the demonstration around Victoria Park didn't help. Daniel only got a few blocks from his apartment before he became glued in a traffic jam. A long line of red brake lights streamed into the blackness ahead.

Turning right along Robie Street, he quickly came to an accident, the cause of the stopped traffic. He veered left through the Dalhousie campus to Vernon, then right up to Quinpool. The station was only a right turn and a few minutes' drive away.

An orange sign blocked the way. *More construction!* A mobile crane hogged both directions, the workers oblivious to the suffering drivers around them.

He spun the car around, forced to go west and away from the police station.

Past Oxford Street, traffic thinned out enough that he finally noticed a pair of headlights in his rear-view mirror. They were darting in and out of the traffic line, getting a bit closer each time, until the vehicle — it was a black SUV — was only a few cars behind him. He thought it was a bit odd. Even in a hurry, there was really no point in zigzagging in and out of the line. Everybody was stuck. Might as well just listen to the radio. Everyone would eventually get back home to the safe suburbs.

Then the SUV did it again. It swerved out and back in, making it only two cars behind Daniel.

He looked ahead and wondered what was going on.

Who is this guy? How could he find me? How did he know I was in this particular car at this location right now? It seemed highly suspicious.

But his training told him to test any hypothesis. *Let's see what he does when I do this …*

Daniel waited until an oncoming car had just passed, and then he lurched hard to the left into the all-but-empty city-bound lane. If the car were following him, the driver would have to swerve into the next oncoming car, a very dangerous move.

He accelerated as he glanced in the rear-view mirror to see the SUV do exactly as he had predicted. It narrowly missed the oncoming car, only by the car steering right to avoid a collision and instead slamming into a telephone pole.

Daniel's driving skills were a bit rusty. He sized up the SUV looming in the rear-view mirror and matching his hundred kilometres per hour in a sixty zone. Daniel had his beat-up Hyundai. The assassin's SUV was a much more powerful vehicle. Probably a Cadillac of some sort. Likely a V8.

He pulled out his cellphone, pushed redial, and pressed the speaker. He tossed it onto the passenger seat.

He thought about the weaknesses of his little car and those of the massive SUV. The most obvious weakness of the SUV was its high centre of gravity. It would topple much more easily in a tight turn. Although Daniel couldn't outrun it, maybe he could outdrive it — if he could combine high speed with tight turns. SUVs were notorious for being wobbly at high speed; they were often the vehicles flipped over in the centre median during snowstorms. Staying in the city wouldn't help. He wouldn't be able to drive fast enough to pull enough Gs to tip the SUV over in a sudden turn. He needed to get to a highway out of town then to the police station.

A voice crackled from his phone sliding around on the passenger seat. "MacKinnon."

Daniel yelled over the engine whine. "It's me, Ritter. I need help."

He blasted through the Armdale Rotary then right along North West Arm Drive. The exit to the 102 north soon beckoned and he veered onto the exit ramp.

"Where are you?" asked the voice.

Daniel said, "I'm about to get on the 102. Exit 1. Going north."

"What happened?"

"Where's Perry?"

"He should be with you."

"He's not, and he wasn't in his car. The guy who killed Forrestal just tried to shoot me in my own apartment. Now he's chasing me."

He kept it at a hundred, only braking at the last second before almost tilting over to the left as he followed the curve onto the main highway. He glanced at the mirror, and to his dismay, the SUV had made it, too.

"Can you describe the other car?"

"It's a big black SUV. New. Cadillac, I think."

"Licence plate?"

"Didn't have time to see."

"I'm on it. MacKinnon out."

How did this guy know where I was? How is he able to follow me? How does he know I'm in this particular car? Maybe the car's LoJacked with a transponder? No way, he'd have to have placed it on the car while Daniel was at work. *How would he have known my address, the make and model and licence plate number?*

He'd have to try again to lose the tail. He floored the accelerator and downshifted to fourth gear for extra oomph. The car shook spasmodically with the strain. The speedometer hit 150, the fastest the car could physically go, but the growing headlights from behind reminded Daniel that it just wasn't fast enough to outrun the Cadillac.

On the open straight highway, the Cadillac closed the distance in seconds.

Where are the cops? MacKinnon, Perry, where are you?

Daniel kept the accelerator on the floor as he zipped past the Lacewood exit and saw a stream of cars bunching up the lanes ahead, most likely shoppers returning home from Bayers Road. He flashed his headlights in warning and a few cars in the left lane pulled to the right. He sped past the mass of traffic, at least 60 km/h faster than the other vehicles. The engine redlined, screaming in protest, knowing that perhaps this was its final journey. The Cadillac remained close, only a couple of car lengths behind.

The next exit was four kilometres away, according to the sign that had just blurred past. Only ninety seconds to go. He remembered there was a tight exit turn there, too. Maybe that might flip the SUV. He'd have to try.

He slammed on the brakes as one of the commuters swerved into the left lane to pass an even slower car. His car whined. He smelled smoke from the melting brake pads.

A single white flash in the mirror and then his rear window shattered. He heard the zip of a bullet lodging into the passenger seat. The Cadillac was right behind him now.

In the mirror, Daniel saw flashes of blue and red appear behind the SUV.

Finally, Perry!

A police interceptor appeared beside the SUV. On a normal day, he would have worried about being stopped for stunt driving, getting slapped with a two-thousand-dollar fine and an automatic impound of his car. It seemed a rather quaint concern, since he now had bullets searching for his head.

He kept the accelerator on the floor, the engine howling in protest. It would be the SUV versus the police first. He switched from glancing in the mirror to looking straight ahead, swerving between slower-moving cars in both lanes. The SUV suddenly got smaller. It must have braked.

This target is still full of surprises, thought Larch as he slowed the SUV from the not-so-feeble yellow bee of a Hyundai a few car lengths ahead.

Larch swerved left, trying to squeeze the police car that had appeared beside him into the concrete barrier that divided the highway. He used his Cadillac's superior weight to jam the car into the wall, but the driver held fast in the left lane. The concrete quickly gave way to a snow-covered median. He tried again but the car stayed nose to nose. He whipped out his pistol and fired twice at the darkened passenger window. He saw glass shatter, and the police cruiser twisted left onto the snowbank. A tire caught, something underneath sparked like flint on the pavement, and the car flipped, spinning high and left.

In his rear-view mirror, Daniel saw sparks fly, and the police headlights disappeared. The SUV grew bigger, and there was no sign of the police until he saw the interceptor high in the air, spinning until it landed on its roof in the median strip. The exit beckoned. He cut into the right lane just in front of two tractor-trailers and lost sight of the SUV.

But it soon pulled in immediately behind him, forcing itself in front of the first tractor-trailer. The lights bore down on him; the high beams were blinding him and throwing jittery black shadows ahead. He flipped his mirror down. The exit came up fast at 150, more than forty metres a second. He couldn't escape the Cadillac, especially now that they were virtually bumper to bumper.

There were only seconds before more gunshots. And he wouldn't miss this time. He was too close.

Advantage for the hit man. He needed to make it a disadvantage. The Cadillac was so close that the driver wouldn't be able to react fast enough if Daniel did something erratic.

The exit came up fast. He had to make it look like he could go either way. He drove directly on the line that separated the exit lane from the lane that would continue north on the highway.

As the pavement arced to the right, he maintained a straight-line trajectory that would lead in seconds to the cement block that split the road. He held it until the last fraction of a second, twisting the wheel hard to the right, his car squealing in protest.

The Cadillac swerved erratically to the left and then straight along the highway. It would take some time to stop, turn around, and continue the pursuit. Daniel knew he had maybe a minute to lose the tail.

The Hyundai screamed and lurched as he dropped down two gears to gain some control along a sharp turn designed for no more than sixty. But Daniel was topping a hundred, and he could feel the right wheels begin to lose contact with the ground. He struggled with the wheel at the maximum g-force point and then regained control as he straightened out toward the intersection and its stoplight ahead.

He didn't wait for the light to turn green, just ploughed to the right along Kearney Lake Road. Once tucked in between two cars, he slowed to match their speed and checked the mirrors to see if he could spot the pursuing vehicle. He saw nothing of the SUV.

Looking over his shoulder, he saw no one in the left lane or in the opposite direction. Without signalling, he spun the car around in a smoky trail and drove back toward the intersection, where a brown-and-red Tim Hortons sat like a plump cat. He parked the car at the rear, hidden from view from the road and the access ramp.

He switched off the smoking engine, swung the door open, grabbed his bag, slammed the door, then ran into the Tim Hortons, where a dozen or so patrons lounged at the scattered tables. He pulled out his cellphone and ordered a taxi. It arrived in a few minutes.

Daniel climbed in and ordered the driver to take him to the police station. He called MacKinnon.

MacKinnon answered gruffly, "Where are you?"

"I'm on my way. He was following me. I think I lost him. Where's Perry?"

"He's not responding to our calls."

"I think he crashed on the 102 a few kilometres back from here. He tried to stop the hit man."

"Shit. So it was him, then?"

"What do you mean?"

"I just overheard a call for fire and ambulance dispatch to an accident on the 102."

"It must be for Perry."

"Jesus. Get yourself over here, now."

"Already in a taxi. Be there in twenty minutes or less." He switched off the phone and took a breath. The radio was turned down, the driver curious about the conversation, aware that he was privy to something important.

Daniel sprawled across the back seat and thought about what had just happened. Someone had successfully predicted his movements, followed his car in traffic, defeated a police pursuit, and nearly killed him. The hit man was skilled and professional. The same one who had killed Forrestal and the hotel manager. And he was coming for Daniel now, the last witness. Two questions nagged. How did he know that he was coming home at that particular time? The killer could have easily found his address on Google or in the phone listing. No surprise there. But his habits? He must have studied his habits. He must have been following Daniel for some time. And how was he able to track Daniel's car? Was it equipped with a hidden GPS transmitter? If so, he must have known which car was his. *How could he have known?*

His cellphone chirped. Area code 514. "Vanessa?" Her timing sucked, as usual.

"What's happened this time, Daniel? You're weaseling out of taking care of Emily again, aren't you?"

"I can explain. I've got a ticket for tonight. But I can't make it."

"I've got plans of my own. I need you to come and take Emily for a few days."

"I'm really sorry, but something's come up."

"I don't care. I don't care. I don't want to do this anymore." Her voice sounded squeaky with tension.

"I can explain. I can't leave Halifax right now."

"What is it this time? Another 'business trip' you can't talk about?" He could hear the quotation marks as she said "business trip."

"I retired from all of that, remember."

"So why can't you come?"

"I'm under police protection. Someone *is* trying to kill me. It's not my fault."

There was no response from the other end.

"Did you hear me?"

"Jesus, police protection? What did you do? I knew it. You're back to your spook shit, aren't you?"

"No. I promised you that I would never go back. But someone is trying to kill me."

"I'm stuck holding the fuckin' bag again. You're so heartless. Well, this is the last time. I swear."

The line went dead.

Daniel held the phone as if it were a lifeless object. Vanessa sounded more frustrated than usual. He cursed under his breath. The taxi driver stared ahead and said nothing.

Daniel stared out the taxi window, wondering. Meanwhile, kilometres away, the man in a dark Cadillac cursed under his breath. Slowing to the speed limit, travelling north to the next exit on the 102, Larch vowed not to underestimate this target again.

THIRTY-ONE

MACKINNON CALLED to say that Perry was in the hospital with life-threatening injuries. Daniel replayed the crash that he had seen in his rear-view mirror. It was a miracle that Perry had survived the spinning, the sparking, the crashing, and the inferno afterward. MacKinnon didn't dwell on the news. They had a BOLO out on the Cadillac. Daniel's car had been towed and would spend the evening in the forensics lab.

As soon as Daniel arrived at the station and saw MacKinnon standing, waiting, he shot him a look of concern. "How's the pizza guy?"

"He suffered from shock and some bruising. He's being treated at the hospital. He already gave us a description of his assailant."

Daniel nodded. "The same one I saw at the Westin? The one who tried to run me off the road."

"It would seem so. We need some help, then." He pointed to another officer who approached, one Daniel didn't recognize. "This is Detective David Touesnard, who will be taking Perry's place while he recovers." Touesnard was about the same age as MacKinnon, but taller and fitter, sporting a thick cover of black hair and a trimmed beard. He appeared strong. His arms barely fit into his shirt. Daniel thought he seemed like a good choice for a personal protection officer.

MacKinnon turned to Touesnard. "I'll let you know if I get a call back."

"Understood." Touesnard looked at Daniel. "He's got another assignment."

Touesnard fiddled with his cellphone before stuffing it into his jacket pocket. "Smugglers."

MacKinnon changed the subject. "We have an ID on the man from the demonstration."

That caught Daniel's attention. *Who was that mountain of a man who attacked me?*

"We got help from the RCMP. His name is Max Pitt. He's a member of the Alberta Independence Movement, a small-time fringe political group in Alberta."

Daniel didn't register the answer at first. "How fringe? Like a neo-Nazi?"

"Sort of."

"What was he doing in Halifax? At that rally? Was he after me?"

"Don't know yet. He's not saying much."

Touesnard accompanied Daniel back to his apartment to collect his essentials. He wouldn't be allowed to stay there while the hit man was free. They put him in what they called a safe house, a room at a moderate downtown hotel facing the harbour, with Touesnard nearby. MacKinnon told him to stay put.

* ✳ *

Daniel didn't sleep much that night. The unfamiliar hotel room felt like a prison. He was trapped between two worries that his mind swatted back and forth like a tennis ball. Vanessa — what was she up to? — and Forrestal's murder. He needed to do something proactive, but he was stuck in this hotel.

He needed to see for himself what was going on with Vanessa and Emily. Flying back to Montreal would be the best thing to do. But the police wouldn't give the all-clear until they could track down the hit man.

Daniel tried to rewind the last few days of his life. His problems began with Forrestal's call. *Why did he want to talk with me when he could have talked with anyone else? How did he even know who I was?*

And Lloyd, that egotistical big fish in a small pond, knows him. But he won't help me. I'm on my own. He calmed his mind for a moment to still the rushing questions and emotions linked with Emily, the worry about Forrestal, and the stress that arose thinking about Lloyd. When in doubt, one of his undergrad teachers had told him, return to first principles.

His troubles started after the call from Forrestal. So his first question was clear. Who was Patrick Forrestal, really?

He returned to Forrestal's investment company website that he had found before his failed meeting Tuesday morning. He clicked on the "About Us" link and moved to a new page with a professional photo of the founder, chairman, and CEO, Patrick Forrestal. There was a short bio. Forrestal founded the company twelve years ago and had increased sales and profits every year. Daniel's curiosity piqued. The page didn't quantify the profits or anything else about the company's performance. The CFO and VP of marketing were listed, but Daniel didn't recognize their names.

Daniel searched SEDAR next. Canadian securities law compels every publicly traded company to publish key financial and personnel information. To manage this information, the securities industry created a simple system with a complicated 1970s-style name: System for Electronic Document Analysis and Retrieval. Although Fireweed wasn't publicly traded, Daniel assumed that Forrestal, being such a prominent business personality, would sit on the boards of other companies. As a director, he would be asked to review and approve the company's strategy, key investments, and top executive appointments. Daniel didn't find a single document with Forrestal's name.

Daniel's curiosity shifted into overdrive. Forrestal was famous for "rescuing" high-tech failures and transforming them into winners. Thousands of people owed their livelihoods to his financial wizardry. He demonstrated an uncanny ability to team up with local experts who could master completely unrelated technologies. He had purchased a company that made video display cards for computers, another that developed a vaccine that the World Health Organization hailed as a lifesaver for the Third World, even a Calgary restaurant that had just won its first Michelin star. A few years ago, he had bought a start-up that developed and sold a smartphone application that teenagers around the world used to maintain private chats out of the purview of their governments and their parents. All winners.

But he wasn't listed as a director with any of these companies.

Why didn't Forrestal join the boards of companies that he had saved? They would have been grateful and certainly would have offered him a board seat. Or they would have been vulnerable, and he could have just taken a seat. But he hadn't. Daniel wrote a note on his pad to figure out the answer.

Daniel couldn't shake a nagging feeling. *Who is Patrick Forrestal?* He had started his company twelve years ago. That was all Daniel knew so far. He got the distinct impression that Mr. Forrestal had liked to keep his life private. Now he was curious to know why. Private and rich spelled trouble.

A new Google search revealed nothing else of substance about his life. All links returned to his corporation's bio page. He tried other search engines, with similar results.

Forrestal's main business wasn't technology. It was akin to company "first aid": identify the patient, diagnose the disease, treat the disease, make the patient presentable, and then sell the patient to the highest bidder. This was his formula for business success. And judging from the Google search results, he had done it at least a dozen times over the past decade or so in several countries. A stunning track record of success.

The money to pay for the companies he fixed came from his second business: stock portfolio investments. He had some proprietary combination of stocks on all of the major exchanges around the world. He consistently outperformed the markets by a few percentage points. Even the 2008 financial crisis barely dented his spectacular track record of generating profits. And it was these profits Daniel assumed that he channelled into his company "first aid" business.

Daniel decided to search for news clippings mentioning the man. Being so prominent, he must have been noticed in the media. A Lexis-Nexis query revealed hundreds of articles in the national news. After reading a sample of them, Daniel knew no more about the mysterious Mr. Forrestal than before.

As far as he could tell, Mr. Forrestal sprang into life twelve years ago.

THIRTY-TWO

CLAIRE, DRESSED IN HER SPOTLESS white uniform, with one colourful ribbon over her left breast pocket, stood at attention while three naval captains entered the small room. Beside her stood her appointed defence lawyer, Commander Colin Rowe, whom she had just met. In the hallway earlier, he had counselled her to just tell the panel the truth. He did not expect any sanction. Worst case, maybe a letter in her personnel file. He would fight to keep her captaincy, but he warned her to be prepared for the possibility that it might be her last.

She put on a brave face as the four-stripers sat at the table at the front of the room. Claire and Rowe remained standing at attention until she heard "Please sit."

"Lieutenant Commander Claire Julie Marcoux, we have reviewed the evidence to determine what, if any, action the navy should take regarding the events of last Monday morning. Recommendations range from nothing to court martial. Do you understand?"

"Yes, sir."

"There is no one present from your immediate chain of command. This is an external review of the events. We will now begin asking you questions."

Claire sighed as she resigned herself to a long and tortuous hearing to save her career.

After a long shower, Larch changed into a black jacket, white shirt with a sharp collar, blue jeans, and his brown cowboy boots. Sandrine said that he cleaned up well. He looked whole again. Reporting to his antsy client about his missed opportunity to clean up the mess would wait. His customer didn't need to know just yet. He would fix it soon anyway.

The night before, he had cleaned the Cadillac and ditched it in a ravine, then caught a cab back to the hotel. He wasn't worried about being linked to the SUV, as he used a credit card in another name: Walt Kowalski. The home address was in Michigan.

It was time to figure out the situation.

He went to Starbucks to get a coffee and checked what Sandrine was up to. She had left two emails. The first asked when he was coming home. A week was too long. The second said she was going with her friends Monique and Estella to St. Thomas for some snorkelling. It was boring all alone at the villa. He tapped a short reply. Have fun. Back next Wednesday for sure. Almost done. Miss you. It was a short but affectionate answer that gave no hint of what he was doing.

He looked at the coffee mug and realized that he shouldn't drink so much caffeine. His aim degraded after too many cups.

His cellphone buzzed in his pocket. The number, with its 403 area code, looked familiar. "What's the situation? Is the problem solved?" Garth didn't wait for "hello."

"Almost."

An uncomfortable silence lasted way too long. "That's disappointing. What are you doing about it?"

"The target is full of surprises."

"He's a bookworm. A professor. How difficult can it be?"

"Are you sure you know his whole background?"

"He did some industry work then went back to school to become a teacher. There's not much to tell, frankly."

"I'd say there are some important gaps in that story."

"A reliable source told me."

"It's not the whole story."

"It's a reliable source."

"I need to know everything."

"What happened?"

"He drives like a madman."

"So?"

"I had him dead in my sights and he got away. By jumping off a fucking balcony. He just leaped off as if he'd done it many times before. It was a reflexive action for him. Then I had him again, and he drove away. I need to know how he can do that."

"Okay, okay. I'll find out."

"Why are you calling me?" Lloyd seethed. The surprise of Garth directly challenging him had yet to dissipate. His stress level spiked when he saw the Alberta area code on his desk phone display.

"I left you three voice mails this morning. You didn't reply," said Garth.

"What's so important?"

"Are you sure you told me everything about Ritter?"

"Of course."

"I have information that suggests he's not who he seems to be."

"Give me a break. He's not even a professor. He's an assistant professor."

"What's the difference?"

"He's junior. Untested."

"How long have you known him?"

"Since he started here."

"How long ago was that?"

"A couple of months."

"What did he do before?"

"Like everyone else, he taught a few courses some-where else. Did well enough. Now he's doing it here."

"And before that?"

"I don't know. Some industry work. He's a bit older than our regular professors, but that can be good in a business school. It doesn't matter anyway. I want to put our project on hold. Without Forrestal, we really don't need Ritter anymore. Take the money and run, I say. Forget him."

"It's too late for that."

Lloyd took a deep breath and looked at the snowy land-scape outside his office window. "What have you done?"

"Nothing you need to worry about. Do you know what he did before he worked there? I need to know."

"Something about consulting."

"Do you know what he did as a consultant?"

"Not that I remember. I'm sure he told us in his interview. But nothing stands out. I can check his CV. I'll call you in a few minutes."

Lloyd replaced the phone, opened a window on his computer, and searched for the CV Daniel had used to apply to the university. He called back.

"Got it," said Lloyd. "Like I said, he worked for a business consulting company based in Montreal."

"Tell me about it."

"Duhamel, McWhirter & Lin. Worked seven years in their Montreal and Beijing offices. Before that, he taught English in Sapporo, Japan, for a year. That's it."

"Doesn't tell me much. What else?"

"He claims to have several years of experience dealing with offshore acquisitions in several countries."

"Which ones?"

"The States and China. It makes sense, though. Nothing special about that."

"Tell me about China."

"It doesn't say much. He was in Beijing. Does that mean anything to you?"

"No, of course not."

"Why are you asking so many questions? What's the problem? He's a junior professor. Nothing to get excited about. I met your guy. Calls himself Larch. He asked a lot of the same questions. Seemed a bit gruff."

"Don't worry about him."

"I'm not. Look, I've done my part. We don't need this deal. Without Forrestal, we don't have a front man. Let's just cash out and close up shop."

* * *

Daniel remained quarantined in the hotel room, unable to leave for his own protection, with his new protection officer, Detective Touesnard, looking bored on the sofa. Daniel continued to browse the web on his laptop. He gasped as he scanned the news websites.

The picture was not flattering at all. There he was with Claire on Amoeba Man, who was clearly knocked out. Daniel's gaze focused on his elbow squishing the man's face on the sidewalk. He seemed to grimace in a distorted, Tony Blair sort of way, while Claire, looking to the right, appeared freaked out. Their expressions were etched raw, overexposed. The picture had been sold to Canadian Press, who distributed it to all of the national news sites that he checked.

CBC quoted a witness as seeing a man and a woman taunt and attack a man who only wanted to be left in peace. It was unprovoked aggression, they were quoted as saying. The *National Post* headline blared "Anti-Alberta Aggression." On the front page of the *Toronto Sun*: "Strong-arm tactics against democracy."

People from Vancouver to St. John's would read that two anti-Alberta protesters, one of whom was a professor named Daniel Ritter, had attacked a bystander. Claire was called the "unidentified woman." The Canadian Press article said he harboured "radical, left-wing political views" and strongly hinted that those views were what prompted him to attack the bystander. Daniel reeled from the article on his screen as if it were contagious. He felt bile bubbling up, producing an acid taste in his mouth.

He pulled out Claire's card and dialed her cellphone. She should know about this. When she didn't answer, he left a message telling her to check the news and call him back.

An image of her face flashed in his mind and he felt transported into another state of anxiety, this time more pleasant. She smiled. She leaned closer, breaking his invisible shield of personal space, where he would only let those closest to him enter. She did it naturally. She began to whisper. And the image dissolved.

He caught his breath and surprised himself by calling again, this time leaving a message asking her out for dinner.

How did the reporters get the story so wrong? Somebody gave the press that innuendo. One name sprang to mind.

In the business school building, which hogged one corner of the campus like an overgrown mushroom, Daniel ran down the hallway, laptop in his left hand, freeing his right to punch the asshole in office 225. Touesnard, running by his side, counselled keeping his cool. He had agreed to this short, supervised visit to campus to get at least one answer, since all other inquiry tracks had so far proved fruitless. Daniel didn't knock, just swung the door open and walked right in. Touesnard stayed outside, watching the hallway.

"You did this." He slapped the computer on the desk, opened it, and turned it so Lloyd could see the photo from the CTV Atlantic website. "Why?"

Lloyd moved in slow motion, lifting his glasses off, blinking at least twice, and taking a long look at the picture, exaggerating each reaction. He scowled, looked pensive, and finished his performance by raising both eyebrows in a look of feigned disappointment. He replaced his glasses and spun around in his chair to face his own desktop computer.

"Why are you bothering me?" He started typing, keeping his back to Daniel.

"I saw this on several news sites. My name is there."

"So?" More typing.

"How would they know?"

"They have reporters. I assume they do research. They're clever."

"That research included you?"

The only sound was his typing. Then he spun around to face Daniel. "A reporter called me, asking to confirm your name. What's the big deal?"

"So the reporter already knew who I was in the picture?"

"Yes. He wanted a confirmation."

"How did he know?"

"Your TV show? How should I know?"

"And what about this horseshit about me having radical, left-wing political views?"

Lloyd glared directly at him but said nothing. The accusation in his stare was clear. Daniel understood the chasm that divided them. Lloyd's animosity was no longer limited to affairs of the academic department.

Touesnard wedged the door open, cutting the tension.

"Yes, Detective?" said Daniel, still engaged in a staring showdown with his new nemesis.

"You need to come back to the station for some further questions. We have new information from our colleagues, and we hope you can help us interpret it."

Lloyd returned to typing on his computer.

Daniel turned to the detective. "This is not finished."

Daniel looked out of the cruiser window as they pulled away from the campus and onto the road north toward the police station. *Why would Lloyd discredit me to the press? Is this no longer just about academic jealousy?* He felt angry. Of course, none of this compared to his other problem. *The hit man's still out there, waiting for another chance to kill me. He's tried twice and failed. He'll try again.*

As they drove back to the main road, Daniel glanced at a solitary man in a Chevrolet sedan, parked just outside the campus limits. But deep in thought, he ignored him.

The clerk emerged in the hallway and beckoned them to return. The hearing had lasted just shy of two hours. The captains had spent a further three hours in closed door deliberations, and they were now ready to render their verdict. Claire re-entered the room, with Commander Rowe in tow, and saw the official-faced senior officers were avoiding looking at her. She stood at attention and awaited her fate.

She tried to distract herself for a moment so she wouldn't burst into tears or lunge at the nearest officer in a fit of rage.

"Lieutenant Commander." The grey-haired captain, seated at the centre of the row of officers on the far side of the table, rose. "We have reviewed the events with your testimony and with that of your direct superior,

Captain Hall." He cleared his throat. "Your actions in the attempted rescue on Sunday were clearly irregular, unorthodox, and even aggressive. However, we commend you. We unanimously agree that you demonstrated the necessary leadership in such a challenging situation."

Claire wheezed. Her throat felt dry.

"We do not concur with the assessment of the situation anonymously provided by one of your crew members. However, we believe that you clearly lacked the requisite experience to deal with such a complex combat situation. You are ordered to undergo further training in combat operations."

She blinked. She could hear the stream of words from the captain, but her brain took a few seconds to process them.

"And you are hereby reassigned as captain of the *Kingston* with immediate effect. Congratulations, Lieutenant Commander, and well done. Captain Hall will be instructed to accelerate your training at his earliest possible convenience."

She turned to look at Rowe. *Did I hear that right?* He didn't move.

"Dismissed," the captain said.

She saluted sharply, turned, and marched out of the room with Rowe. *I'm back!* The joy felt as if it would burst through her chest at any moment.

It was during precious victories like these when she felt loneliest. She needed to talk to someone. No one waited for her in the corridor outside the courtroom. Her parents would find some way to transmit their eternal disappointment at her choice of vocation and lack of partner. Her brother would be no help, no doubt running to some beach and brothel in Thailand to drown his disappointment at not being invited to hockey training camp. So, family was off-limits. And she had no real friends since she'd started her new command.

Then her mind drifted to a surprising image. It was Daniel, picking himself off the sidewalk, about to be pummelled. He was vulnerable, but not. And strong, but not. And when he looked at her, he looked *through* her. That man, certainly unlike any professor she'd ever met, the one she helped at the demonstration. Daniel. Could she share this one with him?

Rowe stared at her.

Was I staring into space? she wondered. She gave him a brief hug. Yes, it was unprofessional, but she had to share this win with someone.

Any trace of a smile evaporated as she thought of the next step: a meeting with her commanding officer who had ripped away her "home" but would soon be ordered to reinstate her.

THIRTY-THREE

BACK AT THE POLICE STATION for a third time, Daniel felt more comfortable now that he knew he was no longer a suspect. However, he was surprised as he was led once again into an interview room. He leaned back in his chair, tilting his head back. Two rows of fluorescent light bars buzzed on the ceiling.

"Dr. Ritter, what offshore financial accounts do you have?" MacKinnon began.

Daniel felt his mouth open wide in surprise.

Touesnard continued, "We found an account linked to you."

MacKinnon crossed his arms. "In the Cayman Islands." They were tag-teaming, like Abbott and Costello. But with guns in their holsters.

"With your name on it."

"And a recent deposit of ten thousand dollars." Touesnard dropped a thin folder on the table.

"Can you help us understand what this all means?"

"I don't know what you're talking about." Daniel opened the folder and saw a deposit receipt in his name. MacKinnon and Touesnard stood near the door, arms crossed. Daniel knew he would not be allowed to leave the room without a satisfactory answer.

"Tell us about your finances, professor."

"There's not much to tell."

"Apparently there is," Touesnard said.

"I've got a chequing account at Scotiabank. Probably have about two paycheques' worth in it at any time."

"How much?" MacKinnon consulted his notepad.

"About five thousand. Unless the rent has gone through. Then it's fifteen hundred less."

"Anything else? Anything offshore?"

"GICs and some mutual funds all locked in. My pension. About four million. The accounts are all in Hong Kong."

MacKinnon nodded. "So your answer is yes, you do have offshore accounts."

"That's where my bank account was when I lived and worked in China."

"Why there?"

"There were tax reasons, of course. But more importantly, there were political reasons."

"Political reasons?" said MacKinnon.

"The Communist government's policies changed unpredictably. It depended on which faction in the government was in power. One minute you were fine; the next, your money could be seized, or you could be arrested, facing a life sentence for moral corruption. It happened to two people I knew over there. The police just took them away, sending a clear message, in a very public way, to everybody. After that, it was company policy to use non-Chinese banks for business transactions and for their employees."

"You had an exceedingly well-paying job there. Followed by no income at all for seven years."

"I lived on my savings when I went back to school. I told you, it was China. Back then, there was so much money and very few controls on what you could do. It was the Wild West."

"With so few rules, was that when you set up the account in the Cayman Islands?"

Daniel smiled. "Nice try. I don't have an account there. Only in Hong Kong. You can check with the company."

"We will."

Touesnard smiled back. "So tell us again, how did you get the one in the Caymans?"

Won't anyone believe me?

THIRTY-FOUR

THIS WAS THE MOMENT she had dreaded. It was frigid in the captain's room, the result of a typical military snafu at work: mid-winter and the air conditioning was at full blast. But she was still sweating under her uniform. Rowe had shook her hand and wished her good luck before disappearing back into the bureaucracy the day before. Captain Hall had revoked her command, effectively accusing her of misconduct, of panicking, and of sabotaging any chance at the career she longed for. The board reinstated her, against the wishes of her boss. And now to get back her ship, she had to report back to him. She hoped he took orders as well as she did.

More than her career was at stake. Since childhood, she had been laser-focused on not becoming one of "those" girls. She would not be dependent on someone else for her identity. She wasn't just someone's *blonde* from Montreal, a francophone in an anglophone's world. Sitting in the captain's chair of the

Kingston for the first time, she had finally understood what she wanted to be, instead of what not to be. While stripped of her command, she hadn't known who she was.

Hall burst into the room, swinging the door wide open. She sprang to attention. The door slammed shut. He plonked a stack of reports on the only table in the cramped room and dropped into the chair behind it.

"At ease, Lieutenant Commander." His growl remained frozen on his face. "You are reassigned to the *Kingston*," he seemed to slow down for effect, "as captain." Another pause. "Congratulations."

She tried to read his face, to see any emotion: anger, frustration, anything. But he knew how to hide his feelings well. Maybe that was another skill she would have to develop.

"Sir?"

He shot her a look full of — well, she wasn't sure what it was. It seemed perfectly balanced between rage and relief. "Isn't that enough?"

"Permission to speak freely."

He glanced behind her at the closed door. "What's on your mind?"

"I'm not sure that I have your trust, sir. Now that I'm the captain again, you've made me responsible for the *Kingston*'s crew; I feel I need to know where I stand with you."

He stood up, startling her. He folded his hands behind his back. "Lieutenant Commander, I have my orders, too."

"Did you want to replace me as captain? I know that I'm young and inexperienced, and that the situation was not one that either of us expected. But I did my best. And, if confronted again, I would do the same thing."

She saw a smile start to form on her boss's mouth. Maybe not much of a smile, but a perceptible rising of the right side of his face. Or perhaps he was holding in his frustration.

"I appreciate that. You need to know where you stand? All right. You're not just young. You're much, much younger than the other captains in my squadron. You're not just inexperienced, you have no experience. You are also the only female captain under my command. So, you see, you stand out quite a bit. You need to understand that."

She gulped. Of course she knew that.

"The review was a necessary step. To protect you. To show my impartiality toward you. You don't know what's going on. And I hoped to shield you from it for a while longer. But circumstances have changed."

He's glad? "Sir?"

"I have received orders from the commodore to implement a surprise readiness exercise for the entire Atlantic Fleet."

Claire restrained a smile. *Another chance to prove myself.* "Where to this time, sir?"

"Grand Banks. I have ordered the *Charlottetown* and the *Montréal* to rendezvous with the *Ville de Québec* there."

"And what about the *Kingston*?"

"I have a special assignment for you, Lieutenant Commander. It's low profile, but important. I hope I can count on you."

THIRTY-FIVE

DANIEL FELT TOUESNARD'S suspicious gaze all the way back to the hotel. He sensed that MacKinnon might just believe his story, but not Touesnard. Who would send ten thousand dollars to an account with his name and not tell him? He hadn't done any consulting work worth that much. And any job he did do was strictly above board and official. He had seen too much corruption and had vowed not to turn to that dark side. Looking at the detective, Daniel didn't know if Touesnard thought he was a victim to be protected or a con man who had convincingly duped the authorities.

Daniel's cellphone chirped with a call from Vanessa. *Finally!*

Daniel's words, pent up for so long, burst through, as though he were continuing their last conversation without a pause. "Won't be long now. This police stuff should settle down in a day or so. Then I'll be right over to help with Emily."

She let out a sigh that seemed to empty the pain she had accumulated in one go. "I'm sorry." He tensed. Her voice sounded different. Not angry, more resigned to a destiny not of her choosing. "Sorry? For what? What's happened? Is Emily all right?"

"Yes, she's fine. She's with me."

"As I said, I think this police stuff will finish soon —"

"Don't bother."

"What do you mean?"

"Don't bother coming back."

Daniel stopped. "Of course I'm coming back. This is only temporary."

"For you, maybe. But I've had a lot of time to think."

Oh no.

"I don't want to stay here anymore. I'm lonely. I hate this fucking winter. You're never around. You said you'd retire from that fucking job that you could never talk about. But it's clear that it's back. It's time for this to stop."

"What are you saying?"

"It's time to end this, Daniel. To end this perpetual state of waiting. We started out so well, but there's only Emily left between us. And I have to live my life. I've waited for you for years. And I've got nothing to show for it."

"I'll talk to the police and come right now. I'll ask for an escort back to Montreal."

"We won't be there."

His heart almost stopped. "Where are you?"

She let out a big sigh. "Vancouver. We're about to catch our flight to Auckland. It's boarding now. I'm taking Emily to stay with my parents until I can figure out what to do next."

His mouth felt dry. "When are you coming back?"

"We're not."

He felt the world melt. "You can't do that. I need Emily, too. You can't take her all for yourself."

"I have her passport and travel document that you signed, by the way." He heard a muffled announcement in the background. "They're making the final boarding call. I have to go."

You can't take her away! "Can I talk with her?"

A pause. "I don't think that would be a good idea."

"I want to talk with her."

"Daniel, she's scared and confused. And your voice will only stress her out."

"Please."

"This is so typical. You can't just disappear doing God-knows-what and then parachute back and assume that our lives have been on pause since the last time you were here."

"But you left me." He felt his voice crack.

"You left me first." The line went dead.

His scream startled Touesnard, who called the Vancouver RCMP, but by the time the court injunction came, the plane had already taken off. Without it, the RCMP had no legal reason to prevent Vanessa from taking Emily to Auckland.

Emily. On his cellphone, Daniel scrolled through the few photos of them together, always with goofy smiles. Maybe over the Pacific, she would ask where her father was, and why he didn't come with them. He wanted to scream again.

He needed to talk to someone, needed to hear a sympathetic voice telling him it would all be okay and that he'd see his daughter again. His mind sifted through the people he could call. It was a short list. No one. Then her face came into view. Claire. He barely knew her but …

He went to his phone, checked the number that she had written on his card, and sent her a short text message to call him.

"We'll get this sorted out, and then you can see your daughter," Touesnard promised. "But it's just too dangerous for you to leave right now."

Emily is gone.

THIRTY-SIX

POWERED BY TWO STRONG COFFEES, Claire strode into a room buzzing with overlapping conversations, chirping cellphones, and keyboards being tapped. An array of large TV screens covered one wall. The operations room in CFB Halifax was full of activity. It was the nexus of the effort to track down the smugglers, whoever they were. She recognized multiple uniforms: navy, of course — but also Halifax Police and RCMP. She was also the only woman in the room.

Her phone buzzed. She turned it off without checking to see who had texted or when.

A civilian stood beside Captain Hall.

"Sir," she said, saluting, "you wanted to speak with me?"

Hall turned, returned the salute. "This is Cliff Whitby. Detective Inspector. RCMP." Whitby, dressed in a grey uniform, looked like a retired park warden with dark secrets behind his eyes. Claire thought of *Deliverance*, which she had seen in film class.

Whitby smiled. "I've heard a lot about your encounter, Lieutenant Commander."

Hall seemed to be waiting for her to respond. When she didn't say anything, he continued. "I want you to sit in on the briefing. We're coordinating all of the information we can gather, and then we'll decide what our next step should be."

She followed the two men to a separate room with glass walls. There was a long table with eight chairs, a projector on one wall, and a whiteboard on the other. Two seats were already taken. Hall and Whitby took places next to each other. She sat opposite Hall, feeling that, although she was the most junior, she was the one everyone most wanted to talk to.

Hall called the meeting to order. "Thank you for coming at such short notice. Let's begin with a round-the-table update. I've asked the captain of the *Kingston* to join us to answer any questions you might have." He motioned to Claire. "Lieutenant Commander Marcoux."

Nods all around, but no one said anything.

Hall grabbed a marker and started writing on the whiteboard. "Let's summarize what we know so far. The *Atlantic Mariner* is seen leaving Boston early Sunday morning. It's identified by a coastal patrol flight from Greenwood Monday evening. It doesn't respond to radio requests. The *Kingston* encounters it. It fires on a search-and-rescue helicopter. The *Kingston* is forced to sink her." Hall glanced at Claire. "No debris was recovered. That's what the navy knows. Cliff?"

Whitby stood and watched Claire as he spoke. She didn't like the way his eyes bored down on her, a suggestion of violence behind the stare. "The FBI sent us what they know. The ship was owned by a shell company listed in Barbados. IRS can link the account to a former Blackwater operator who's serving ten years for manslaughter. He was a private military contractor who killed a local family while on duty in Iraq. He disappeared after that. But the account is still active. We think it belongs to someone higher up in the company. Probably used it to cover operational expenses. It suggests there's an operation underway right now. But we don't know for whom. The company owns another ship still in port. Boston Police are watching for anyone to show up. That's all we've got."

Whitby sat down and Hall read from a piece of paper in his hand. "Thanks, Cliff. Mr. MacKinnon?"

The next man stood up, the police detective she had met with Daniel, after the demonstration. He was early forties, with dark hair and alert eyes. He turned toward Claire and nodded in acknowledgement. "Matt MacKinnon. HRM Police." Then he swung toward the others. "We've detected nothing suspicious in either the Halifax or Bedford docks. Wherever that ship was going, it wasn't to Halifax. We've added patrols along the coastline within city limits, just in case it was going to Sambro or one of the other outports. So far, nothing of interest." He took his seat.

Hall tried to keep the momentum going. He motioned to a trim, dark-haired man in his late thirties, sitting at Claire's right. "Brett?"

Brett stood up. "Brett Lansdowne, CBSA." Claire nodded at the Canadian Border Services Agency agent. Lansdowne didn't acknowledge her nod. He talked to the others as if she weren't present. Maybe he thought she should get them all coffee.

"We have a Zodiac on standby in case we need to intercept," he said. "Homeland Security suspects drug smuggling. The cartels have restricted supply for the last few months; now they're trying to feed the demand, raise prices, and ship a lot of product north. We think that Halifax was only a transit station, and that most of it was to be shipped west to bigger cities," he concluded. He returned to his seat.

Hall stood. "Thank you, gentlemen," he said. "Now I would like to ask Lieutenant Commander Marcoux to tell us what happened out there." He looked directly at Claire. "You're the only one who has had direct experience with these people."

She stood, trying to calm her nerves and not let her nervousness show. She knew she would be doubly judged — once as an officer, once as a woman. She tried to blur the men around the table, but Lansdowne stood out. There was something familiar but unsettling in the way he looked at her. She sensed dual messages from him, and she wasn't sure if she wanted to know what the second message was. She took a breath. "Well, it was a brief encounter. They tried to hide. They didn't acknowledge our hails."

Lansdowne waved his hand. "So you obviously provoked them."

"No, sir. I gave them time to respond."

"You lost your cool, perhaps?"

"They fired at us first. Then they tried to ram us. It wasn't me who lost their cool."

"You could have given them a chance to surrender."

"I did. But I don't think that they wanted to be rescued at all."

Lansdowne turned to face the other end of the table. "I think we need someone cool at the helm if there's going to be a next encounter. We lost a critical opportunity to gather intelligence." He turned to Claire. "All we have from you is a story. No boat. No suspects in custody. No evidence. Just a story."

Claire controlled her anger. "I was cool, Mr. Lansdowne. And we have more than just a story. Have you ever commanded —"

Hall cut her off. "Brett, I am satisfied that navy protocols were followed. Lieutenant Commander Marcoux took appropriate action."

Lansdowne pressed on. "So you won't assign another officer? Someone more seasoned? Now is not the time to have someone prone to emotion."

Claire glared. *What an asshole.* He knew virtually nothing about her, but he felt qualified enough to judge her actions? She opened her mouth, prepared to launch into an impassioned rebuttal, but then she looked at her commanding officer at the far end of the table. His eyes could have shot twin laser beams at Mr. CBSA.

"Brett, this is not your call. I don't tell you how to do your work. Don't tell me how to do mine."

Claire watched Lansdowne deflate. He nodded, and that was the end of the dispute.

Whitby broke the tension. "Lieutenant Commander, what do you think was in that boat?"

Claire turned to face Whitby and to block Lansdowne's leer. "Hard to say, sir. It must have been quite valuable. The crew took on a navy warship. They had serious firepower with an RPG, and they knew how to defend themselves."

"Speculate."

"Can I ask you all a question first? How many kilos of drugs could fit on a ship like that? A fishing boat."

Mr. CBSA spoke first. "A few hundred at least."

"What would that be worth?"

MacKinnon said, "Tens of millions of dollars on the street. An impressive catch for sure."

Claire looked at MacKinnon. "Do you believe that a drug gang would fight to the death to protect a shipment worth tens of millions of dollars?"

"What's your point?"

"Why wouldn't they just give up, throw their cargo overboard, or abandon ship? Why fight? Ten million dollars may be a lot, but it seems to me that amount would be small potatoes for a multinational drug syndicate. They'd recover the loss somehow."

"It was drugs. Homeland Security says so," Lansdowne said.

Claire grinned. "Do you always let them do your thinking for you?"

She heard a few snickers. Lansdowne's look implied that he'd like to commit some form of serious, maybe sexual, violence. "It was drugs. Case closed."

"If not drugs, then what?" said MacKinnon.

Whitby answered with a serious look, "Something worth a lot more."

"What's worth dying for?" Hall added.

The answer came to Claire immediately. "A cause." Her sociology class replayed in her mind.

"You mean like global warming or save the seal pups?" said Lansdowne.

"Maybe, but the more I think about it, the more it

seems to me that they reacted not so much to save prof-its but to save their cause, their fight."

"Eco-terrorists, then?" MacKinnon said.

Whitby was nodding. "Sounds plausible. It wouldn't be the first time radical environmentalists took on a navy. I've read that they've tussled with the Japanese navy sev-eral times."

"But never fired an RPG at them," added Hall.

Lansdowne leaned forward. "You can't be serious. What would their mission be? Take down a navy vessel to save seal pups?"

"No, I think they were just unlucky with the weather, unlucky running into you," Whitby said.

Claire stiffened. "No, sir, they weren't unlucky. They weren't sailors at all. Any sailor would have known about the storm and how to avoid it. These people sailed deliberately into the storm. They did it on purpose."

Lansdowne flung his arms high. "So they're crazy and amateurish."

"I think they were hiding."

Arms in the air again. "Jesus, why would anyone take a boat *into* a winter storm?"

Whitby seemed to be at a loss. "Research?"

"It could have been part of lying low," Claire said. "Maybe they didn't want anyone checking in on them or following them. A storm makes that all the more difficult."

Whitby leaned forward, both elbows on the table, head cradled in both hands. "So if they were hiding, what was their mission?"

"Delivery of something very time sensitive. Other-wise they could have waited until after the storm. They saw it coming, but they had no choice. Their cargo had to be delivered on time. And unobserved."

"Definitely dodgy," said Lansdowne, checking out her figure.

"If they were eco-terrorists, it could be explosives. Maybe they wanted to blow something up." Whitby looked at MacKinnon. "But you said their destination wasn't Halifax."

"If it's time sensitive," Claire said, "when does the clock strike zero?"

Whitby grinned and turned to face her. "That, Lieutenant Commander, is the right question to ask."

"So what's the plan, then?" Claire said.

Captain Hall nodded. "If it's a cause, as you say?"

"They will try again. And soon," Whitby said.

"And they'll be more desperate than before," added Claire.

Hall said, "When they move, the navy boxes them in. RCMP or Border Services picks them up. If they're found in HRM, you nab them." He pointed at MacKinnon.

Nods all around. Lansdowne continued leering at her. She knew what he was thinking.

Hall looked across the table at Claire. "Now you know what to do."

Keeping Lansdowne in her view, she said, "I certainly do."

THIRTY-SEVEN

TOUESNARD LEAPED FROM the sofa and rushed to the door, past Daniel, scattering dozens of papers with notes about Forrestal's curious background on the floor. "Someone's out there." He pointed to the door and warned Daniel to crouch low and behind the wall into the bedroom. Touesnard hugged the wall beside the door, pistol in hand.

"It's me. I've got coffee." Daniel recognized MacKinnon's tired voice. Touesnard holstered his gun in relief then opened the door.

Daniel gathered the leaves of paper and stood from the table as MacKinnon lumbered into the room. "Now you come to see me?"

MacKinnon was looking quite pleased with himself. He held a coffee in one hand. "Busy morning. Perry is out of intensive care. We'll get an update in a day or so."

Relief washed over Daniel. He felt as if he owed Perry his life. "That's wonderful news." He noticed Touesnard's muted response. "Did you know him?"

"Not really. Poor dude."

MacKinnon pulled off his coat and dropped his notebook on the little table still covered with empty pizza boxes. "We have work to do. The best thing we can do for him is to find his assailant." He let out a long sigh as he sat down in the chair. "In the meantime, you might find this interesting." He opened his notebook. "Forensics believe that the gun that was used to shoot at your car was the same type as the one that killed the hotel manager."

Daniel raised his eyebrows.

"So there *is* someone trying to kill any potential witnesses to the Forrestal murder," said Touesnard.

MacKinnon nodded. "And we have our first lead in the case. Last night, I spoke on the phone with Forrestal's lawyer and a woman named Gabrielle. She claims to be Mr. Forrestal's ex-wife."

"I thought Forrestal wasn't married?" Daniel threw MacKinnon a quizzical look.

"They weren't legally, but she said they'd been together for six years. Anyway, she was contacted by someone saying he was a cop looking for our Mr. Forrestal."

Touesnard shook his head. "Not a cop?"

MacKinnon snorted. "Of course not. No record of this guy anywhere."

Daniel said, "So someone was looking for him. To kill him?"

MacKinnon hunched his shoulders. "Whoever it was, he was a pro. Pretended to be a cop. Must have done serious research to find the ex-girlfriend."

"So who was looking for him? A pissed-off business partner?"

"No idea. The lawyer didn't say much except that the value of his assets had yet to be determined. He was very cagey and vague."

"If we only knew what assets he had."

"We'll find a way. What have you found?"

"Nothing earlier than twelve years ago," said Daniel. "There's no trace of him before he started his company."

Touesnard nodded. "Calgary Police are checking. They'll let me know what they find."

"So there is more to him than we thought." MacKinnon crossed his arms.

Touesnard's phone chimed. He read the message. "I had a constable do some more digging into that Cayman Island account of yours."

Daniel glowered.

MacKinnon looked at Daniel as Touesnard said, "The money was wired from another account in the Caymans. But we can't identify the owner. They have strict privacy laws down there to prevent us from finding out who the account is registered to."

"It's not mine." Daniel crossed his arms. "So let's see if I understand what's going on. There is a killer out there trying to eliminate any witnesses to Forrestal's murder, and I seem to be the last one alive. Forrestal might have been killed for a deal gone bad. A deal that we can't find. He might have a family, at least one former girlfriend, but he just appeared out of nowhere twelve years ago. And someone wired ten thousand dollars from one Cayman Island bank account to another one with my name on it."

MacKinnon rocked back and forth in his chair, keeping his gaze on Daniel. "I'll contact our financial crimes unit to figure this out. But it will take a while to get an answer. They're pretty overwhelmed with work."

Daniel picked up his phone. "Don't bother. I know someone who can give us answers faster."

THIRTY-EIGHT

GARTH FELL INTO HIS SEAT at the front of the bus, exhausted from the mounting pressure of the non-stop tour. He'd hardly slept, and he cursed the rising sun under his breath. The campaign would soon reach its climax at the sold-out spectacle at Rexall Place in Edmonton on Sunday night. The Saddledome speech last night had garnered all of the right headlines. "Premier Confident of Victory." "Brewster Nation-Building Speech Caps Successful Campaign." "What to Expect in an Independent Alberta." "Americans Interested in New State."

The key op-eds were now in and they were positive. Both the *Calgary Herald* and its sister paper, the *Edmonton Journal*, argued for a cautious Yes vote. Garth knew that this was a major victory for the premier. The media initially thought the referendum was political suicide. They called it unwinnable, especially when those advocating for independence were being confronted with the overwhelming power of the federal government, which would naturally argue for the No side. But Ottawa had been reassuringly silent on the key points in the campaign. The Feds didn't argue about Alberta's ability to go it alone. Nor did they question any of the economic arguments about diversification away from oil revenue dependency. The Conservative federal government wasn't too happy about the referendum; as the ideological twin of the Alberta Conservatives, they seemed to participate only grudgingly, trying half-heartedly to support the No side and preserve the Confederation they were constitutionally bound to protect.

Ever the practical campaign manager, Garth couldn't take chances, though. He had to plan for the worst possible scenario and, at least officially, hope it would never arise.

Alberta flashed by outside the bus window. They continued their way north toward the provincial capital. Each flash of light between the long periods of darkness drew him closer to the final goal, to final victory. Except that he knew that even this victory wouldn't be the end of the struggle. It would be just the start of building a new country. His job would be to put in the foundation pieces of the nation.

What does every nation need? A government, laws, diplomatic recognition, maybe even a currency. Brewster had other people to arrange those parts. Garth had a special mission for a special piece of the puzzle of state. It was especially sensitive. Done correctly, the citizens of the newly independent Alberta would never even know about its existence, but if done incorrectly, he could see armed intervention from both

Canada and the United States. The stakes were high, and he had to get it just right.

The premier stormed toward him from the back of the bus. "You're not cleaning this up too well."

"Wait for the headlines. The local ones are good. The No side is being blamed for the disturbance at the protest in Halifax." He rubbed his eyes.

"Get over there and fix it."

"The final loose end is being taken care of as we speak. And you need me here on the campaign trail."

"If you don't clean this up, there won't be any campaign trail left."

THIRTY-NINE

DANIEL SWIPED SEVERAL TIMES through his contacts until he saw the name Lu Xiao Ping. He smiled, remembering their special relationship — forged across numerous business deals, some very rewarding, others harrowing disasters — and his final mission where he crossed a personal Rubicon he thought was inviolable. He had vowed never to kill, a vow he had been forced to break.

Then he dialed and waited for a voice to answer in a time zone twelve hours ahead.

"*Wei*?" Her voice sounded tired and warmly familiar, even after so many years.

"Xiao Ping? It's me, Daniel. Daniel Ritter."

Several seconds passed. "Well, well, Daniel." A long pause before she said, "In trouble again?"

He smiled. "Sorry for calling you so late. Yes, I need your special access once again."

"Hmm. And what will it be this time?"

Daniel glanced at MacKinnon, who sported a surprised look. "Dinner at the Hyatt Beijing?"

"We did that already. How about Hong Kong? The Peninsula?"

"Good choice."

"Who will be paying this time?"

"This one's company-free."

"So you're still retired?"

He cracked another smile. "True. I'm a professor now. I'm respectable. I teach. I write academic papers."

"Are you saying you're harmless now?"

"I'm trying to be."

A pause. "Is it working?"

"Until yesterday, yes."

"What happened?"

He took a big breath. "It's complicated. Let's just say I'm under police protection now."

"How ironic."

"Like I said, I'm really trying. Can we change the subject?"

"Get to the point."

"Do you still have access to banking information for private clients?"

"For official use only, Daniel." He could hear her stir in her seat as she thought. "Are you retired, or aren't you?"

"Yes, I'm retired. But I need to understand all of the banking details for a Canadian dealmaker. Patrick Forrestal." He spelled out the name.

"Who is this person?"

"Was. He's dead, and I need to find out why."

"Not because of you, I hope."

"Of course not."

"Another case of financial foul play?"

"I don't know."

"An unhappy customer?"

"That's our working hypothesis."

"'Our?' Is it connected to your police protection?"

"Oh, most definitely."

"I'm intrigued."

"I'll tell you more when you call back with the goodies."

"Nice to work with you again, Daniel. I hope it's as productive as our last assignment in Hong Kong."

A smile spread across his face. That assignment involved helping a Canadian auto parts assembler that suspected their Chinese supplier of embezzling, skimming at least 20 percent off the top of any contract. Calls to the Chinese authorities went nowhere. So the Canadian company's CEO called around for someone who could manage the labyrinth that was the Chinese business world. They hired Daniel, through his consulting firm, to hunt down who was doing the embezzling. He and Xiao Ping caught the executive vice-president of the Canadian company receiving fat envelopes of U.S. hundred-dollar bills from the owner of the Chinese firm. It turned out that the VP had also sold company technology secrets to the Chinese.

"He was so surprised to see us," said Xiao Ping. "Just another case of corporate and security espionage, wasn't it?"

"Yes," said Daniel, "we finally got to do both of our jobs at the same time."

"A very satisfying case, Daniel."

"Can't hide from us."

The man was serving twelve years in a federal prison in Manitoba, Daniel recalled. "Can't hide from you." They even got a special commendation for their work from the minister.

"Ready for another one?"

She paused. "It has been a bit quiet recently. Maybe I have a bit of free time."

"Can you also check a bank transfer between two banks in the Caymans? I've got the SWIFT code of the receiving account. It's apparently in my name."

"You getting greedy?"

"Believe me, it's not mine. But someone set it up to make it look like mine. I want to know why and who is responsible."

"No problem."

He emailed her all the information MacKinnon had.

"Call me when you have something."

"Will you be in town anytime soon?"

"Not for a while, unfortunately. You coming back home for a visit?"

"My posting is for another year."

"It would be nice to see you again. The Peninsula, Hong Kong, when I'm back?"

"Or at the Château Laurier when I get back."

"Either way, I'll look forward to it."

He remembered her smile, confidence, and curves. They made a great team. Both on and off duty. Of course, that was before Vanessa. Before he knew why he was doing what he did. And before Emily, who was now thousands of kilometres away.

FORTY

CLAIRE SWIVELLED IN HER captain's chair and swore under her breath as Brett Lansdowne lectured her again on the radio. "Just keep them from escaping. We'll keep them on our side of the border. They won't be breaking any U.S. laws, just ours."

With her command reinstated, she had crash-sailed the *Kingston* overnight, only to putter off the east side of Grand Manan Island at the entrance to the Bay of Fundy, the shortest sea path between Maine and Canada. She wanted to be closer to shore, but Lansdowne valued concealment and the chance to surprise the suspects. The *Kingston* had to remain invisible.

She had blown a gasket when Captain Hall ordered her to support a CBSA mission to capture the smugglers. Her superiors had wind of a second attempt, somewhere in southern New Brunswick. Of course, that would put her too close to the blowhard Lansdowne, who said, "Your orders are to stay put and let the professionals deal with the smugglers. Right?"

"Yes." She crushed her teeth as she said it. *Idiot.* Border Services should let the RCMP take the lead. The Mounties had more resources in the area. Lansdowne would be too slow to catch the smugglers in their little dinghy, but he was too arrogant to see it. She was sure he would never let a woman tell him what to do.

Wiseman gave her a brittle look. Was it because some unseen bureaucrat was lecturing his captain, or because he wanted to do it, too? Claire couldn't tell. Sullivan watched his radio console, Barry his navigation screen, but she could feel their gaze as well.

This isn't going to work, she thought.

Twenty minutes later, Claire slammed her clipboard onto her armrest while she spat into the microphone in her other hand. "They escaped?"

The voice on the other end was gasping. "They're making a run for the border."

"You said they wouldn't be able to squeeze through."

The wheezing crackled on the radio.

"You made us wait on the wrong side of Grand Manan. So we wouldn't be seen."

"Look —"

"But that also meant that we wouldn't be able to catch them if they escaped. *Merde de tabarnak.* Where are they?" She faced Sub-Lieutenant Barry, the navigator.

The nav muttered while he scanned the radar display. "Less than five kilometres from the border. Moving fast. Only minutes to American waters."

She stood up from her captain's chair, looked at the radar screen for a moment, and turned to the helmsman.

"Steer three zero zero. Ahead flank."

Wiseman repeated the order. The bridge banked to the left as she was slammed into her chair by the sudden acceleration.

She steadied herself, grabbing the handle on the ceiling, then shot a look at Wiseman. "Prepare for boarding."

He winced. "It's going to be close, ma'am."

"They're not at the border yet."

Claire saw Sullivan, the radio operator, wave his hand. A low voice over the speaker: "This is the United States Coast Guard station Boothbay Harbour. Please identify yourself."

Claire clutched the microphone. "Coast Guard. This is the captain of the HMCS *Kingston*. We are in pursuit of suspected smugglers now returning to your waters at high speed."

"*Kingston*, understood. You do not have authorization to enter United States waters. I repeat. No authorization."

"We are working with the FBI and RCMP on this —"

"Captain of the *Kingston*. We'll take it from here. Stand down."

She slammed her clipboard on the floor. Its clang echoed for a moment, like the frustration in her head.

Câlice. They won't do a fucking thing.

FORTY-ONE

THE PREMIER WAS ANGRY with him again. "I haven't heard from you. This better be good news, Garth."

Garth's hand shook as it held his cellphone to his ear. "It is. We have taken direct action and I am waiting for confirmation that —"

He could hear the premier's snarl over the line. "I don't want to hear 'waiting for confirmation.' I want to hear that it's confirmed."

"We've got him this time. There won't be any more surprises."

"Your confidence worries me, Garth."

"I've learned."

"The stakes are too high now. You have to be sure." He paused. "I want you to personally deal with it."

"I am."

"No, I mean in person. I already told you I want you to fly over there and oversee the operations yourself."

He couldn't leave when he hadn't yet fixed the weapons shipment problems. He had to convince the premier without exposing his plan. "But you need me *here*."

"There's nothing more to do here. And the most important thing you can do for the campaign is to make sure that no bad press comes from your cleaning up your mess out East. I don't want any more surprises."

"This is ridiculous. The East Coast doesn't matter for us. I don't need to go over there. Everything will be under control soon." *The weapons are coming here. I need to be here.*

"This is not a debate. We need good news. Your inability to control the situation has given me pause, and a new idea born out of necessity. We do need to better promote our message of hope across the country, not just here in Alberta. The opinion of Canadians will count when we negotiate with the Feds. When you've cleaned up your mess, I want you to do a fast coast-to-coast tour." Brewster paused. "Start out East. Halifax will do just fine. Then do one in Montreal, Toronto, Winnipeg, and don't forget Vancouver."

"But the vote is in less than two days."

"Take the campaign plane. It will be waiting for you. Use my stump speech. Don't get too creative with it. Stick to the talking points. I'll make sure the media show up."

"There's not much time."

"Do it."

FORTY-TWO

CLAIRE TAPPED HER PEN on the armrest of the captain's chair. *Tat-tat-tat.* Everyone in the bridge heard it. *Tat-tat-tat.* No one said a word.

Thoughts about her orders, the man she had met, that idiot Lansdowne, and most of all, the crew member who had complained threatened to overwhelm her. *Who was it?* She wanted Captain Hall's trust, but she also wanted to trust her own crew. And that macho moron Lansdowne had screwed up. Fury at him spun in her head. Captain Hall told her that he tried to pin the blame for losing the smugglers on her. Said she had positioned the *Kingston* too far for pursuit. Said she hadn't followed his orders. Said that he wanted another officer to work with. Hall got her side of the story over the phone, with plenty of expletives in both official languages. He told Lansdowne that Claire would remain the navy contact.

Now a third vessel had been spotted sneaking up the coast.

She had no time to process everything. Her life suddenly spiked with activity after weeks of training, criticisms from the fleet captain, more training, and her first solo as captain of the *Kingston*. She sank a suspicious ship then capped it off with the failure with the CBSA. And now, this new hunting mission with clear operating instructions: box in the suspect ship, prevent them from escaping, and wait for police to arrest them. This time, navy takes the lead.

Her crew had only been given one hour to assemble on board from whatever lives they had suddenly been forced to give up, at least for a few more days. She had gathered the group of twenty-two and told them their mission was to intercept a third suspected smuggler vessel similar to the one they had sunk. It had been spotted leaving Boston. She had explained that she expected everyone to focus on his or her job and the mission would be successful.

The ship curved around the tree-tufted coast and entered the Bay of Fundy.

Claire realized her tapping had accelerated.

Wiseman, standing near, reminded her in a whispering voice that they shouldn't be sailing into this particular bay, at least not too far. There was something special about it. It wasn't that it was ringed by countless pretty fishing villages, or swarmed by flocks of squawky seagulls. What made the bay truly special was its tides. They were the highest in the world, and they could spell doom for the ship and her career.

In just over six hours, the sea level dipped sixteen metres. More water than flowed in all the rivers in the world rammed into the bay, and then, six hours later, went back into the open ocean. The tides were generated by a curious and fortunate series of coincidences. The floor of the funnel-shaped bay descended a staircase toward the ocean. The moon pulled on the water, just at the right time as it flowed in, then out of the bay. Together the moon and the peculiar shape of the bay created a natural resonance, like pushing on a swing. If you pushed at the right time, the swing rose higher. But in this case, what rose was the water level.

Her potential problem was therefore one of subtraction. The bay's depth hovered around twenty-five metres at high tide. At low tide, only eight. The bay was also shallower along the eastern Nova Scotia coast than along the western New Brunswick side. Toward Truro and Maitland, it was very shallow, essentially becoming a mud flat for a few hours. But the *Kingston*'s draught, the minimum depth of water needed for the ship to navigate, was just over three metres. So at low tide, there wasn't much margin of error. If she miscalculated, the multi-million-dollar ship would be stranded on a suddenly exposed sand reef.

Tat-tat-tat.

Of course, she would never jeopardize her ship and career by chasing smugglers deep into the bay. She only had to prevent them from escaping.

Preventing the smugglers' escape was the main problem, but there was also the fact that someone in her crew had been complaining directly to Captain Hall about her decisions. How to expose the mole? Who could she trust? She should be able to count on her number one, Wiseman, the XO. He was biding his time on the *Kingston* until he could get his own command. No way he would jeopardize a strong recommendation from her when the time came.

Although they had only sailed together for a few months, she had come to rely on her bridge crew. They had performed as an amazing team during each exercise and certainly when they encountered the hostile ship two days ago. The engine crew below deck she was less familiar with. But they gave her a rock solid ship that did everything she had ever asked, even when under fire — the ultimate test for any crew.

As the setting sun glowed through the window on her left, and the coast, ablaze with snow tinged red and orange, lazily passed on the right, the printer wheezed out a sheet of paper. The radio operator, PO2 Sullivan, handed it to her. "Ma'am. A message from Maritime Command." *Maybe he's the traitor*, Claire thought. She shook her head in disgust at her rising suspicion.

The report updated what was known about the suspected smugglers. The FBI had advised the RCMP that a second boat had left the Boston pier under surveillance. The report warned that the smugglers probably had sophisticated weaponry, maybe even machine guns or Stinger surface-to-air missiles. Most importantly, the report said that the smugglers had evaded police on both sides of the border.

Her orders had changed; Maritime Command ordered the *Kingston* to intercept the boat as it entered Canadian waters.

She showed the communiqué to the XO.

"So what do you think?" He was at least a head taller than her. *The ship must feel cramped to him*, Claire thought.

Wiseman cleared his throat. "Looks straightforward. But …"

She eyed him. "Tell me. I need your opinion, especially if we might be putting the ship and crew in the line of fire once again."

She noticed the bridge crew perk up.

"Our approach is high risk. Maybe higher risk than it need be."

"Spell it out, X." She swivelled in her chair, where only the captain could sit. When she wasn't around, it stood empty, a powerful symbol of her sole authority on the ship. The XO was a year older than her and just as ambitious. She saw the way he longed for a chair of his own. She liked that; he wouldn't hold back. *But would he rat on me to move me out of his way to a promotion?*

"Do we really need to enter the bay? We could wait here, at the entrance, until after they off-load whatever shipment they have. RCMP nab the haul and we catch them on the way back."

She nodded slowly. "I want to force them to act. At a time of my choosing. To catch them off guard. Then catch them red-handed. And vector in the police. To do that, we need to be close."

"But the bay. The tides. It's tricky to manage the clearance. We could be stranded with no warning."

"That's why I'm counting on you and the rest of the crew. I want navigation calling out sounding depths and three spotters at all times." She swivelled away to look at the front window. "But I appreciate your counsel, X." She offered him this gentle termination of the conversation. It was her ship. Her decision stood. He got the hint and said no more.

All she had to do was contain the smugglers, send out the *Kingston*'s rigid-hulled inflatable boat, or RHIB, to hunt them down, box them in at the bay, and tell the RCMP where to pick them up. And at night, the *Kingston*, with its high-tech imaging system, would have the advantage. The only real problem was the tide, maybe giving her insufficient water to navigate. But, unlike the unknown mole on board, at least it was predictable.

Tat-tat-tat.

FORTY-THREE

"DEPTH SOUNDING," said Claire. She crouched over the map spread out on the small table in the centre of the cramped bridge, compass set in her right hand, her other hand tapping her pen. Her navigation officer, Sub-Lieutenant Barry, nervously looked outside as the jagged black wall of trees rushed by in the moonlight.

The junior bridge officer read the echogram on the green electronic display. A stream of vertical lines spilled from right to left on the screen. The lines were getting shorter. "I read eight metres sixty and shrinking fast, ma'am."

The tidal current was fierce near this point, as water squeezed between the narrow peninsula on the Nova Scotia side and the New Brunswick mainland only a few kilometres away.

"Ma'am," said the radio operator, "Hotel-one-oh is reporting movement on the New Brunswick side."

Claire grabbed the microphone dangling from the ceiling. "This is the *Kingston* CO. Report Hotel-one-oh."

"O'Brien here. Nice to be working with you again, *Kingston*. Hope this mission goes better than our first one."

"I hope so, too, Captain. What do you have for us?"

"Infrared shows suspicious movement on the New Brunswick side. I've given the coordinates to your radio operator."

Claire saw Sullivan nod.

"We have to leave. Low on fuel."

"Roger, Hotel-one-oh. Thanks for the heads-up."

Claire motioned to Sullivan to cut off the call. After he flicked a switch on his radio console, he sat tense, motionless, for a moment. He scribbled on his pad then swung in his chair to face Claire. "RCMP has cordoned off the area and is requesting our assistance to ensure that the suspects do not escape by sea."

"Where?"

"Coordinates coming in now. Five kilometres west of Fundy National Park. Same area that Hotel-one-oh reported suspicious movement."

Claire whipped around to the navigator. "Can we turn around here?"

Barry consulted the map, mumbled a few calculations, and said, "Yes, we have enough clearance. But we'll have to hurry. The tide's still going out fast."

"Seven metres," said the officer watching the echogram.

Time to turn, she thought. "Quarter speed. Helmsman, steer two seven zero, rudder thirty."

"Aye aye, ma'am. Quarter speed. Steering two seven zero. Rudder thirty."

The ship lurched in a high-g left turn, tilting the floor at a steep angle. The hull shuddered under the strain.

Claire grabbed the overhead handle to steady herself. As the ship righted itself, she said, "Ahead full."

"Ahead full, aye aye, ma'am," said the helmsman.

She felt the slap of the ship's sudden thrust. "ETA?"

The navigator looked at his chart. "Twenty minutes, ma'am."

"Sullivan, advise the RCMP of our ETA." She slouched a bit in her captain's chair. She could relax for a moment.

Time to get some pre-authorization from HQ, she thought.

"Then contact Maritime Command. I want to speak with Captain Hall. In my ready room. XO, you have the bridge."

"I have the bridge, ma'am," said Wiseman.

She hopped up from her chair and walked to her cramped room directly behind the bridge. She closed the door, sat on her chair, and waited less than a minute before Sullivan called. "Captain Hall on the phone, ma'am."

His voice was stern. "What are you up to?"

"Sir, Lieutenant Commander Marcoux. We are approaching the location of the second shipment. We have a few minutes before contact, and I want to know what options I have."

"Be specific."

"If I get into another RPG situation."

"You know what you can use."

"I want permission to use the Bofors, sir."

"You cannot fire that cannon on Canadian soil without ministerial approval. You know that, Commander."

"I don't intend to use it, sir. I just want to know that I can use it if I decide I need it to protect the ship."

"You can't use it. Period."

"I expect to face at least the same kind of resistance as before. But the opposition may have access to more weaponry on shore than on the first boat we encountered."

There was a long pause before Hall said, "Your orders are not to engage. Just prevent them from escaping. Let the police do their work."

"Police already en route. But we don't know where they will land. We will be positioned to keep them from escaping at sea. But considering the fight they put up before, I expect fiercer resistance, especially if they feel trapped."

She had thought a lot about the situation. When she heard no sound from Hall, she continued, "Wherever they go, we will pin them down on land, at their most vulnerable. When they're transferring the cargo from ship to car. But timing is tricky. We are shadowing a suspicious vessel. I estimate maybe a ten-minute window to act. The police may not have enough time to catch them."

Another long pause from Hall. "I'll see what I can do. Until then, you do not have permission. Not. Understood?"

"Yes, sir. *Kingston* out." She replaced the phone. A feeling of jitteriness grew in her stomach. Those people, the smugglers or whatever they were, would be better prepared this time. Defending their mysterious shipment would be easier on land than on a small fishing vessel alone in a snowstorm.

And this time, they would be expecting trouble.

She returned to the bridge, busy with electronic bleeps and the bustle of the six-bridge crew watching and reacting to an ever-changing situation. She had to trust them all. And they had to trust her. In another fire-fight, it would be a lot easier if she could use the cannon.

"Sounding. Six metres eighty," called out the navigator. *We're losing manoeuvring space*, Claire thought. *I'll have to move fast.*

She'd been given a little wiggle room to deal with the threat. And she intended to use all of it. It was time to implement the plan that she had been working out in her head since they had left port. If it worked, she'd get both the smugglers and the mole.

FORTY-FOUR

THE FAINT GLOW from a fat crescent moon bathed the landscape beyond their van's headlights in a soft grey tinge. It was close to three in the morning, and they were the only people on the two-lane road a dozen or so kilometres from the turnoff on the Trans-Canada Highway. They'd passed a few scattered houses, all dark.

Gus slowed the van until the headlights pointed to a dirt road that led to a blackness that must be the ocean. "Are you sure this is the place, Zeke?"

Zeke checked the directions on his phone once again. "Think so. Didn't Ash say it was a place that no one would notice?" He pulled out a wrinkled provincial road map, one of several stuffed in the side pocket on the door. Another paper map, this one of his home province of Alberta, tumbled to the floor. He shoved it under his seat. Then he compared the image on his phone with the paper map and nodded.

Gus stepped on the gas and heard snow crunch under the tires as they bobbed over well-worn ruts that led to the coastline. The path rose over a small ridge, and then they saw in the fan of their high beams a neat bay with a thin beach protected by a thick layer of trees and the ridge. It was a perfect low-visibility spot for transiting shipments from boats to trucks. He checked his watch: 3:06. Ten minutes to kill before the boat arrived, and then the hard work would begin.

Gus yanked the phone from Zeke and dialed the familiar number. It rang only once.

"Yes?"

"We've arrived at the destination."

There was a short pause before the low, raspy voice on the line continued, "Describe it."

"Well, it's a small bay. There's a beach, trees. Snow. There's no one else around."

"Look at the sea. What do you see off the coast?"

Gus grabbed the binoculars and scanned the black void ahead. The black morphed to a lighter grey at one spot directly ahead.

"There's a small island."

"Right. Stay there. Shipment will be there soon."

"Will there be any trouble?"

"It's been taken care of."

Gus heard the click on the other end and gave the phone back to Zeke.

"So what do we do now?" asked Zeke.

"We wait."

Two minutes later, the phone buzzed, jolting Zeke and Gus from their seats.

"Change of plans. You'll meet the boat at another location."

"What happened?"

"They think they might have been followed. It'll be safer to unload farther along the shore. I'm sending you the directions."

Gus was an Alberta boy and tides meant little. There was no chance that the prairie would ever heave up and down on a daily basis. But he had heard that the tides here in the Bay of Fundy were special. And in the beam of his flashlight, he could see why. In the short time they had been waiting, he noticed the beach was bigger, the water now a foot lower than when they had arrived.

"We're leaving," he said.

"Where we going?" Zeke scrunched his eyebrows as his phone beeped with the new directions from Ash.

"Farther into the bay. The boat will unload over there."

Zeke had trouble describing the route Ash had sent. Five minutes into the drive, the map on his phone pointed to a lonely road that went off to the right. Gus turned the truck and drove until it ended with a small "Dead End" sign, mostly hidden with snow-covered branches that drooped from tall trees nearby. The headlights didn't expose any other part of the route. Gus cut the engine. They spent a minute staring at the silent blackness outside until their eyes adapted to the darkness and the surroundings materialized into view.

With his watch flashing 3:17 a.m., Gus knew the boat they were supposed to meet would arrive in a few minutes.

Zeke looked at Gus. "What do we do now?"

"We wait."

Zeke clicked the door open. The interior light flicked on, nearly blinding them.

Gus squinted. "Stay in the van. We don't want to attract attention."

Zeke closed the door and the darkness returned. He began to fidget, shaking his knee, then tapping his fingers. *He's not good at containing his feelings*, Gus thought. Not for the first time. Such a weakness could be dangerous in their line of work.

"Do you really think we're going to get our own country on Monday?"

Gus stared at Zeke in disbelief. Zeke had never before expressed any interest in their cause. He hadn't shown any evidence of commitment beyond signing up as an AIM recruit two months ago. He recalled the rally the week before, when Mr. Haynes, who had stepped down as AIM leader when he joined the government, had spoken to all of the senior military staff. Haynes was well respected and was now the premier's trusted lieutenant. He explained their objective, and how each of their jobs would contribute to victory. Gus knew that victory required their mission to be a success. Many people in the organization depended on him to finish the job. He didn't need to know more. "Yes, I do. And we need to be prepared."

"So you think it's right, then?"

Gus sighed. "Independence? Why not?"

"But there hasn't been much action. I signed up for action. And so far, there ain't been much."

"Be careful what you wish for, kid. Action is not fun. In fact, it's grim."

"You've been in a fight?"

"Yeah, lots."

"But nothing's happened so far."

"Before all this. Bosnia. Afghanistan."

"You were in the army?"

"Three tours of duty."

"What did you do in the army?"

"I was a platoon leader. I retired as a sergeant."

Zeke's eyes grew wide. "Wow. You kill anyone?"

He's such a kid. "Next question."

Zeke was about to ask the question again but thought twice about it and changed the topic. "So why did you join?"

Gus turned away and stared at the night sky and its countless points of light. "I've seen too much pointless death."

"You could've joined private groups. You could be rich."

"I didn't want to be a mercenary."

"You'd be rich, though."

"I don't fight or kill for money."

"We're getting paid for this job."

"Yeah, but there's much more to it."

"Our own country?"

"Our own country. We have to win."

"Didn't we already win?"

"Win what?"

"Didn't we stop those bad guys in Bosnia? Who were they again?"

"The Bosnian Serbs, you mean?"

"I guess."

"If you don't know who the bad guys were, then we didn't win, did we? Look up Srebrenica sometime."

"And Afghanistan? We won that one?"

"No. More like a draw. We stayed, they went away. We left, and they came back. We left the government in charge and crossed our fingers."

"Oh, I get it. You're oh, one, and one then?"

Gus looked at him.

Zeke continued, "No wins, one draw, one loss."

"I hadn't thought of it that way but, yeah, I guess I'm looking for a win before I retire from this job."

FORTY-FIVE

GUS POINTED ON THE MAP that glowed from Zeke's phone. "It's time. Get the gear. We'll go to the beach and wait there."

Zeke hopped up and opened two small boxes from the back of the van. He gathered two encrypted walkie talkie VHF radios, a pair of Celestron 10x70 binoculars, a flashlight, and two Glock handguns, each with extra ammunition clips.

Gus scuttled down the shallow embankment that separated the end of the dirt road from the beach, while Zeke walked awkwardly cradling the gear in both hands. Gus scanned the horizon to the west and south in search of the boat, but all he saw were two shades of black with a fuzzy horizontal line separating sky from sea. Zeke handed him the binoculars, a radio that he stuffed into his pocket, and a pistol, which he jammed into the rear waistband of his pants.

Gus looked up. A pair of red-green navigation lights appeared next to the leftmost cliff. The boat was coming and it was on time. Maybe this job would be easier than he thought. All he had to do now was wait, load the cargo into the truck, and drive very, very carefully back to Airdrie. Redemption was now a distinct possibility.

He handed the binoculars back to Zeke. "They're coming. Gimme the flashlight."

Zeke tossed the light over, and Gus aimed it directly at the incoming boat. He turned the beam on and off several times. One long flash followed by two short and a long. The letter X in Morse code. A similar on-off flash, long, short, long, long — Y — was quickly returned from the boat now only a hundred metres or so away and approaching fast.

A moment later they heard the growing whine of a small outboard engine; soon, a short bald man appeared in a small dinghy. He jumped out and dragged the craft onto the beach. He did not approach but instead put his hand into his right pocket and said coolly, "Who sent you?"

"Ash," Gus replied.

"Right," he said, more relaxed. "Here's the first part of the shipment. There are two others. We don't have much time. We're being followed."

Gus motioned for Zeke to begin unloading the wooden crates, each about the size of a small refrigerator. Zeke took the first one and was surprised at its weight. He dragged it, straining with effort, swearing with each step until it lay in front of the open van. Gus grabbed the second one. As the crate passed through his flashlight beam, he noticed the markings on the box: Property of the U.S. Army.

He loaded several similar crates into the van. As Zeke walked back to fetch the next crate, he stopped and looked out to sea, where another set of lights had appeared. He turned to Gus. "There's another boat out there. And it's coming this way."

Lieutenant Commander Claire Marcoux clutched the rope that held her within the bucking RHIB as it knifed through wave after angry wave. Its twin engines roared, shattering the silence of the night. Wrapped within her heavy Kevlar armour and helmet, she felt the buzz that accompanied impending action.

Her orders were that the *Kingston* could not confront the smugglers. But they said nothing about sending out their motorized Zodiac, the rigid-hulled inflatable boat. She knew she was taking a risk in interpreting her orders creatively, but she didn't want to waste the opportunity to stop the smugglers now that they were in her sights.

Directly ahead, the shoreline glowed pale green through her night vision goggles, with flickers of white light from three tiny people who scurried between a small boat and the bush.

She looked at the other three sailors with her in the boat. The massive bulks of Petty Officer First Class Steven Burns and Petty Officer Second Class Maddie Kershaw squatted at the front, each clutching black Heckler & Koch MP5 sub-machine guns, while Leading Seaman Ferguson steered and controlled the throttle from the back of the boat. All were in full battle gear. Claire felt her heart rate increase and the sharp intake of air with every breath. She wanted answers. She'd left the XO in command of the ship.

Fifty metres, she estimated.

"Okay, everyone," Claire screamed into the mike over the roar of the engines, "safeties off. Remember, I want them alive."

She flicked the safety off her SIG Sauer 9 mm pistol and clutched it tightly in her right hand.

"Roger, ma'am," said Burns.

Twenty metres.

Time to start the show. Claire raised the bullhorn with her left hand and said, "Stop where you are. Drop your weapons!"

"This is the Royal Canadian Navy," boomed the voice from the sea.

"The navy? Are you fucking kidding?" Gus barked to Zeke.

Gus pulled out his Glock and twisted behind the tree nearest the beach. But Zeke froze in terror. Zeke had never been in combat. If Zeke wasn't going to fight for their noble cause, he would get captured. Then he would spill his guts and expose their plan. Zeke couldn't be allowed to jeopardize the plan. Gus shifted his aim from the Zodiac crashing onto the beach and aimed at Zeke, just as Zeke suddenly awoke from his stupor and darted toward another tree. They now had some cover, but it was different for the man at the dinghy.

The RHIB slammed to a stop ten metres or so to the left of the dinghy. Claire saw two figures hide behind trees, but the third ducked behind the dinghy on shore and opened fire. She could see one, two, three muzzle flashes. But she had no idea how close the bullets flew because of the engine noise and her helmet. She assumed they had been close. Burns stayed crouched in the boat and returned fire with two short, controlled bursts, flame belching from his MP5, a few tracer bullets streaking toward the dinghy. The man jerked awkwardly backward and crumpled on the sand.

Kershaw and Burns sprang onto the beach and ran for the nearest tree. Once there, they fired a few rounds toward the presumed location of the other two men, as Claire pivoted off the side of the RHIB, thumped onto the beach, and dove behind a tree near where Kershaw crouched.

At least two targets were still out there. Probably armed.

Ferguson slid onto the sand directly behind Claire. She turned toward the dinghy and saw a heavy-set man in a checkered jacket run from behind a tree and deeper into the forest. Kershaw fired a rapid one, two, three, four shots from her MP5, an orange tracer darting into the night.

Claire wheezed heavily, weighed down by her Kevlar armour and her helmet with its night vision system. She held her SIG Sauer, as she knelt on the sand and scanned the glowing green scene ahead. Trees, rocks, beach, and abandoned boat as expected. The dark forest began only metres from shore. The targets were hiding in there somewhere. The rest of the team spread out to her left maybe ten metres apart, slowly approaching the forest edge.

A blur at the far edge of the view. "Movement at eleven o'clock. Fifty metres," she said into her commlink.

"Roger," two of her team replied. She ran to the line between beach and forest, slammed against the first tree she encountered, and peered cautiously around it. She saw a second figure running away, farther into the trees.

"Suspect moving, two o'clock. Fifty metres," Kershaw said.

"Roger," Claire replied. "Proceed with caution."

She took five steps and ran to the next tree, only a few metres ahead. Two flashes from the forest were followed by two whizzes as bullets narrowly missed her. She slammed onto the ground and held her pistol toward where she thought the flashes had been. With no clear target, she didn't fire.

"Two targets, twenty metres. Kershaw, I'm on their left. You take the right," Burns said.

"Roger. There in ten seconds," Kershaw replied.

"Ma'am. Come up straight ahead," Burns added.

"Copy. I want them alive," said Claire.

"Understood."

Claire saw Kershaw approach low, taking advantage of the forest cover. She took one, two slow steps at a time. Claire sprinted to the next tree and waited, peering quickly around. When she saw no movement, she ran to the next tree ahead, closing the distance toward the two targets. With their night vision goggles, Claire and her team had the advantage. They formed a triangle that would soon strangle any potential escape route for the doomed pair of smugglers foolish enough to mess with the navy.

One figure broke cover behind a tree not ten metres away, then ran amazingly fast away from Claire. He slipped past both Kershaw and Burns and out of range of her goggles.

There was one left. They had to get him alive.

Claire heard Burns's voice both live and, with a fraction of a second delay, over her commlink. "Do not move. Do not fuckin' move. Royal Canadian Navy. There are two machine guns pointed at you. You move, you die."

"Don't shoot. Don't shoot. Don't shoot." The figure was on his knees, both hands in the air. His shaking hands were empty.

Claire approached cautiously, one step, then another, her pistol rigid, straight out, aimed at the man. "Where's the gun? Point to it."

The man gestured to his left.

"Found it." Kershaw held up a pistol in one hand.

"Name. What's your name?" Claire ordered. It was good that he was alive, although the one who escaped worried her. First things first.

No answer.

"Who's your friend? And the one at the boat?"

No answer.

Ferguson's voice on the radio. "I'm by the boat. Found one male, deceased. It's one of the suspects, ma'am."

Claire holstered her pistol and spoke into her radio headset. "Roger." She turned her head away and walked a few steps. "This is Marcoux. Calling the *Kingston*. Over."

A voice crackled in her ear. "This is the *Kingston*, ma'am. Over."

"Inform the RCMP that we have one person of interest in custody. One deceased. And one missing." She turned to face the prisoner on his knees. "We've called the RCMP. They're on their way and will be picking you up for questioning. You should know that smuggling military weapons is an act of terrorism."

Burns approached the man from behind, cuffs in his hand.

Zeke couldn't stop shaking. *I'm no terrorist. What am I going to do? I have to escape.* The soldiers terrified him. Gus was right. Action was grim. One of the soldiers looked smaller than the others. It was his chance.

The man on his knees suddenly bolted up. He curled his fist and launched it right at Claire's face. She guessed he was about six foot one and two hundred pounds. Huge compared to her relatively measly five foot nine. The man probably calculated that in order to escape, he only had to incapacitate the smallest and most vulnerable target.

Zeke launched an uppercut punch toward Claire. With his massive bulk, his punch was clearly aimed at crushing her jaw by striking under her helmet. But she had seen his upper lip begin to tense along with his shoulders, and her head had already moved the few centimetres necessary to avoid contact. And, as Zeke realized that his punch was about to miss, he felt a throbbing pain in his right elbow as she locked it with a short, sharp hold. He fell over on his right side and realized that his right arm was hyper-extended in the wrong direction. Moving in any direction produced searing stabs of pain. He flailed his other arm but it was pointless. Her knee was at the back of his neck. His stomach pressed into the ice and dirt.

"Relax," Claire said. "One more move like that and I'll snap your arm in two. Got it?"

Zeke screamed in pain and nodded as someone grabbed his wrists from behind and cuffed them using plastic straps. His right arm still throbbed, but remained reassuringly intact.

The other soldier, another woman who had just appeared from the darkness beyond, leaned over Zeke and said matter-of-factly, "Don't fuck with the captain."

Claire flipped him over.

Burns seemed a bit surprised. Claire could sense a new-found respect from the two petty officers. They had never seen this side of her. Yes, she was smart, determined, and ambitious. But she was also strong and fierce, even in the face of a very fit and aggressive two-hundred-pound man. He wasn't going anywhere until the RCMP arrived.

Gus sprinted through the shadowless forest cast in a pale glow by the crescent moon directly overhead. He circled back to where they had left the van. In the moonlight, he saw a lone sailor holding a machine gun, standing on guard beside the dinghy the assault team had arrived in. How many had there been in the assault team? At least four. The van was at least thirty metres away. Could he sneak into the van without attracting the sailor's attention, or should he just shoot him now?

The experience of being hunted at night drew him back to the trauma of Afghanistan. Helmand province. But now, instead of the Taliban, it was his own navy wanting to capture or kill him. This was so fucking messed up. He could accept being hunted by the police, but it hurt knowing that people he may have served honourably with in the armed forces were now pointing weapons at him. He resolved to only shoot the sailor if there were no other choice. He would do his best to escape undetected. He wasn't like Zeke, killing indiscriminately. He had principles.

He knew what he would do in a similar ground situation: outflank, encircle, and contain. Time was critical. He had to break out before the trap was set. He crawled back to the van, one arm ahead of the other, his face in the snow and mud, and his pistol in his right hand. He cleared the forest cover and continued. He could easily be seen if the sailor turned to face him. But the sailor kept his focus on the forest far to the left, one ear tuned to his radio, no doubt. There was a body at his feet on the sand.

Gus crept forward, arms and legs burning with effort, until he touched the front tire. He stuffed his pistol into his belt until he felt it dig into his back. He hoisted himself onto his knees, opened the driver door, looked back toward the sailor, and froze.

He hadn't been noticed. The rear door was closed. He had no idea how much of the cargo was inside. They had been surprised early. He hopped into the driver's seat and glanced back to see at least a half-dozen crates in the hold. Good enough. He took a second to catch his breath and try to close the passenger door that swung lifelessly as a gust of wind blew into the cab. Zeke had been caught and would likely spill the beans. *He's such a kid.*

So success of the mission relied on him escaping, switching vans, and getting the weapons back home on time. He clicked the door shut, flicked the key, and the van roared to life. It would immediately attract the attention of the navy. He had to escape before they encircled him. He floored the accelerator. The rear wheels whined in protest, coughing up mud, snow, and rocks, as the van darted forward along the rutted path they had followed to get here. Freedom was only a few minutes away.

* ✳ *

"Ferguson," Claire yelled into the commlink, "we have one prisoner. Check out the van."

Claire paced in front of the prisoner and thought out loud, "You guys steam undercover from the Boston area, close to the coast where no one would notice. You carry a shitload of weapons. And it's a repeat attempt at smuggling, I assume." She turned to Zeke. "Who are you working for? Who ordered the weapons? Where were you going?"

He stayed silent.

"Ma'am," Ferguson radioed back, "the other suspect just took off with the van."

Claire swore silently. She pushed her commlink button. "*Kingston*, this is Charlie Oscar, come in."

Wiseman's voice crackled. "*Kingston*, acknowledged. Over."

"One suspect is fleeing in the van along the shoreline. Track and prepare to pursue. Inform the RCMP."

"Aye aye, ma'am."

"We'll clean up here and return to the *Kingston* in a moment. Out."

Ferguson called on the same channel. "Ma'am. You should have a look at this."

Claire motioned for Kershaw and Burns to follow her back to the beach and to bring the prisoner. They walked a few paces behind as she raced back to the beachhead where Ferguson pointed to two crates that had busted open, spilling their contents onto the snow and sand. One had long wooden boxes marked "U.S. Army"; the other was packed with machine guns and pistols.

"RPGs?" Claire said, pointing to the first open crate.

"Yes, ma'am. Two dozen of them. Two crates of Claymores. And five boxes of C-4 sticks, too."

"Who would want that?" Ferguson said.

"Someone equipping an army, I suppose," said Claire. She turned toward Kershaw and Burns and pointed to Zeke. "Bring him over here."

Kershaw tried to pull the prisoner up and shove him over to the van. He continued looking at the ground. Burns ordered him to move, but he barely registered the command. Claire thought he was in shock. He stayed seated.

Claire walked up to the prisoner. He stared at her, trying to look cool and intimidating. His shaking betrayed his fear. *He's not the leader*, she thought. "Who are these for? Who's your customer?"

He said nothing.

"Found some more, ma'am."

Claire walked back. Four more crates, all ripped open to reveal their shocking contents. Machine guns, grenades, sniper rifles, land mines, countless boxes of ammunitions, and Stinger surface-to-air missiles. She nodded. Enough to equip a small army.

"Where were you taking them?"

"Ma'am," Ferguson called out again, "I think I know where they were going."

Claire approached near where the driver's side door had been. A few maps lay in a loose pile in the mud. Ferguson retrieved the top one, a well-worn hiking map of Fundy National Park.

"They used this map to find this location." He dug out the other ones: tourist maps of Quebec, Ontario, Manitoba, Saskatchewan, and Alberta, each with a yellow trace over a route taken. There was no map of B.C. "I think they were taking this shipment to somewhere in Alberta," Ferguson said.

Claire turned to gauge the prisoner's reaction. He began to squirm and look down at the snow in the moonlight. Ferguson was on to something.

"Can you be more specific?"

He flipped the map, brushed off the loose earth, and carefully noted every hand-drawn line, circle, and scribble. The yellow trace line ended just north of Calgary. There were numbers on the right edge of the official provincial map of Alberta. A seven-digit number was circled.

"I think here." He pointed to the end of the yellow trace.

"Airdrie?"

The prisoner turned away. At least until Kershaw, who stood behind, guarding him, shoved his face hard onto the ground.

"Yes, ma'am. Look here. There's lots of notes around Airdrie and see these? Phone numbers, right?"

"I think you're correct." Claire called into her commlink, "*Kingston*, we're on our way back. Prepare to pursue the van."

Gus didn't let up on the accelerator. He powered past the darkened ghosts of tree after tree until he broke through onto a gravel road. He felt for the map on the passenger seat, but he couldn't find it. And Zeke's phone had the map and the directions. *Which way to go?* He turned left and silently prayed it wouldn't prove to be a fatal mistake. A few minutes later, he realized he had driven right back to the navy. He whizzed by a parked police cruiser. *Jesus, RCMP, too?* In the headlights, he saw figures and shadows, and one of them was Zeke, slouching, handcuffed. He would spill the beans for sure. Gus had to be sure that Zeke wouldn't compromise their mission. Whatever it took.

He braked hard, veered to the left side of the path, and spun the wheel to the right. The van screeched as it pivoted in the narrow path, walled in with ominous forest on both sides. He opened his door, pulled out his pistol, aimed, and fired.

Claire stormed back onto the *Kingston*'s bridge.

"Captain on the bridge," said Barry. Claire dropped into her chair. She tossed one of the sailors her helmet, slimed with sweat and salt, and her flak jacket.

"Status?" Her pulsed raced. She gulped air.

Wiseman stood and faced her. "Petty Officer Kershaw is holding the prisoner on shore. She's waiting for pick-up by the RCMP. Anchor retracted. All personnel accounted for. Ready to get underway. Sounding depth five metres fifty."

"Ma'am," said Sullivan, "RCMP confirms they've arrived on scene."

The radio hissed and popped. "We found the other one. Under fire."

Claire grabbed the mike. "Kershaw. Report."

The voice was out of breath. "Ma'am. RCMP arrived. They were taking the prisoner when the other suspect just showed up" — the voice cut out for a moment — "and we're now in pursuit."

"Kershaw, do you need assistance?"

"Uh, I think we found him —" The radio cut off. Sounds of gunshots echoed from the speaker on the bridge. She counted four sharp cracks.

"Kershaw. Report." Claire barked into the microphone.

No sound came from the speaker for what seemed like minutes. Claire scanned the black horizon with her night vision binoculars, looking for movement. She saw small, sporadic flashes trace vectors to the right of the landing zone on shore. A gunfight between Kershaw and the RCMP on one side, the suspect on the other.

She put her binoculars down for a moment just as the shore was lit up by a bigger, brighter blaze. She whipped the binoculars up to see the outline of a police cruiser in the dying flare.

She heard muffled sounds on the radio speaker. "Kershaw here, ma'am. Officer down. Officer down. Call an ambulance."

"Copy." Claire looked at Sullivan He picked up his cellphone and dialed.

Kershaw came back on. "Suspect escaped. Driving a dark van to the east. I cannot pursue. He is armed and very dangerous."

"And the officer down?"

"I'm staying with him. He's hit in the chest. There's a lot of blood."

"Copy. And the prisoner?"

"Unhurt and still in custody. I parked him. He's not going anywhere."

"Copy that. We're sending a RHIB to pick you up." Claire shot a glance at the XO. Wiseman spun around, pointed to two petty officers and together they flew out from the bridge. "RHIB ETA five minutes."

Sullivan said, "Ambulance on its way. ETA eight minutes."

Claire relayed the message to Kershaw.

"Copy, ma'am."

Claire sat back in her chair and digested the new situation. The suspect, the probable leader of the group, had escaped and was carrying military weapons in his van. He had come back to rescue his comrade. He had shot and injured at least one RCMP officer, and fired upon a member of her crew. She wanted the prisoner alive to compare stories with their first prisoner and to explain what was going on. But now, loose with an armoury of military-grade weaponry, he posed a grave threat to the local community. She had to alert the RCMP.

"Navigator, what's the nearest community?"

The young officer scoured the map on the small navigation table. "Alma. Three kilometres east."

Claire pulled the microphone from its hook on the ceiling and was about to speak when someone yelled, "Incoming fire. Incoming fire. Port side from shore." She turned toward the black shore they had just left and saw a white-orange flame streak toward them and whiz by.

"Action stations!" she ordered, and the klaxon alerted the crew to the imminent danger. The missing smuggler was firing at them now. *He doesn't want us to follow*. Another RPG could easily cause a crippling fire or sink her ship. "M2, can you see a target?"

"No. All dark," said a sailor manning the M2 0.50-calibre machine gun and peering into the forest with night vision goggles.

"Gun crew, close up." The crew used the Bofors 40 mm gun. It was different than trying to hit a floating piece of metal in the bay during target practice exercises. They knew she required approval from the brass at HQ before it could be used. "RO, get me Maritime Command."

"Aye aye, ma'am."

"Ma'am, there's movement." A leading seaman with binoculars pointed into the distance. She grabbed her own binoculars and saw red tail lights moving, flickering through the black. It looked like a truck at moderate speed trying to navigate its way through the forest. The one who fired at them. He was trying to get away. She couldn't let him succeed.

"Steer oh nine oh. All ahead flank. We can't lose him," she ordered.

"Aye aye. Steering oh nine oh. All ahead flank," replied the seaman at the helm.

The navigator said, "Sounding depth. Four metres seventy."

The twin diesel engines roared into life with a deep, throaty growl. The sudden jolt of power threw Claire back into her seat as the nose of the ship tilted up and veered sharply to the right.

"Gun crew. Track the lights."

She watched as the lights suddenly stopped. She saw movement but couldn't make it out. Until she saw another flash of orange and white come straight at them.

"Evasive manoeuvres!" she ordered.

The helmsman swung the wheel right multiple times, and the ship groaned starboard, making an extreme arc in the water. The RPG zipped past, missing the bridge by a few metres.

"M2 crew. Aim and target."

The machine gun crew tried their best to find the location the RPG had been fired from, but facing a wall of black on shore, they had nothing to aim at. She couldn't fire blind. This close to a community, there could be innocent people on shore. "No target, ma'am."

This isn't working. "M2 crew. Stand down. Stand down."

"Sounding four metres fifty," the navigator said. "At current rate of decrease, minimum clearance in ten minutes."

She was running out of water. The Fundy tides were sucking most of the water out of the bay at an astounding rate. Only a few minutes remaining until there wasn't enough water to float the ship. But she couldn't let the suspect escape. There was too much at stake.

The RO piped up, "Ma'am. Captain Hall on the satphone."

She grabbed the handset near the base of her chair. "Lieutenant Commander Marcoux, sir."

"What's going on?"

"Sir, we're in pursuit of one of the smuggling suspects. We had one in custody. He shot an RCMP officer. We're in pursuit. Police reinforcements are on their way. We've been fired upon twice. Permission to use the Bofors, sir."

"I told you not to engage the suspects."

"They engaged us, sir. I don't see any other way to stop the second suspect. We have physical evidence that he's in possession of a large amount of military weaponry brought in from the States. We don't want that loose among civilians."

"And the local police?"

"On their way, sir. But they'll be too late. I have the suspect and cargo sighted and we're following them, but I don't know for how much longer, though." The speaker crackled.

"Sounding. Three metres forty. Minimum clearance in four minutes," said the navigator.

"Incoming. Incoming. Port side. Fore. From the shore," screamed the spotter.

Another flash.

Then the ship quaked as a blinding burst of light from the rear of the ship filled the sky. An eerie silence followed.

Time slowed. The bridge tilted to an extreme angle. Objects slid to the right. Claire grabbed onto the rail to stay in her chair.

Then the bridge slapped back level with a loud thud.

The crew stood still, in shock.

"Report!" she barked. She turned aft to see fire, sparks, and smoke. *The RPG must have hit the RHIB launcher at least.* Dangerously close to the fuel tanks, too. And the XO and two petty officers were on their way back there.

"Ma'am," the XO's voice came in on the commlink, "direct hit on the RHIB launcher. Aft quarter on fire. Fire suppression team on their way. Fuel tanks undamaged. Recommend we move out of RPG range."

Claire took a deep breath as the crew returned to their duties, worry etched on their faces. They were under attack with an inexperienced captain.

Claire glowered. Now she was having more doubts about the XO. "We're not going anywhere. Casualties?"

"Still waiting for report."

"Can we manoeuvre?" She looked at the helmsman, who shifted his nervous gaze to the rear door as Wiseman burst through. He was covered in charcoal. His face was tinged orange from the fire behind them.

"Fire suppression team active," he choked.

Claire looked at him with concern. "Can we manoeuvre?"

Wiseman scanned the displays in front of the helmsman. "Yes, ma'am. Engines unaffected. We should move out of range."

"You have a problem, X?"

"We have what we need. We don't need to engage them. We should retreat and let the police handle the remaining suspect."

She spun around in her chair as Wiseman stumbled onto the bridge. "We need to have a talk after, X."

"Yes, ma'am." He stared at his blackened hands.

"Weapons?" Her weapons were on the front of the ship, far from the fire.

The XO hesitated. "M2. And Bofors available."

The RO added, "Radio contact lost with Maritime Command." He threw his hands up in frustration. "The antenna is probably damaged."

Wiseman pointed to Sullivan. "Get out there and fix it. We need to confirm our orders —"

"No, we don't," said Claire. She turned to Wiseman and pointed aft. "Take charge of the fire crews back there. We can manoeuvre. We know they have military-grade weaponry. They have to be stopped. Now."

"We don't have permission to —"

She replaced the microphone, and she could feel the atmosphere change. Was it more tension? Or maybe respect? She had decided to use the big gun. And everyone on the bridge knew it.

Wiseman grabbed a fire extinguisher, pushed through the aft door, and disappeared.

Claire swung to face forward, looking out to the black coast on her left. "Gun crew, aim and target."

"Aim and target, ma'am." They could see the brake lights of the fleeing truck flick between the black of the trees. The road must be near the water's edge. But it must be in poor shape. The truck seemed hampered and couldn't drive at full speed. It was barely moving faster than the crippled *Kingston*, a thousand-tonne warship now at flank speed, knifing through the water at about forty kilometres an hour.

"Warning shot. Aim fifty metres in front of them." She gripped her binoculars. The XO reappeared.

"Sounding at four metres twenty, ma'am." Barry, the navigation officer, sounded stressed. "Running out of room fast."

"Aye aye, ma'am," the XO said, "fifty metres in front. Aim and target."

"Fire."

The cannon flashed, and she felt the compression wave smack her entire body. A moment later, a portion of the forest lit up in an orange blast, sending sparks and trees flying. She could see the truck in the reflected light for a fraction of a second.

"It's not stopping, ma'am," said the lookout. The van didn't slow down. It didn't accept the warning.

"Gun crew. Aim and target. Target the truck."

"Ma'am?" said the XO.

"We can't let him escape. He has military-grade weaponry in that truck. We have orders to stop it."

"Aim and target, ma'am."

"Sounding at four metres. Breached minimum clearance." Panic washed through the navigation officer's voice.

This was the biggest decision of her career. Maybe of her life. If she was wrong, her career was over. Maybe even if she was right, too. The crew held their breath. The cannon could annihilate an entire city block. She might run aground on a sand bar at any moment.

Time to decide.

Unleash.

Or not.

He fired on my crew.

She had to clean up the mess left by that asshole Lansdowne.

No way they were going to get away. The smugglers. Lansdowne.

No way.

She sucked in a breath. "Fire."

The crew didn't hesitate this time. The Bofors roared with orange flame. Four seconds later, a hundred-metre tract of forest vapourized in a blaze of white light, followed seconds later by a rumbling, growling roar. It was a direct hit on a vehicle. Whatever weaponry and ammunition it contained detonated with the blast. The explosion was spectacular, throwing shadows everywhere for a few seconds before dying as quickly as it appeared, leaving a twisted collection of glowing red metal and shattered tree stumps burning beside the shoreline.

The crew stared in awe.

Now she had two suspects dead, a hell of a mess near a national park, and one prisoner who better have some of the answers.

She turned the *Kingston* around just before they ran out of navigating room. With the onboard launcher now a pile of twisted metal from the RPG blast, she couldn't send the RHIB to pick up Kershaw after she had transferred the prisoner to the RCMP.

The RO got the message over the radio. Kershaw would get a ride back with the RCMP. "Police reinforcements have arrived," Kershaw said. "They confirm they have the prisoner, ma'am. They've begun interrogation. So far they said he's only a low-ranking member of a white supremacist group. In Alberta. The maps were right."

"Roger." That got Claire's attention. Why would white supremacists in Alberta want military weapons? Who were they going to war against? If they were battling another white power group, would they really need RPGs and Stingers? Their enemy must be substantially more powerful. Did they want the weapons to even the odds? Why smuggle them along the Atlantic coast? Why not just bring them over the border from Montana? Someone went to a great deal of effort to conceal their activity.

Too many unanswered questions.

And the XO is toast.

FORTY-SIX

DANIEL SIPPED HIS COFFEE and watched the faint morning sun creaking over the sleepy, snowy town. Breaking his contemplation, there was a knock on the door. MacKinnon, right on time.

"How are you two getting along?"

Touesnard grunted from the stupor of another restless night on the sofa.

"Glad to hear it." MacKinnon turned to Daniel. "Does the name Sharon mean anything to you?"

Daniel shook his head. "No. Why?"

MacKinnon held up a plastic bag holding an iPod. "This was Forrestal's. It was the password. Must mean something important to him."

"Wife's name?"

"Nope. That was Gabrielle."

"Daughter's name?"

"No children."

"New girlfriend?"

"Nobody we could find."

"Boyfriend?"

MacKinnon threw him a look of surprise. "It would be an odd name for a man."

Daniel rubbed his nose. "There's something important that we're missing about Mr. Forrestal."

"I agree," said Touesnard.

"What did you find on his iPod?" said Daniel.

"Music of someone in his late fifties. Beatles, Rolling Stones, Led Zeppelin, Jimmy Buffett …"

"Jimmy Buffett?" Touesnard tilted his head.

"'Margaritaville.' It was a big hit in the seventies, remember?"

Touesnard shrugged.

"It looks like a pretty generic hit list to me," Daniel said.

"Except it's not." MacKinnon's face tensed.

"He could have downloaded it from dozens of music sites."

"No, this list is unique. It's Denise Michael's *Sunday Night Rock Royalty Top 100*. Says so right here." He showed Daniel and Touesnard the image on the iPod display.

"So?"

"This show is from Cay Rock 96.5 FM. Cayman Islands. We've already confirmed with the radio station. This was their list from two weeks ago."

Daniel and Touesnard looked at each other in surprise.

MacKinnon continued. "I think he spent a lot of time down there. He wanted something to remember it by."

"So. Forrestal had a connection with the place where someone set up an account with my name on it. It *could* be a coincidence," said Daniel without any conviction.

MacKinnon cradled the iPod. "You don't believe that, and I don't believe in coincidences either."

Daniel's cellphone buzzed. He answered right away and put his phone face up on the table.

"Hi, Xiao Ping. I'm putting you on speaker. The police are here."

"Back in the thick of it, Daniel?"

MacKinnon looked surprised. "Is that your friend from China, again?"

"Detectives, this is Xiao Ping Lu. She's the one I called before. She's in Beijing. Xiao Ping, I'm working with Detectives MacKinnon and Touesnard on this end. Trying to get to the bottom of things. It's been a busy few days —"

Xiao Ping interrupted. "What happened?"

"Just like old times. Almost run off the road, among other things."

"How is your driving holding up?"

"A bit rusty."

The two detectives looked puzzled.

Daniel explained. "I took a high-performance driving course. All senior managers in our Beijing office had to take it."

Touesnard said, "Didn't you have taxis or a driver?"

"Sure. But we were all potentially high-worth targets. Kidnapping was common, and bodyguards couldn't protect us all the time. The company had insurance policies on us, and the insurance company insisted that we knew how to defend ourselves in case something bad happened. Remember, it was the Wild West out there."

Xiao Ping said, "He was a crazy driver."

"The training was good. But it was a few years ago." Daniel took a deep breath. "Glad you're enjoying yourself, Xiao Ping. What did you find out about our mysterious businessman?"

"He's an interesting person, Daniel. Competent."

"That's the good news. I'm after the bad news."

"As I said, he's interesting. Regular transactions."

"Shell company?"

"No surprise there. On paper, it looks like a real company, but it exists only as a post office box number to hide the real owner and his money from prying eyes like ours."

"Where is it located?"

"Cayman Islands. They have strict secrecy laws to prevent disclosure of the owner of any shell company."

Daniel and MacKinnon nodded at each other. Daniel said, "Did your contact cough up the details?"

"Of course. Looks like the company hid a series of bridge loans."

"So he had big bills to pay and came up short on cash to pay them?"

"Yep."

"What did he have to pay?"

"Loans. And lots of them. They cascaded, one loan to pay the prior loan."

"Diversified sources of revenue? Clients?"

"Not really. He seems to have only one income source."

"What about investments? What does he have in his portfolio? Oil? Natural resources? Banks? High-tech?"

"It started with real estate. Then nothing. It's more like a big savings account. One with a regular infusion of cash. The most recent deposit came in last July: 2.7 million dollars."

Daniel tried to recall which acquisition happened last summer. "I remember that he bought Transcon Securitech, a Virginia-based online data management and security company. It was another big success, with more happy investors and more fawning headlines." He checked Google Finance on his laptop to verify the price. "He paid three million and change. With fees, it could easily have netted him a couple of million. So 2.7 million is possible." *No surprises there*, he concluded.

But the lack of a diversified portfolio got his spidey senses tingling.

"So no investments at all? Where did the money go then?"

"There were regular withdrawals. Usually to another shell account, also linked to him."

"And they went where?"

"I've got the pattern breakdown. There were many places, and each time the list of destinations grew. He got around. Canada, of course, then Eastern Europe, Central Asia, then back to Canada and the States."

A growing list of clients. That made sense. He was paying back dividends to his customers. But he wasn't investing any money.

"Can you check to see if any destinations have been there since the beginning? Can you trace back a few years?"

"Only seven years back." Daniel heard keys clicking in the background, then Xiao Ping said, "Yes, there's one account that's been there since the start. The SWIFT code is based in the Cayman Islands, but the company is headquartered in Panama City. And it's not under his name. It's owned by another shell company, LJF Global Investments."

"And who is that?"

"That's another reason we were such a great team, Daniel. You know, people still talk about our bust in Hong Kong. Just a second …"

Daniel felt a twinge of regret. It was so much more than just a bust. At least three people lost their lives because of his decisions that week. And for one man in particular, Daniel was the one who pulled the trigger.

"Got it," Xiao Ping continued. "The only one listed on the proxy form as owner and founder is someone named Lloyd Fanshawe."

FORTY-SEVEN

CLAIRE WAS ONCE AGAIN standing at attention in Captain Hall's spartan office on base. He fumed. "I support you, as always, Marcoux, but now I have to explain myself again to the commodore. He's getting flak from the chief of the defence staff and probably the minister of defence. And he has to explain to the New Brunswick premier why part of a national park was destroyed this morning by the navy. You do have a knack of getting the attention of the top brass."

Her ship had limped back into port two hours earlier. The engineer said he needed at least two months, maybe six, to repair the damage. The crew was denied shore leave to prevent them from recounting their amazing tale to their families for at least a day. She was ordered to report to Hall immediately. Soot, smoke, and sweat streaked her day uniform, and her hair was tied loosely in some random Frank Gehry pattern. She hadn't bothered to change. In spite of her exhaustion, she had sprinted up the stairs to his office.

"That was not my intention, sir, but we have some answers now. And it doesn't look good."

He sat in his chair behind a desk covered with stacks of paper. "I agree that it doesn't look good." He looked at the floor, as if trying to assemble his next thought. "For your career. You take too many liberties with the rules. You attract too much attention. Maybe I've given you too much leeway." He picked up a printout and seemed distracted for a second as he read it. "And you want another XO? What's wrong with Wiseman?"

"He's too cautious."

He leaned forward, his hands on his desk. "That's why he's an XO, not a captain. He's your second-in-command. Deal with it."

Startled, she sat back. "I don't know if I can trust him when we're under pressure —"

Hall cut her off. "It's your job to make him trustworthy. You're the captain. Act like it." He dropped back into his chair. "You'll figure it out. Your main problem is what to do about the commodore and the CDS. They're not pleased with what you did to a significant patch of New Brunswick coastline."

"It was a special hunting mission, while the rest of the fleet was on exercise. You said so yourself."

"There are some aspects of your mission that you are not privy to. To protect you. I also said that it was supposed to be a low-profile hunting mission. The key words were 'low profile.'"

Claire thought before she responded. "It worked. The smugglers were clearly surprised."

He spun away from her for a moment, his back to her. "No, it didn't work. I wasn't talking about the smugglers. There were others who I didn't want to be aware." He swivelled his chair back and looked directly at her. "And now they know."

FORTY-EIGHT

FORRESTAL AND LLOYD. The names echoed in Daniel's mind. To avoid the Chinese government censors, Xiao Ping used an encrypted VPN to send files of the banking details to Daniel's email address. He owed her another big favour. They had evidence of a financial link between Forrestal and Lloyd. It explained a lot. But just because Lloyd made money with Forrestal didn't mean he was part of something nasty. He and Lloyd didn't like each other, and Daniel suspected it was because he made Lloyd nervous, jealous, and unsure about his position in the department. *But was jealousy enough to kill Forrestal and now to try to kill me?*

Daniel pulled the PDF up on his computer screen for everyone to see. "So now we know how Forrestal made money," he said. He was still stunned by the connection they'd unearthed.

"You seem to have an interesting past, professor," MacKinnon said. "Care to explain what she said to the rest of us?"

"His first investment was in real estate in Ontario. He built it up in a few years into quite a portfolio of properties."

Touesnard said, "So he was a real estate developer then?"

Daniel kept scrolling and reading the document. "Sort of. More of a property speculator. He bought for prestige."

"Where did the money come from? He didn't come from a wealthy family," Touesnard said.

"Looks like he convinced some wealthy investors to go into the real estate business with him." Daniel kept reading. "Interesting. He's highly leveraged."

"Which means?"

"That he borrowed a lot of money. For every dollar he had, he borrowed another ten."

"How could he ever pay that back?"

"There's always another investor coming in with new money."

"To bail him out?"

"To pay the earlier investors." Daniel began to slowly nod.

"He was a good negotiator, everyone said so," added MacKinnon.

"And he saved those companies."

"True. He knew how to turn around a company. But he was always only a step away from total collapse."

"So was he very good, lucky, or a crook?" Touesnard sneered.

"Maybe a bit of all three. He was brilliant."

"So what interests you about his finances, professor?" MacKinnon said.

"He just brought in money from new investors to pay the old investors."

"Sounds scammy," said Touesnard.

"It is. It's called a Ponzi scheme. Everyone's happy unless you're one of the last investors who buys in before the scam is outed. And Lloyd was in on it from the beginning."

Daniel saw something new in the documents, something more important than the Ponzi scheme. "Do you see the dates of the first transactions, Detective?"

Touesnard swung the laptop to face him. His eyes zigzagged across the screen. "The late eighties. Eighty-eight. Eighty-nine." He looked at Daniel. "So?"

"Earlier than twelve years ago. Now we know what he did *before* he founded the Fireweed Corporation. He used to run a real estate development company."

"Look at when the transactions stop and start up again. There's a big gap there." He pointed to the spreadsheet. "Two years between '89 and '91. All of the other ones are only spaced a few weeks or months apart. But not these two."

Touesnard nodded slowly. "But the early ones are under a different company name. And look who signed them off. A different person."

Daniel looked closer and shook his head. "The same person, the same bank account. Forrestal used a different name then." He turned to face a confused MacKinnon. "Says here he used to be called Robert Haynes. So why did he change his name?"

FORTY-NINE

LLOYD FLIPPED ON HIS COMPUTER. He thought maybe marking a few student assignments would help him get a jump on next week's teaching load. An email notification popped up on the computer screen. He wouldn't normally pay any attention to it, but for the heading: Account activity detected.

He ignored the first assignment and clicked on the link. His Cayman Island bank had received an official request for account details from a bank in China that he had never heard of. Someone was snooping in his private account. The timing was suspicious. His heart rate increased. His forehead began to sweat.

He punched a memorized number, never to be stored, into his cellphone. He didn't wait for the customary hello.

"They've found it."

"What are you talking about?" Garth said. "Remember this is an open line. Someone could be listening."

"Don't patronize me. Someone is poking around in my bank account. The one I don't want them poking around in."

"How would they even know about it?"

"No idea. But they do. What is Larch doing about it? We don't need Ritter anymore. Tell him to back off."

"Don't worry. I'm on it."

FIFTY

"SIT, COMMANDER." Hall's deep voice, at times reassuring, confident, and terrifying for her, resonated in his sparsely decorated office. Claire hesitated, looking at the lone chair in front of his desk. She had always stood at attention, a stark symbol of his authority. "Sit." He pointed.

She lowered herself into the seat, back straight, unsure of what was next.

"Spit it out," he said.

Claire didn't know how to react.

"There's something that you want to ask me." Hall leaned forward, cupping his hands over his desk. "It's consuming you. Get it out."

How does he know?

"Yes, sir. It's about our support for Border Services. Why did you order me to support Lansdowne?"

Hall rubbed his crewcut. "Because I thought he was our mole. And I wanted you to stay close and watch him."

"A mole?"

"The smugglers are a step ahead of us. They knew we were waiting for them —"

"Not the first time I found them."

"No, that was a fluke. But someone has been telling them our plans since then. And I thought it was our CBSA colleague."

"But he's not?"

Hall shook his head.

"He sure is an asshole."

Hall smirked. "And he won't be the last you'll have to deal with. It's part of the deal of being in command."

Claire paused. She considered Hall's statement for a moment. "So who is the mole?"

Hall raised his index finger as his phone chimed. He put the RCMP on speaker.

"Hall? Cliff Whitby here." It was the Detective Inspector whom Claire had met at the operations meeting.

"What have you got for us, Cliff?"

"Congratulations, Captain. We intercepted the smuggler's boat. The other crew member surrendered without a fight. He was terrified after your fireworks display. He's not talking much. Yet. However, the suspect you captured is Zeke Snow. Twenty-four years old. From High River. He's a junior member of the Alberta Independence Movement, a fringe group in southern Alberta. He's got only one prior arrest, for assault. He and his partner were on the beach to pick up a shipment. That's what he said."

"There was also another man," said Claire. "Do you know anything about him?"

"Hello, Lieutenant Commander. Yes, the one who was killed on the beach. We don't have his name yet, but we're pretty sure that he worked for a private military contractor in the States."

"Private military?" said Hall.

"Yes." Claire heard Whitby take a quick gulping drink. "Now, the interesting thing is, I think Mr. Snow was surprised to learn that the shipment was high-tech military weaponry."

"So what are the weapons for?" Claire said, eliciting a surprised look from her superior officer. *Let the man finish.*

"Not for what, but for whom. The military contractor was hired by a middleman. The FBI knows the guy. He does the dirty work for some extreme right-wingers in the U.S. We also know, courtesy of Mr. Snow, that they had a strict deadline to deliver to a location north of Calgary by Sunday night."

"Airdrie?" said Hall.

"Correct." Whitby nodded.

"What's so special about tonight?"

Claire was suddenly excited. "It's a day before the Alberta referendum."

"Could be coincidence," said Hall. "There are probably lots of other things going on at the same time."

"We need to ask the right question," said Claire.

Hall crossed his arms. "Which is what?"

Whitby offered, "Who in Alberta, sensitive to the referendum date …"

Claire finished the thought: "Wants anti-tank weapons and machine guns by the dozen?"

"And can afford them?" said Hall.

"Twice," added Claire. "Remember, we sank the first shipment. They had to order another one. So they've paid twice."

Hall seemed to ignore her. "Cliff, what's your take? You must have seen something like this before."

"It looks like anti-government freedom fighters in the U.S. They believe in the Apocalypse. The biblical one. End of days and all that. They believe that any government is effectively tyrannical. They wait for some sort of government or societal collapse. So they stockpile food, weapons, and ammunition, waiting for the shit to hit the fan. They isolate themselves in small communities to maintain social control and avoid contamination of their values."

"Sounds a bit nuts," Hall said.

"Right," said Claire. "Are there any of these groups in Alberta?"

"Sure, a few. They're small. And they've been pretty quiet, too, except that Mr. Snow admitted to being a member of the Alberta Independence Movement."

"What's that?" Claire said.

"An anti-government survivalist group. They're petty smugglers. But it's usually small stuff. Handguns. Narcotics. They're small-time. We don't know why they would bother to go to the opposite side of the continent to smuggle weapons when the Montana border is next door. This is a very well-financed operation, way beyond their abilities. It's much bigger than these groups could pull off," said Whitby. "If they're that well financed, they might be getting more from other routes. We're checking. And we've increased manpower on all border crossings along with CBSA."

Claire had never seen Captain Hall look so concerned. "So someone is worried that something bad might happen after the referendum."

She leaned closer to the phone. "Or that same someone will make sure something bad *does* happen."

FIFTY-ONE

BACK AT THE SAFE HOUSE, Daniel, Touesnard, and MacKinnon scoured the web on their separate laptops to assemble a biography of Forrestal under his earlier name. After four hours and six coffees among them, Daniel sat back. "Have we got enough to put a picture together?"

MacKinnon bobbed his head while reading from his notes. "Forrestal used to be called Robert Haynes and developed real estate in Edmonton in the '80s, during the oil boom. He built strip malls and apartments. It seems he was married to a Sharon Mills —"

"The password on his iPhone," Daniel and Touesnard said simultaneously.

MacKinnon continued. "And he had one child, a boy. In '89, one of his buildings caught fire. The headline in the *Edmonton Journal* mentioned construction short-cuts and sub-standard building material. Tragically, a family was killed."

Touesnard continued, accelerating the pace as if they were speeding toward some important milestone. "Then Haynes went dark. He had millions stashed away in this Cayman Island account by that time. No trace of him for two years until he withdrew money from Belize. Then a few scattered withdrawals to accounts in Eastern Europe, this time under the name Forrestal."

"After the Berlin Wall fell. They were boom years for reconstruction. He's quite shrewd," added Daniel.

MacKinnon said, "So, let's see if I understand. Mr. Forrestal runs an offshore business in the Caymans, out of the reach of the Canadian and U.S. authorities. He runs this with Professor Fanshawe, who joined in 2002. Two days ago, the account paid out the ten thousand dollars meant to be given to you." He motioned to Daniel, who grunted in reply. "It also issued money transfers to three other people in the last month. Dave, any leads?"

Touesnard continued as he read from his screen. "One was for three million paid to another offshore account. Ms. Lu just sent us the owner information. It's owned by a Calgary lawyer named Evans."

"Alberta comes up again," said Daniel.

"Another was to a second account, this one in Bermuda, generic name, Express Wilderness Inc., withdrawn at a Canadian bank in Alberta. Airdrie branch."

"How much?" MacKinnon rubbed his forehead as if he had a headache.

"A million and change."

"Any idea what for?"

Touesnard and Daniel shook their heads.

MacKinnon said, "What about the third money transfer?"

"This one was given in two pieces. Ten thousand, three weeks ago. And another five on Tuesday. Same destination. A company called Professional Solutions Inc. based in Mustique, an island in the Caribbean."

"Wait. I have a website for Professional Solutions," Daniel said, typing on his computer. A website came up. He swung the computer around so MacKinnon and Touesnard could see. "It's cute. They talk about contract disputes and professional conflict resolution. But it's a euphemism, just a polite way to say professional killers. Lloyd Fanshawe paid for an assassin."

The two officers eyed Daniel. Touesnard said it first. "How do you know that?"

Daniel cleared his throat. "Because I used to have to deal with them. Not this particular company, but others like them."

"As a professor in a Halifax business school?" MacKinnon choked on his words.

"Before that. When I was in China. I told you I negotiated complex business deals between Canadian and Chinese manufacturers. Sometimes one side would resort to extreme ways to up the pressure on the other. Sometimes that included violence."

"You're joking."

"I had to deal with them a couple of times."

"And how exactly did you 'deal' with them?"

"Professionally."

"You're being evasive again, professor."

"They threatened me and my partner." Daniel hesitated to recall the images of that final assignment. Mr. Wang's car, a Bentley, malevolent black to hide in the night, narrowly missed ramming into him and Xiao Ping walking on a sidewalk in Kowloon. The car screeched to a halt a few metres ahead, and Mr. Wang's driver burst out from the right-side door, waving a pistol in one hand, ready to finish the job. He only took four steps before Daniel put two rounds from his Glock into the man's chest. His mind fast-forwarded to the final scene, with a surprised Mr. Wang sweating and standing still at the far end of the same pistol held firmly by Daniel. "I had the training. I knew what to do. I removed them from the picture."

The officers' mouths were agape.

MacKinnon snatched his phone and dialed. "I have to tell the command team about the money trail."

FIFTY-TWO

LARCH WAS A PATIENT MAN, but his client was not. Mr. Haynes had phoned with more details of his target and needed it dealt with by midnight. Larch didn't ask why, and Haynes didn't explain. Haynes only repeated the importance of securing the target and not missing the deadline. Larch began to worry. There were more surprises than normal with this contract. He had already accomplished his first task. But still there was a loose end. Now a second, surprise target. With less than nine hours until the client's absolutely-must-be-done-no-excuses deadline, he felt he had no choice but to pursue riskier options, involving non-targets if necessary.

The target was well protected, always accompanied by a plainclothes cop. To find a protection gap, he brought his mobile device identifier, essentially a cellphone sniffer. A small box connected to his phone, it intercepted the unique electronic identity number of any cellphone. Police used them regularly. He obtained his through his regular American channels. He had already tracked the target's phone to several locations. He could also read the numbers of the people he called and could listen to unencrypted calls. Tracking calls since Tuesday revealed a number in Montreal, several calls to the local police, and a reoccurring number to a woman living downtown. Text conversations suggested a possible girlfriend and an upcoming date. It was unlikely the cop would stick close by when the target and the girlfriend were together. He was running out of time as his client, ever more nervous, wanted the target dealt with now. He had failed twice with his regular tactic: detect, hunt, and eliminate. It now seemed like the highest percentage play he could devise would be to make the target come to him.

An easy search revealed the location: the apartment that he now faced across the street. She finally came into view in her green hatchback. She scooted into a parking spot near the main entrance of the apartment building he had been watching. He had been meticulous researching the professor. But his client insisted on rapid action this time. He didn't know much about her, and he didn't like improvising. She walked to the main door with a confident stride, wearing a black parka, dark pants, sunglasses, and with a grocery bag in each hand.

He timed his arrival at the front entrance of the building with Swiss accuracy. He dropped his two Superstore shopping bags and pretended to search for his door keys while she fumbled for hers. She jabbed and twisted the key into the lock, opened the door, and moved straight to the elevator. Larch followed and stood beside her as the elevator door opened. She pushed 2 and he pushed 3. It was unlikely that she would be very familiar with anyone living a floor higher, since she probably either went straight to her apartment or took the stairs. A building with four floors was big enough to provide a distant, formal atmosphere, where few tenants would recognize each other. Her lack of suspicions proved his instincts correct.

At her floor, the door pinged open, and the woman walked out. Larch peeked around the corner and confirmed that she stopped at number 211 before the elevator door hissed shut. He darted out at floor three, bounded down the flight of stairs, and peered through the small window of the fire door at the end of the hall. No police officer in the hallway.

He would have one chance to do this right. He sensed rising urgency in his conversations with his client. He was beginning to dislike Mr. Haynes very much. He resolved that this would be his final mission for him. An image of his pastel-coloured beach house on Mustique flashed in his head. Sandrine would be waiting for him. Maybe it was time to slow down a bit. Spend more time with her. She had been very patient, too.

He shook the images from his head and returned his attention to the stairwell and the task at hand. From one of his shopping bags, he pulled out a pair of work gloves, a short black box, and his lock pick tools. He closed the briefcase and opened the fire door. He only needed sixteen steps to reach the door of suite 211. He waited, listened to the silence, looked at the gap between the door and the floor to check for any movement of the shadows. Nothing. She must be stationary somewhere in the apartment.

He jammed the lock tool, flicked it to the right, and after a few moments of feeling the pins, heard the lock cylinder click into place. He kneeled, weapon pulled from his jacket pocket in hand, and gently swung the door open.

Satisfied. Claire felt drop-down-in-your-chair-and-cross-your-arms satisfied. She had stopped the smugglers and had showed Lansdowne how it was done. Hall was on her side. He seemed pleased and ordered her to go home and recover. Emerging from her bedroom, she was dressed in a dark brown T-shirt that matched her eyes and black Roots track pants. She felt refreshed after a short but deep sleep, a quick trip to the store to stock up on food, and a military-speed shower. She stared at herself in the bathroom mirror. Were those worry lines around her eyes? Thirty-one and she still didn't look like a ship's captain. But yes, she had the respect of the people who counted on the *Kingston*. Except one.

And Daniel had texted again. Dinner date in a few hours. She offered to come over to his hotel where he was holed up. After his protest and plea for escape, she invited him over. Not something she would normally do, but he did come with his own police escort. Did she even have enough of a romantic track record to have a "normal"? A few rebuffed offers from a paltry five men, mostly navy, inappropriately positioned somewhere in her chain of command. Then there was Alexandre, but he took off when she signed up. There was something about Daniel she liked. Yes, he was handsome, but there was something else, a future perhaps, waiting to burst out from inside. At a minimum, he was worthy of further investigation. Did she dare hope for some sort of a connection tonight? She would take it slow and boot him out if she saw any signs of —

She froze.

Was that a noise from the front door?

It might be Mr. Skyler, the nice retiree who regularly forgot that he lived in 213. He would fiddle with the lock, and when it didn't respond, he would realize his mistake. But this sounded like the door was opening. The landlord? Maybe she should have listened to her voice messages after all. She didn't remember any messages from him. She shoved her head into the hall to see what was happening at the door at the far end.

It was barely open, but moving, and there was a hand low, pushing it open —

Larch saw a shadow veer to the left. He had been spotted. He darted into the room, holding his pistol straight out, ready to face anything.

The girlfriend stood alone in a T-shirt and track pants a few metres away, looking surprised, transfixed, and unbelieving.

Claire didn't know what to make of her situation. She was still dripping and a stressed man just busted open her door to her apartment. And he was holding a pistol, what looked like a Beretta. How to react?

"Get out," Claire ordered. "*Vas-t'en, maudit* —"

She didn't wait for an answer. Always on the offence, her training reminded her. She lunged at the man with her comb as her only weapon. It was, after all, a row of sharp plastic spears.

But the man was ready, his body and centre of gravity low, the pistol in his right hand. He shifted to his left to avoid her assault, but she anticipated his move, and her foot slammed into his chest. His body thudded into the wall beside the door, her lone framed picture crashed, and glass splintered on the floor. She grabbed the gun's muzzle and wrenched it away and out of his hand. The gun spun across the floor, out of reach.

Another flurry of fists and she scratched his face. As she retreated and anticipated his counterattack, his hand found blood from his cheek. The pain shot to his brain just ahead of the feeling of surprise.

Then, he saw what she held in her hand. A plastic comb. Another surprise. He would be more careful now.

She came at him again with a ferocity that surprised him. A slash with the comb, then a blow from her elbow onto his nose. She kicked at his knees. She knew they were a weak spot, easily broken. Any fighter was swiftly weakened with a broken knee.

He saw the move, shifted to the right, and slammed his own elbow down onto her extended left arm, frozen for a moment as her strike missed its target. The scream he heard confirmed that he had hit the right nerve, and her arm was immobilized.

But she didn't stop.

She retreated a step, swept her hand behind her, and used her familiarity with her space to search for another weapon on the low living room table. Larch lunged across the floor away from her and spun around to face her.

Claire was breathing heavily, as if she were engaged in a boxing match. She grabbed a small bowl. It seemed made of porcelain or something else potentially lethal if she managed at high speed to make contact with his head.

She threw it but missed his head. It smashed with a loud crack on the wall instead. He lunged at her, tackling her headfirst. She fell backward, her head smacked the floor, and then her world collapsed into black.

Claire awoke, suddenly aware of the whirr of the refrigerator and the slow tick of a wall clock. A buzz pulsed through her body. She heard a loud ringing in her right ear. How long had she been out? She opened her eyes. She tasted the salty sting of blood. She was sitting on her bed, her head propped up against a pillow. The stranger sat in a chair directly in front of the bed. He looked relieved. He held a pistol loosely in his right hand.

"Miss Marcoux. It's nice to finally meet you." He dropped her wallet on the table between them. She saw the contents of her purse scattered on the kitchen counter behind him. "I see why you were so effective in fighting me." He waved her navy ID card.

"*Qui êtes-vous?* … Who are you?" She noticed that the man tensed immediately as she tried to move her hands to rub her eyes. Her hands were bound with several layers of duct tape. As were her feet.

"My name is not important. What you have to say to me is."

"What do you want?"

"Where is Mr. Ritter?"

"I have nothing to say to you."

"When are you expecting him back?"

She said nothing.

"Don't take it personally. It's just business. And you're just the latest impediment to the completion of my duties."

He pulled out his cellphone. He knew how to use her to meet his deadline.

FIFTY-THREE

MACKINNON HAD NEWS that couldn't wait. Touesnard placed his cellphone on the table and put it on speaker so Daniel could hear.

MacKinnon's voice was raspy with tension. "I just finished meeting with my RCMP colleague, Detective Inspector Whitby. We think we've found some disturbing connections."

"Lloyd is an asshole? That's not news." Daniel sniffed.

MacKinnon was unfazed. "Let's start at the beginning. Remember how Forrestal changed his name?"

Daniel and Touesnard nodded.

"He had a son. I did some digging. The son's name is Garth. Garth Haynes."

"So, what does that have to do with anything?" Daniel asked.

"The son is involved in politics as the head of the pro-independence campaign going on right now in Alberta."

"Yet another link with Alberta," Daniel said.

"There's more. The RCMP interviewed the smuggler the navy captured. In an operation led by your friend, Lieutenant Commander Marcoux, by the way. He admitted being a member of a white supremacist organization called AIM."

Daniel smiled as he pictured Claire for a moment. They would soon be on their first date.

MacKinnon continued, "He was trying to smuggle a lot of weapons. Military weapons. Enough to equip a small army. Guess who was a founder of the AIM organization?"

"Mr. Forrestal? No." Touesnard crossed his arms. "The son, Garth Haynes?"

"Yes. You have been paying attention. So now we have a connection between Mr. Forrestal's money trail and weapons for a white supremacist group."

Daniel scratched his head. "Didn't Forrestal's money also pay for the hit man? The one trying to kill me?"

"The one who killed Mr. Forrestal himself?" added Touesnard.

"So Forrestal bankrolled his own killer? That doesn't make sense."

"Unless he didn't know he was paying for an assassin," said MacKinnon.

"So Garth pays for the murder of his own father?" Daniel shook his head. "That's really messed up."

Touesnard raised his hand. "Or the instructions came not from Mr. Forrestal but from the professor."

Daniel's mouth was agape. "Lloyd wants weapons? And he paid someone to kill Forrestal, his mega-successful business partner? I don't believe it."

MacKinnon took a deep breath. "So we have quite a few questions for Mr. Haynes and Professor Fanshawe."

"You'll arrest them?" Daniel said.

MacKinnon paused before answering. "Not yet. The RCMP wants to see how this plays out first. It might be a white power gang issue. Or it might be something much bigger tied to the referendum campaign."

The puzzle was beginning to fill in for Daniel. Forrestal had changed his name to hide from a stained past. *Coward.* Instead of facing up to his mistakes, he fled. Then there was a financial link between Forrestal and an offshore bank account used to transfer money in Daniel's name as an attempt to blame him. And Lloyd had paid for the man now trying to kill Daniel.

But who wanted Forrestal dead? Was it Lloyd or Forrestal's own son? And why did Forrestal want to talk with him? Too many questions with no answers.

Lloyd was the one person with connections to both Forrestal and to the hit man, and Daniel had an idea about how to get him to talk.

"Know your enemy," Daniel repeated to himself as Touesnard drove him back to campus. They were running out of time. *Weapons, enough for a small army, MacKinnon had said. Lloyd's in on it, too. Whatever they're up to, the timing with Monday's referendum is key.*

Lloyd was where he always was after teaching a Saturday MBA class: at his desk, sending emails. Daniel didn't knock this time. He walked right in and sat in the empty chair facing Lloyd's sparsely covered desk. It was so neat, with papers properly stacked. Even his coffee mug was clean. A perfectly ordered life. Nothing out of place.

Daniel took a big breath. "I have a proposal for you."

Lloyd closed an email window and looked at Daniel, as if he were trying to imprint an image of him, knowing they would never cross paths again. "I'm busy."

"Don't you want to hear it? I thought you liked a good deal?"

He glared at Daniel. "Have the police found Patrick's killer yet? I haven't seen anything on the news."

"Murder. Remember, he was murdered."

"Of course. Do the police have any leads? Any suspects?"

"Yes, they do. They expect to have the main suspect in custody soon. The suspect is here. Close by. Following me. He's been following me since the murder."

Lloyd didn't react.

Daniel thought about the telltale signs of lying. TV shows showed polygraph tests, sweating, and nervous looks. But they were only partly correct. The real test of lying was in putting together multiple cues. Nervous looks alone were not enough. However, lying might be present if combined with the extra brain processing necessary to cross-check the fib with facts that the interviewer might already know. It was this short delay in response, or stalling by overtalking, that Daniel waited for in Lloyd. If Lloyd were lying, he would take longer to provide meaningful answers as Daniel wove the story into something ever more complex. He had used this technique before, with good results.

"In fact, he seems to know where I am," Daniel continued. "Even now, I bet he's watching me."

"Have you called the police?"

"Yes, a police officer is standing outside the door, but somehow I feel that protection isn't needed now. I don't think he'll try anything."

"Why not?"

"Because I'm with *you*. And whatever happens to me has to remain far away from you."

Lloyd's eyebrows folded down in the middle. He glowered at Daniel. "What are you saying, Daniel?"

"I think you have a problem, Lloyd. A problem that I can help you solve. There is a man, a professional contract killer, looking for me. He's tried to kill me twice so far, and being the pro that I'm sure he is, he'll try again soon. I'll be fine, though." Daniel pointed to Touesnard, who was sitting passively on the bench, visible through the open office door. "I have police protection. But you don't."

"Why would I need any?"

"I think that I'm being hounded because I can identify Patrick's killer. I saw him just after Patrick was gunned down. If I'm dead, no more witnesses. Just a grainy hotel video. And the killer goes free."

Lloyd said nothing, but Daniel noticed raised shoulders and a stiffening posture, signs that he was paying closer attention.

"Whoever is giving orders to the hit man has one goal. No witnesses alive. That means anyone else who might know of whatever plan was behind the killing. At first, it seemed like retribution for a deal gone bad. But we both know that Patrick never made a bad deal. So there's something else going on. Whatever it is, when I'm gone, you'll be the next target."

"Are you delusional?" Lloyd sputtered.

"You've known Patrick for a long time, haven't you? Yet he calls me."

"What's the big mystery?"

"You gave him my name."

Lloyd's face didn't move.

"I kept asking myself why you'd help me. You've never helped me before."

"Aren't you a business professor?"

Daniel nodded.

"People listen to what you say. You've got your own prissy TV show."

Daniel gave only the slightest nod.

"So Forrestal might listen to you, too."

Daniel folded his arms. "No, this was never about helping me. It's all about helping you. So my question became, How can a relationship between Forrestal and me help you? Or more precisely, help Fireweed, your offshore company."

Lloyd flinched. "How do you know about that?"

Daniel pressed on. "You and your financial dealings have attracted quite a bit of interest. Not just mine, but also the police."

He waited for a reaction. Lloyd was cool, maybe overconfident in his ability to conceal what he had done. Daniel aimed to break his resolve. "You two have been in a very successful business for at least a decade. I guess it started when you were in Calgary."

Lloyd's lips tightened.

Daniel tried hard not to smile. He pressed on. "You must have become close. He must have learned a lot from you. Like how to buy companies, flip them around, and leave before the mess appeared?"

Daniel uncrossed his arms. "Whoever killed Forrestal and wants me dead will be coming after you next. You want help? Protection? Then you need to talk." Daniel saw a change in how Lloyd glared at him. The look morphed from hate or indifference, he could never tell, to cool calculation.

Lloyd switched off his computer screen and looked directly at Daniel for the first time, nervously twirling a pen around his thumb.

Daniel pushed harder. "Let's see if I've got the complete picture. You and Forrestal have a tidy business buying up struggling companies in precarious situations and turning them around. Each one is a winner. You cash out of each deal before something bad happens. It's an amazing track record, even if you don't actually do anything with their money."

"We know what we're doing."

"You have only two accounts. One for money coming in, the other for paying your dividends to your existing investors.

"Surprised I know?" Daniel noticed a few beads of sweat on Lloyd's forehead. "And they're all happy with, I would guess, ten to thirty percent returns on their investments. Which is quite extraordinary in this inflation-free market."

Lloyd didn't move.

Daniel raised his arms high. "You don't give a shit about anyone but yourself." He leaned back in his chair. "That's why I think you should take this offer. I bet you think you're usually a step or two ahead of everyone else. So I'm surprised you haven't asked yourself the most important question."

He waited until he saw anticipation on Lloyd's face.

"If I can find out this information about you and Forrestal, he can, too."

Daniel was enjoying this moment.

"And when he's ordered to take you out, he won't be as forgiving as me or the police."

FIFTY-FOUR

LLOYD, NORMALLY A SLIPPERY EEL, didn't budge in his chair. For Daniel, that was proof of his interest in the deal. They waited for MacKinnon to arrive. He parked himself, arms crossed, against the wall beside the door. Touesnard stood beside him. They looked skeptically at Lloyd.

Daniel locked onto Lloyd's squirming face, his eyes shifting between Daniel, the two cops leaning near the office door, and his computer screen. "What did you need me for?"

Lloyd remained still.

He's trying to make up a story. Daniel knew how to push. "Remember, no co-operation, no deal, right?" Daniel looked over his shoulder at MacKinnon, who nodded.

Lloyd's words seem to bubble up from some abyss in his personality. "High-tech start-ups. Spinoff companies from universities."

Daniel needed a moment to find the words to respond. "Wow, I'm flattered. You and Forrestal must think highly of me."

"You'll do."

"Which universities?"

"Dalhousie and Calgary."

Calgary. *Another coincidence with Alberta.* "But that doesn't answer my question. What was I supposed to do?"

"Not much."

Daniel leaned back in the chair and crossed his arms.

"You're just supposed to talk about the project," said Lloyd.

"But I don't know anything about it."

"That's what Patrick was going to explain when you saw him."

"It never happened. He was dead before I saw him."

"That's why Mr. Larch wants to see you. To get you on board."

"Are you serious?" Daniel tipped his chair forward onto all four legs with a bang and leaned over the desk, collapsing the physical and psychological distance between him and Lloyd. "He wants to see me for only one reason. He wants me dead. Our encounters so far have made that clear."

"No," Lloyd snapped, "his job is to convince you to sign up to front the projects."

Daniel turned again to the detectives. "What do you think? He wants me dead or he wants me as a business partner?"

MacKinnon spoke first. "Oh, I'd say dead. He's a contract killer. He has an impressive resumé."

Touesnard joined in. "Once you identified him, we checked out his Interpol file. At least ten professional hits. All big-time political targets. Whoever hired him knew to hire the best."

Daniel could see that Lloyd was genuinely surprised.

"Impossible," Lloyd protested, "Garth sent him personally. I talked with him yesterday myself."

Daniel smiled. They were getting somewhere. "You mean Garth Haynes?"

Lloyd nodded.

MacKinnon leaned forward. "What is your relationship with Mr. Haynes?"

"A business one. A private one."

Daniel stopped. "This is weird. Forrestal abandons his life in Edmonton after the fire. The photo you showed me before." He looked at MacKinnon. "He had a family. A son. He changed his name. Jesus, he just didn't abandon his business, he abandoned his own family, his only son —"

Lloyd's face reddened. "Are you people fucking nuts?"

MacKinnon sprang away from the wall. "This Larch guy killed Mr. Forrestal. And he doesn't want witnesses."

Daniel saw the beginnings of doubt on Lloyd's face. He pushed harder. "So you don't know everything that's going on, do you? Did you know about Patrick's relationship with Garth?"

Lloyd shook his head. "You're making this up. Garth's father passed away when he was a child. He told me so himself."

Touesnard said, "We have a credible source."

Daniel edged closer to Lloyd. "He didn't pass away, at least not until two days ago. He abandoned his family, including Garth, when a deal went bad. He's been hiding ever since. But Garth found him. And sent Larch to exact revenge. You've been working with a professional killer, Lloyd. He's just waiting to off me, before he gets new orders to take you out, too."

Lloyd said nothing.

"So you wanted me to talk nicely about your new projects in Halifax and Calgary?"

"You're only for the Halifax deal."

Daniel frowned.

Lloyd continued, as if the revelation about Larch forced him to question other assumptions. "People know you. You're on TV. They ask for your opinion every time there's a big business story that affects the region. You know powerful people in government. But you're not too close to them to be thought of as co-opted or corrupted."

"And you have someone else lined up for the Calgary project?"

"Of course. And he's been much less trouble than you." He flicked a glance to the officers. "So I have my protection now?"

MacKinnon pushed away from the wall near the door. "We can certainly discuss the details at the station. You'll have to come with me."

Lloyd stood up and grabbed his jacket, fanning one neat stack of papers on his desk onto the floor. He walked out with MacKinnon.

Daniel grabbed Lloyd's arm. Something sounded a bit too coincidental. "What's the Calgary deal about, really?"

Lloyd glared at Daniel's hand on his arm. "We develop the neighbourhood for the spin-off companies from the university. And sell it to the government."

"At a substantial risk premium, no doubt. You're waiting for the referendum to pass. Then a new and in-experienced Alberta government takes power. They'll be desperate to buy, trying to make a big splash to show their new citizens a shiny new future. They'll have no bargaining leverage. They'll pay whatever you want."

"Timing is everything, as they say."

Daniel hissed at Lloyd's pompous airs. "You're a greedy and selfish bastard. When's the sale?"

"Why do you care?"

"Humour me."

"Next week."

Daniel released his arm and watched Lloyd and MacKinnon walk down the hall and out of the business building.

Touesnard accompanied Daniel. "What was that about?"

"Don't you find it odd that Alberta keeps coming up? Lloyd and Forrestal send a lot of money to some lawyer in Calgary. MacKinnon said the intercepted weapons were destined for a right-wing fringe group in Alberta. The founder of this group is now the leader of a referen-dum campaign that concludes in two days. Larch takes his orders from this leader. And now, Lloyd has been working on a property development project to be sold to the government in Alberta."

Touesnard nodded.

"And there's something special about the timing of the deal, too. Another coincidence. Right after the ref-erendum. Do you believe in coincidences, Detective?"

"I wouldn't be alive if I did."

FIFTY-FIVE

AT THIRTY-ONE THOUSAND FEET over Saskatchewan, the ride was smooth. The Yes campaign's Bombardier Global 5000 soared over the world, leaving everything behind as it flew swiftly forward. *Into the future*, Garth thought. With a strong tailwind, it would be a six-hour flight from Edmonton to Halifax. It was insulting that the premier didn't trust him to finish the job. But he would finish it, and he would demonstrate how valuable he was to the new government-in-waiting. Direct, decisive action would make him the perfect defence minister. And after a respectful period, leader.

His official cellphone buzzed with a text message from Brewster.

Why does the RCMP want to talk to you?

No idea.

What did you do?

What did you tell them?

It better not affect the campaign.

I don't know what you mean.
I told them you were flying out East.
Yes.
Don't fuck it up.

Garth swore at the blue sky out the window. He tossed his phone onto the neighbouring seat. His other, non-official cellphone buzzed immediately. He grabbed it as if it were a weapon. Larch.

Waiting for target. Have leverage. Will advise when target terminated. Instructions?

Garth thought for a few moments. Decisive action. Direct. The answer was simple.

No loose ends. Do it now.

Five hours to landing and to some good news.

FIFTY-SIX

DANIEL FELT A WARM CONTENTMENT. He had finally dealt with Lloyd and his persistent hostility. While MacKinnon escorted Lloyd to the police station for booking and questioning, Touesnard drove Daniel back to the hotel room, in spite of his protests. He worried that Larch was closing in, and he didn't want Daniel exposed. No question he would be safer at the hotel.

On the wall-mounted TV, CBC News reported the latest referendum polls. The gap between the Yes and No sides was shrinking, with the Yes side gaining momentum from the premier's rousing promises. Daniel flicked the TV off, dialed, and listened to six rings on his cellphone before he hung up and tried again. He had sent several text and voice messages to Claire, saying he would be right on time for their dinner date.

But there was no reply from her.

He could easily walk the short distance to her apartment, but Larch was out there still. Claire should have answered. She would have texted if she had been re-called to duty. Claire should have responded by now. *Why isn't she answering?*

He should go straight to Claire's, only a few blocks away. But Touesnard had told him to stay put.

Daniel's worry spiked. He grabbed his coat, slipping out of the hotel room and into the gathering evening gloom while Touesnard was in the bathroom. He ran a few minutes through the damp despair, squishing the grey slush on the sidewalk with every step. Rounding the corner onto Brunswick Street, he could see light leaking from what he assumed was her apartment on the second floor. She had given her address to him on an earlier text message. *She was there. So why didn't she answer?*

His mind came up with several possible answers. She was in the shower and couldn't hear the phone. She heard it but decided to not answer it. She was busy, cooking a nice meal with the radio turned up loud. No, that was supposed to be his job tonight. He struggled to come up with answers as he climbed the staircase along Citadel Hill. Halfway up, he could see through her apartment window on the other side of the street. It looked like she was there. A couple of lights had to be on. He saw a shadow move. And another one.

Wait.

Why *two* shadows?

He wasn't expecting anyone else. Maybe she had a friend visiting. She hadn't mentioned anyone, though. He stopped and looked at the ground in a flash of guilt; he was spying on her. Would this be his new normal for relationships after his failed marriage to Vanessa? Was he genuinely concerned for her well-being, or merely petty, jealous, and insecure? How could he see who was there without revealing himself? He rushed over and pushed the door buzzer for her apartment in the lobby. No answer. He pushed again. Again, no response. He ran outside to discover that the blinds had been closed so he could no longer see inside the apartment.

His mind gravitated toward the worst-case scenario.

He approached the main entrance, found the buzzer panel, double-checked her apartment number on the card he pulled from his pocket, and pushed the right button. No reply. He walked across the street to get a better view.

Touesnard appeared out of the darkness, slightly out of breath. "Don't do that again." He scowled between puffs.

Daniel pointed at the second floor window. "Remember I have a date tonight? I'm supposed to be there soon. Something's wrong."

"Aren't you overreacting?"

Daniel shot him a look. "I've called her several times, but she hasn't answered. I saw her through the window. And someone else is there, too. She didn't answer when I buzzed her apartment. I don't like it."

"I don't see anything."

Movement behind the blinds was reduced to a single blob pacing to the left then to the right. "The curtains are closed now. I can't see the window, and Claire's not answering her phone or the door buzzer."

Touesnard rubbed his beard. "It's probably nothing, but I don't want you sneaking out again. Let's settle this now." He dialed a number on his cellphone. "Hang on."

Daniel could hear MacKinnon's tinny voice from the phone. "Daniel, Professor Fanshawe said that Larch asked a lot of questions about you. He's been studying you, following you, looking for weaknesses, knows about your interest in Ms. Marcoux. You might be onto something. MacKinnon's on his way."

Daniel sat on a bench outside the main entrance, his phone quiet in his hand, while Touesnard kept his focus on the apartment above. A life Daniel might be beginning to care about was on the line.

A man emerged from a darkened car. He carried an oversized bag in each hand and ignored the scattering of tourists admiring the clock tower at the Halifax Citadel. Unlike the group of fifty or so sightseers from a dozen countries, he didn't much care that King Edward VII commissioned the clock when he was but an earl. He didn't marvel at the colourful flags flapping in the stiff ocean breeze. Instead, he turned his gaze to the apartment building across the street. While the group continued their tour around the hill, the man hurried across the street and stopped at the entrance to the Maritime Foundry Apartments.

Daniel was pacing at the front door and heaved a sigh of relief as MacKinnon handed one of the bags to Touesnard, who continued to watch the window above. MacKinnon pulled out a key. They silently stepped into the vestibule. Opening the inner door, they marched straight into the elevator, and MacKinnon pushed the button for the second floor. MacKinnon and Touesnard dropped their bags and the deep bass thud betrayed contents that were much heavier than the bags suggested.

In apartment 211, Larch sent a text and then tossed his cellphone onto the bed beside his captive. He moved his bag to the floor and walked to the end of the bed so he could see her in one clear view. She was bound with duct tape around the hands and feet, and her mouth was now taped shut. A stream of coagulated blood traced a wavy line down the right side of her head, matting her blond hair.

"I'm sorry for the inconvenience. You're not my target. I'm waiting for Mr. Ritter. I know that he'll be here soon. I believe you agreed to meet him for dinner." He patted a small box with wires attached to a short antenna.

Claire shook and squirmed on the bed. *How does he know that?*

He took two steps, picked up his bag, opened it, and pulled out his pistol and the silencer. He spoke to the gun. "Miss Marcoux. I need you to understand a few things first. I'm a professional. I mean you no ill will, personally. This is just business."

She had ceased squirming by the time he finished twisting the suppressor onto the pistol barrel.

In the elevator, MacKinnon flipped the emergency stop switch before they had reached the second floor, freezing the door closed, and the men opened their gym bags. Touesnard reached into his and removed a jet-black SIG Sauer pistol that he stuffed into his holster. He pulled out a Kevlar vest and slipped it over his shoulders.

MacKinnon slid his vest over his head and secured the Velcro straps around his waist. He turned to face Daniel. "Remember, stay near the elevator. There is probably an innocent explanation, but after what Professor Fanshawe explained, we should just check it out. Maybe nothing will happen, but maybe something will. The best way you can help us is to stay out of the way." He put his right hand on Daniel's shoulder. "I don't care what you did in China. We know what we're doing."

Daniel nodded, but it wasn't the tension about the situation they were about to face that caused his stomach to churn. Finding himself once again in the orbit of guns brought memories of his time in China flooding back. Another piece of his old world had crept back, bringing with it the potential for terrible violence. For a moment, he was in another elevator with Vanessa, shortly after he revealed his shadow career as a trade attaché for the intelligence agency.

"You had a gun?" Vanessa had asked with a frisson of fear.

"They trained me. I needed to protect myself."

"So it was like the driving training, just part of the job?"

"No, it was different. When you carry a gun, you can't just put it in a drawer at night and forget about it. You're never not thinking about it."

Waves of confusion and worry spread across her face. "Just part of your work uniform, then?"

"A jacket is a part of a uniform, but a gun is a perpetual threat. You're always aware of its terrible power to destroy." He sighed. "I hated carrying it around. Even if I never used it."

She looked deeper into his eyes and saw something disturbing staring back. "But you did use it, didn't you?"

Daniel stared at the floor and sighed at the images, the faces, the carnage that spun in his head. "You have no idea how relieved I felt when I returned it."

Now, in the elevator with two cops, the guns had come smiling back, as if waving to him and welcoming an old friend. He felt trapped in someone else's cycle of violence once more.

Daniel saw MacKinnon and Touesnard flip thin fabric bibs with the word "POLICE" on the front and back of their black Kevlar vests. They stuffed radio earpieces in their right ears. After a quick adjustment, MacKinnon said, "Base, we're about to approach the residence at 1651 Brunswick, apartment 211." They each pulled back the slides of their SIGs and holstered them.

Daniel tapped his foot on the floor. *Hurry!* The addictive adrenalin rush returned.

He could barely make out the tinny voice leaking from MacKinnon's earpiece. "Base. Acknowledged."

"Copy."

Touesnard flipped the switch on the wall panel, the elevator lurched upward, stopped a short moment later, and the doors burst open. He walked first, the laser from his SIG pointing straight ahead, pointing left, then right, then painting a jiggling red dot on the door to apartment 211. They crouched at opposite sides of the door and listened to a silence from within the apartment.

"Whoa!" said a startled voice down the hall near the elevator. Both men swung their weapons toward it. A rotund man in his midtwenties wearing an olive *M*A*S*H* T-shirt dusted with orange Cheezie stains, black shorts, and flip-flops stood holding a small green garbage bag in his right hand. His mouth froze open at the sight of two armed police officers in his hallway.

MacKinnon ran up to him and motioned "Shhh" with his index finger to his mouth. "Get out of here, buddy," he whispered. "Police operation." The man didn't respond for a moment, body paralyzed with surprise, and then he slowly nodded.

"Can I drop off my garbage in the chute?" He motioned to the small door in the far wall.

"No."

The man scurried back to his apartment, MacKinnon observing him while Touesnard kept watch at Claire's apartment door. The man locked his own door with an audible click.

Daniel wanted to join the two cops, but he stood against the wall beside the elevator. He then flicked his gaze back to MacKinnon. No sound. Touesnard stood directly in front of the door. He gave Daniel and MacKinnon a look. *Should we buzz and identify ourselves?*

Touesnard moved beside the door, hugging the wall, and knocked once, twice, three times.

No sound from within apartment 211.

He knocked again. "Hello, Ms. Marcoux?" He looked at MacKinnon, who twirled his fingers over and under each other, indicating that he should keep talking. "Are you there?"

Inside, Larch pivoted his head to face down the hall toward the door. He saw flickering shadows under it.

"You are indeed fortunate," he whispered to Claire.

Larch walked with deadly purpose to the door, gripping his pistol tight, and looked through the peephole.

From the other side of the door, Touesnard glanced back again, and got the same reaction from his colleague. "It's Frank from two …" — he looked down the hall, past MacKinnon, at the number on the door — "fourteen." He moved directly in front of the door, faced it, put his hands behind his back to hide what he held, and smiled.

Daniel's training warned that the killer could be on the other side and that such a flimsy wooden door wouldn't stop any bullets. Touesnard would know this, too. *He's a very brave man*, Daniel thought.

Larch peered through the peephole to see a distorted image of a man, fortyish, sporting a trimmed beard around a broad smile, evidently eager to see his attractive neighbour.

It's not Ritter. The situation just got a lot more complicated.

Touesnard continued his high-stakes acting. "Claire, are you angry at me? I'm sorry for what I said to you before. I'd like to apologize." He tried to look penitent by looking at his shoes, careful to keep his hands out of view. He saw a shifting shadow through the crack between the door and the floor. Someone was watching on the other side of the door.

Larch's brain whirred through possible ways of getting rid of this annoying neighbour who posed a direct threat to his ability to complete his mission. He had realized the first part of his plan; since he had difficulty in following Ritter with the constant police shadow, he anticipated where the target would go. Waiting at the apparent girlfriend's place, Larch would be able to finally catch Ritter when he appeared for dinner. But this bothersome neighbour threatened to expose his trap. Miss Marcoux would never be allowed to answer. He would wait it out until the neighbour gave up. He peered out again at the visitor. Good, the man was leaving —

Touesnard saw the shadow under the door move again. He turned away from the door, looked at MacKinnon, nodded slightly, backed up against the wall opposite the door, accelerated over two steps, extended his right boot, and smashed the door with a bass-heavy *whomp*. The door splintered at the deadbolt and whipped around on its hinges.

They heard the low thump of a person hitting the floor and a hiss as the air pressure equalized between the room and the hallway. The air felt stale and metallic with fear.

Daniel saw Touesnard run into the apartment, and MacKinnon follow right behind, guns drawn.

He heard a voice yell "Police." *Sounds like Touesnard*, thought Daniel —

Then MacKinnon's voice, "Don't move. Drop the gun. Drop it." A silence. Then, "Drop it!" followed by a pop, then another, then a cacophony of bangs. The air in front of the open door crackled with bursts of light, the charcoal tang of gunpowder, and the angry staccato of concussive sounds. The wall opposite the open door splintered as bullets knifed into the cement. Daniel ran from the exposed position in front of the elevator and crouched in the doorway of the neighbouring apartment.

He heard a scream of pain in between shots. Next, a thud. Then the sound of something heavy sliding along the floor.

MacKinnon emerged, crouched, panting, attempting to fire his pistol with one shaking hand. His face strained as he dragged a motionless Touesnard into the hallway and tried to veer out of the line of fire. Directly in front of the apartment door, they had no cover from the onslaught coming from inside Claire's apartment.

MacKinnon staggered backward as another bullet slammed into his Kevlar vest. He stumbled against the hallway wall directly opposite the open door while his damaged hand released Touesnard. He managed to fire again toward the unseen assailant just as the force of the impact against the far wall knocked the pistol from his hand.

It spun wildly until it stopped beside Daniel's left foot.

The gun called to him. Daniel grabbed it on instinct.

The handle was still warm. It felt comfortable, like the company of a long-lost friend who you could just pick up a conversation with, as if no time had passed since the last time you met.

Daniel's brain shifted into a well-worn routine. He pulled the clip down and saw that three rounds remained. And one in the chamber. He shoved it back in until he heard the reassuring click and pulled the slide. Ready to go. He scanned the situation. MacKinnon lay dazed in the hallway, trying to get up, and frantically looking for his gun. Touesnard was unconscious in the middle of the hallway, blood seeping from a wound on his neck. He had been hit just above his Kevlar vest. Poor guy. His weapon was nowhere to be seen.

Daniel marked the important information: there were two guns he couldn't see.

He approached slowly, shuffling his feet while holding the SIG with both arms outstretched and keeping it level, his right eye tracking a simple, straight path for any bullet he might launch.

His brain searched for any movement or threat. A shadow emerged from the apartment. It advanced in small steps until Daniel saw an arm, outstretched, holding a pistol, aimed directly at MacKinnon, ready to finish the job. But the man stopped, surprised to see someone else standing on the extreme left side of his field of view.

Maybe Daniel saw the face of a surprised Mr. Wang, the last person he targeted with a gun. Perhaps he didn't want a repeat of the mess in Hong Kong. So Daniel didn't shoot, just ran straight at the assailant. After four steps, he crashed his right shoulder into the man's chest, surprising him, throwing him off balance, and knocking the man's gun into the air. The man slammed into the edge of the open door. He grunted with the pain of his back crunching on the sharp corner of the doorway. He bounced back and shoved Daniel backward from a football tackle position. Daniel crashed onto his backside, and struggling to get up, lost control of his weapon. It dropped to the floor as the man regained his balance.

There was a moment as each man processed his memories, trying to identify the other.

Larch saw his final witness at last — a more important target than the wounded policeman on the ground.

Daniel came face-to-face with the soulless killer who had been trying to hunt him down.

No words were spoken. They recognized each other simultaneously. Survival would depend on who had the fastest reflexes.

Daniel, already on the floor, lunged for his pistol three feet away. Now on his stomach, he extended his arm, gripped the pistol, rolled onto his side, and raised the gun.

Larch was leaning down, fetching his weapon.

Daniel, with his gun already aimed straight, had the advantage.

He squeezed once, slowly, holding the far end steady despite his shaking hands. He fired into Larch's right side, as close to the centre of mass as he could estimate, where the heart would be. His body shuddered from the gun's recoil.

Larch looked down, surprised, at the point where the bullet struck him, his body trembling from the impact. He continued moving his gun higher, closer to aiming at the prostrate Daniel.

Daniel didn't flinch and fired again. And again. Each time, a spent cartridge hopped away from his pistol, and Larch's body quivered until it thumped against the wall beside the open apartment door. The gun dropped from Larch's limp, lifeless hand as he crumpled, with a sickening crunch, headfirst to the ground into an expanding crimson puddle.

MacKinnon had seen everything from his prone position on the floor and looked as surprised as Larch had been. He pulled Touesnard closer and tried to stop the bleeding with his hand. He struggled to talk, barely whispering into his commlink, "Officer down. Shots fired. Need medical assistance."

As Daniel hopped up, he could hear the response through MacKinnon's earpiece. "Copy. Backup ETA two minutes. Ambulance dispatched to your location."

MacKinnon gestured toward the apartment.

One gun was still unaccounted for. Daniel didn't know if there was a second shooter still hiding in the apartment. He popped the magazine from the handle and confirmed one remaining bullet before jamming it back in and pulling back the slide. Ready to fire.

He burst in, hugged the wall in the kitchen, and faced a small living room. No one there, but the furniture was scattered, the chair on its back, a broken lamp.

There had been a struggle. He picked up the pistol on the floor. Daniel quickly examined the kitchen on the right and then darted straight ahead to the bedroom.

Claire was trying to worm her way off the bed, her arms and legs tied up, face covered with sweat and dried blood, her mouth covered with silvery duct tape. Her eyes were wide, scared, but also relieved.

She's alive.

"Anyone else here?" He was still holding the SIG at the ready.

Claire shook her head.

He peeked into the bathroom, just in case. No one.

He knelt down, put the SIG on the bed, and removed the tape over her mouth with a quick tug.

Claire screamed in pain.

"You got that *maudit* fucker?" she said.

Daniel nodded.

"Where are the cops?"

Daniel gestured toward the hall as he searched for and then found a knife on the floor. "They're hurt. Help is on its way." He cut the tape around her hands.

"Since when do you know how to handle a gun, *câlice*?" She looked up at him as she rubbed her wrists.

He continued cutting tape, freeing her feet. "It's a long story."

"*Hé*, I'm not complaining." She was breathing fast.

He looked directly into her eyes. "Are you okay?"

She considered the question for a moment. "He was waiting for you." She seemed angry with him, but Daniel assumed this was the adrenalin talking.

"Yes, I know."

He looked at the puffy pink log that was her left arm.

"You look like shit. Your arm's in bad shape. You're going to need a medic. Ambulance is coming."

She smacked his arm as she stood up. "So now we're even."

With Claire safe, and no other threats about, he remembered MacKinnon and Touesnard in the hallway. "I have to help them. You stay put." He grabbed a towel from the bathroom and ran back to the hallway, where he wrapped it around Touesnard's neck.

MacKinnon knelt beside Touesnard, concern etched on his face. He looked at Daniel. "Thanks."

Daniel nodded but kept his focus on Touesnard. Two police officers, guns drawn, sprang from the stairwell, followed by two paramedics, each holding orange bags of gear. MacKinnon gestured for the officers to reholster their weapons. One paramedic made a beeline for Touesnard, while the other checked out Larch. He quickly moved on to Touesnard.

MacKinnon said as he pointed to his colleague, "I'm okay. He needs help. Gunshot wound in the neck."

"We've tried to stop the bleeding," Daniel said to one of the paramedics, "and there's someone else who needs your help." He motioned to the apartment. "Hostage we just rescued. Her arm needs attention."

MacKinnon wobbled as he stood up, pushing against the wall to steady himself. "You going to give me back my weapon?"

Daniel gave a sheepish look before spinning it around and handing it to MacKinnon grip first. MacKinnon popped out the magazine, confirmed the remaining round, jammed it back into the gun, and slipped the pistol back into his holster.

MacKinnon said, "So that's what you did in China."

Daniel nodded as he sprinted back to Claire, who was examining a wallet while a paramedic examined her arm. She dumped the wallet's contents on the bed. "This is his." She pointed back to the open front door, where she could see Larch's leg jutting out from the hallway.

"California licence. Nick Pulovski." She found some tickets, stubs, and a hotel key card in the front pocket. "Looks like he was staying at the Westin. He's got a rental from Enterprise. Had a meal at the Bicycle Thief. Wow, two hundred dollars for dinner." She held the credit card receipt in her shaking hand.

Daniel took her hand, steadied it. "Big spender."

"Not anymore."

Claire pulled her hand away. Daniel leaned over, picked up the man's pistol, popped the magazine, and ejected the lone bullet still in the gun, rendering it safe.

"I've been staring at this damn thing for too long. Beretta with a silencer. He was very cool. Professional." She looked at Daniel.

Daniel said, "You think he would have killed you?"

"Definitely. He didn't tell me that exactly — he wasn't a big talker — but he made it clear ... He didn't talk much to me, but he was texting someone."

Daniel found Larch's phone on the bedside table beside a small box with a cable.

"He kept texting someone for instructions." He tossed the box over to MacKinnon. "And he's been following us with this phone thing."

MacKinnon looked at it carefully. "Wow, an IMSI-catcher."

Daniel looked at him, not understanding.

"Each cellphone has a unique number. With this gadget," he said, patting it, "you can track the user and listen in on calls. Very sophisticated. We have to borrow ours from the RCMP."

Daniel returned to the cellphone in his hand. The text conversation was with someone called "Client." He reviewed the short conversation, which ended with No loose ends. Do it now. The hit man took orders from this person.

MacKinnon took the phone and saw the phone number had a 403 area code.

"Alberta," said Daniel.

"Not so fast," said MacKinnon. He saw the paramedics hoisting Touesnard onto a gurney in the hallway and rolling him to the elevator. MacKinnon opened his own phone and dialed. When a voice answered, he said, "I want an identity and trace on this number." He read out the digits.

In a few seconds, the voice said something that Daniel couldn't make out.

"Keep a trace on it." MacKinnon stuffed the phone into a pocket on his Kevlar vest. "It's a burner phone. A prepaid account. Paid in cash. It's only been active for six weeks."

The hit man's phone buzzed as a new message arrived. Status?

MacKinnon showed it to Daniel and Claire. "What do you think we should we say?"

Claire shrugged. "Give him the answer he wants and see what happens?"

"Sounds good to me." MacKinnon typed Done and pressed *send*.

FIFTY-SEVEN

THE CRIME SCENE BUZZED with activity. Police officers swarmed the hallway, some rolling out yellow "Do Not Cross" tape, others interviewing shocked neighbours about what they had seen and heard. Touesnard's and Larch's guns were sealed in evidence bags. A medical examiner knelt over Larch's body.

"Careful," Claire protested at the paramedics bandaging her left arm. At least she was right-handed.

MacKinnon held up the hit man's driver's licence. "So who was Nick Pulovski?"

Daniel was puzzled. "I think I used to know someone by that name. But I can't remember where or when. The name sounds familiar."

Claire clutched a red passport. "But that's not the name in his passport. It looks like him, but he's Mitchell Gant here. British."

I've heard of that guy, too, thought Daniel.

MacKinnon flipped open his notebook. "There was only one black Cadillac SUV rented two days ago. To someone named Walt Kowalski, using a fake U.S. passport."

"It must be the same guy," said Daniel.

"Odd choice of names," said Claire.

"I've heard these names before."

"Anything else in his bag?"

Claire dumped the contents on the floor. Another passport, American. Ben Shockley.

Daniel flipped through mental images of men with these names. He felt he had met all of them, and though he couldn't recall the exact circumstances, he was sure that he knew them.

He squeezed his memory for one image. Mitchell Gant. In a plane. It was military. But Daniel couldn't recall ever being in a military plane. But the image was sharper now, the face coming into view. A stern face, with a bit of stubble. Sharp, shifty narrow eyes. Eyes with a terrible purpose.

Then a second image. Shockley. He was in the back seat of a crappy car, next to a young prostitute, driving through a scorching desert. The same eyes, the same face.

Somehow they were the same person.

MacKinnon typed the first name, Nick Pulovski, into the Google app on his smartphone. He scowled at the answer. Same reaction after punching in the name Ben Shockley. And with Mitchell Gant.

"They're not real people at all," he said. "They're characters played by Clint Eastwood in different movies."

"Our hit man was a Clint Eastwood fan?" said Claire.

Daniel cracked a thin smile. He felt ahead of the curve for the first time since he had received Forrestal's phone call on Monday morning.

* ✳ *

Daniel's cellphone pinged with a new text message. **We need to talk.**

His heart leaped. It was from Vanessa, no doubt at her parents' house in trendy Devonport, across the bay from Auckland.

Sure.

When can you come visit?

I'll find out. Soon. How's E?

She misses you.

I miss her more. Where are you?

Mum and Dad's. We have things to discuss.

Are you coming back?

That's what we need to talk about. How's your situation?

Improving. Hope to be able to come in a few days. Will let u know.

K.

Daniel wondered if the distance had deadened her anger toward him. Maybe he could see Emily after all, now that the assassin was no longer a threat.

Larch's phone beeped. A message from the client. **Leave town ASAP. Setting up major action tomorrow. Victoria Park. Noon.**

FIFTY-EIGHT

THE MILITARY-GRADE EXPLOSIVE, innocently called Composition C-4, tumbled noiselessly in his knapsack. It had arrived Thursday in the one shipment from the U.S. by sea. Aspen confirmed its on-time delivery, in spite of some interference from the RCMP and Border Services. He expected more, but with the most recent consignment intercepted by a navy patrol, he had to make do with the four kilograms in the bag.

Opening the box, he saw a number of short, rectangular sticks wrapped in black. Inhaling that crisp scent transported him back to a unique summer camp in Idaho years ago for new AIM recruits where mornings were for weapons training. Early one sunny day found him breaking pieces of the malleable material into different sizes, sticking a shiny detonator rod into each, learning how to use it safely, how to judge how stable it was, and how the blast radius varied. That evening, in the arid mountain air, sitting around the campfire, he swapped tall tales of the resulting destruction scenarios with his fellow AIM brothers. One man's terrifying story and bandaged stump of an arm reinforced the most important lesson: keep the nine-volt battery and detonator rod in separate pockets in your jeans.

Today, his task was simple. Garth had instructed his driver, a loyal AIM member — what was his name, Ted? — to park around the corner and out of sight while he strolled down Spring Garden. The street was devoid of traffic or people, apart from the pair of pedestrians leaving the McDonald's beyond the opposite corner. With the jet lag pulling him down, he didn't care if it was seven or four in the morning as he saw the first spray of light from the coming dawn. This was his final chance to derail the opponents of the campaign and save the dream of a country of his own. He couldn't fail. He would do it himself. He imagined Brewster's grinning face as he watched news reports of the carnage in Halifax in a few hours.

When he stopped in the shadow behind the statue to tie up his boot, no one noticed. No one was around to remark on his forgetfulness. They couldn't see when he stabbed the detonator into the plastic, clipped the battery into its holder, and set the timer. As he walked to the garbage can beside the tree, he took another quick glance at the two people on the otherwise empty street. All clear. He closed the small grey backpack and tossed it in the can. He listened to the thunk as it hit the bottom while he felt the pistol in his pocket for reassurance. He covered the backpack with the trash already in the bin. Then he just walked away, lost in his thoughts. Like the two people now at the corner, staring at the sidewalk, waiting for the light to change on a way-too-early Sunday morning.

Nice to be in Nova Scotia. Garth stretched his arms and arched his back. Then he walked to the just-opened Smitty's for a well-deserved breakfast, careful not to stay too long.

FIFTY-NINE

WHERE ARE THEY?

Daniel scanned Spring Garden Road, which carved Victoria Park off from the Public Gardens. Dozens of locals, wrapped in thick coats, raised their arms to shield their eyes from the February gusts whipping up snow. Others held signs. All wormed their way along the sidewalks on both sides to assemble at the statue across the street. He stood under the traffic light where the avenues crossed. He looked at each approaching face, searching for telltale signs of pent-up aggression.

They have to be here.

Lloyd had said as much to MacKinnon. Garth, the person all agreed was probably on the other end of Larch's cellphone, had texted to stay away from Victoria Park. Lloyd thought it was to warn him of the Yes demonstration planned for noon. Coupled with the cryptic message sent to Larch, Claire and the cops agreed the most likely meaning of "action" was a violent counterdemonstration.

It wouldn't be the first time. Daniel remembered his brush with another one days earlier. That man had been sent by the Yes campaign to start a fight with the No supporters. And it had worked, grabbing headlines across the country. Daniel grimaced as he recalled the photograph of him and Claire on the news site.

This time it was a show of support for the Yes side. Daniel had lingering doubts. *Would Garth rough up some of his own supporters to get sympathy from the press?* A few people could do the job, especially if they were eager to use violence to intimidate demonstrators. MacKinnon had refused to take them to the scene. It was a police matter. Daniel and Claire had leaped out from their taxi and rushed to the park entrance, covering the access from the north and west.

Now, with a growing sense of unease, Daniel inspected the gathering crowd spilling along Spring Garden Road. He didn't know who to look for. He guessed it would be another Amoeba Man, someone large, muscular, and threatening. Through the snow that slashed by in horizontal strokes, he noticed a banner that read "Hands off my country!" It reminded him of the earlier demonstration that had trapped him on his way to the police station. He remembered the biker, huge, aggressive, and distracted long enough by a can of tomato soup. He smiled at a surprising sense of irony that enveloped his thoughts.

Do I have Garth and Lloyd to thank for introducing me to Claire?

He shook away the happiness he must have shown on his face and returned to scanning the multitude of parkas, hats, and signs.

How many are there?

Daniel started counting and realized that he was a poor judge of crowd size. There could have been two hundred or four. He couldn't tell by guessing. A thump of frustration hit as he realized his margin of error was 100 percent. He had to admit he could only say that the crowd was big and growing bigger.

Which ones?

"They all look the same," Claire called from behind. He turned to see her watching people surging from the north along South Park. "I can't tell who it might be."

She had a point. Only noses or pairs of eyes peeked out of the mass of parkas, toques, and scarves. The faint light didn't help.

"Are we sure this is their plan?" Claire approached.

Daniel brushed the snow off his watch. Seven minutes before the planned start of the demonstration. "We'll find out soon enough."

MacKinnon's cruiser screeched to a stop in front of Daniel. He opened the door, stood, and pointed at him to leave. Then he pointed at Claire.

Daniel snapped his head around to face the statue across the street. He focused on the sculpture of Robbie Burns that crowned the main entrance to Victoria Park. At first, he didn't know why his attention had been drawn in that direction.

The unnatural disturbance in the flow of the crowd?

The sudden silence?

The collective holding of breath?

Or perhaps a flash of intuition that something didn't belong in the scene?

MacKinnon was first to express it. "Looks like it's about to start." He pointed across the street.

Daniel and Claire continued searching for the expected fight between the agent provocateur and members of the demonstration.

"Something feels wrong." Claire lunged ahead, closing the distance to the crowd in only a few strides.

"I don't see what's going on." Daniel was startled at Claire's evident ferocity in the face of potential violence.

Sound returned to the crowd as it began to disperse, people scattering and running in random directions.

Then the source of the commotion came into view. A garbage can had been tipped on its side. Among the contents scattered on the snow and mud, a small grey backpack, partially open, lay on the snow; something grey-green inside shone in the weak noon light.

Then someone, stepping back from it, said, "It looks like a bomb."

Claire sliced through the crowd until she kneeled beside the bag, careful not to touch it. She looked up at Daniel and snorted. "Fucking C-4." She pointed to the Mylar wrappers.

"Are you serious?" Daniel had never seen the plastic explosive up close. Garth's plan materialized in his mind. They had misjudged him. *Garth isn't going to disrupt the protest with another thug to stir things up. He's going to kill or maim whoever shows up.* He nodded silently to himself. *Would he kill his own supporters to get what he wants?* Daniel grudgingly acknowledged the logic behind the brutal move. *Of course. Better carnage. Better headlines. More outrage.*

Claire was examining the bomb as if it were a miniature crime scene. "Look. It's complete. See the wires, the detonators. How the fuck did they get this?" She positioned her finger close, but she was careful to avoid physical contact. "I don't know how to defuse it."

MacKinnon had already used his radio to call it in. He said, "Bomb squad is on its way. We have to evacuate the area." He looked at Claire. "Can you see the timer?"

The firefight in the bay flashed in her mind. The prisoner. The military hardware in the crates. Clearly they had missed something. "I bet this was part of the shipment I intercepted yesterday. These people are serious." She looked closer at the small digital display connected to one of the wires. "It's set for noon." She leaned back.

Daniel looked at his watch. "That's only a couple of minutes away." He looked at her again, impressed with her calm and methodical approach to a potentially lethal problem. She always seemed to run *toward* danger.

"How big of a blast will it be?" MacKinnon said.

Daniel pulled Claire up. She brushed the snow and dirt from her jeans. "I saw eight plastic blocks. I'd guess three or four kilos. Anyone in this intersection is in danger."

MacKinnon was back on his radio. "We need to evacuate everyone in a two-block radius. We only have a couple of minutes. Hurry!" He turned to Daniel and Claire. "There's not enough time. It's up to us."

Daniel took in Claire's searing brown eyes, sealing an unspoken bond, as police cruisers with their lights flashing screeched to a halt in the out-of-focus background. In moments, cops were deflecting traffic two blocks away.

Only a few stragglers remained in the park. They appeared confused, expecting a large crowd and finding only a few people running away, abandoning their signs in the snow, while a cop and two strangers stood alone at the demonstration site.

Police were clearing out the local café, the Smitty's across the street, and the high-end hotel at the opposite corner. A pair of officers gathered the small crowd's attention. MacKinnon ran to his cruiser, popped the trunk, and grabbed a megaphone.

As he ran back to the statue, he waved his free hand at any people still in the area. "This demonstration has been cancelled. Please leave for your own safety."

The new arrivals reacted poorly, catcalling, jeering, and refusing to budge from their constitutionally protected right to protest. No one was going to prevent them from telling the world that they wanted their own country.

Daniel checked his watch. "One minute."

Claire nodded. "We can't assume that the timer is set to the same time as your watch."

MacKinnon said, "Good point." He raised the megaphone and began to run back to his car. "Run. There's a bomb. Take cover. It's set to go off any second."

The latecomers scattered. No one screamed, as if the effort to do so would sap their ability to speed away from the epicentre of the expected explosion. MacKinnon quickly shepherded a few protesters along Spring Garden.

Then Daniel saw another protester, a young man, emerging from some trees behind the statue, looking surprised at the emptiness before him.

Daniel ran over to him. He saw Claire do the same from the corner of his eye.

"Get out of here. There's a bomb," she yelled.

The man turned and began to run.

Daniel grabbed Claire's hand. They turned to flee.

It would be the absence of sound that surprised him when he retold the story to MacKinnon.

He saw the flash first.

A bright burst of white orange tore at the base of what used to be the Robbie Burns statue about twenty metres away. The park vanished in a blinding fireball. Then the pressure wave punched Daniel, ripping Claire's hand from his grip. A deep, deafening roar scooped him up from the street and shoved him through a large window. He bounced off the edge of a counter, showering straws, napkins, tables, and fragments of concrete throughout the room.

Daniel slammed into the far wall. He couldn't move. He couldn't feel anything. His ears throbbed with a sharp pain. He heard no sound. Lying on his back, he saw the ceiling scorched with streaks of black fanning away from the front of the café. Smoke swirled in the air above him. He tried to raise his head to see his surroundings. He nearly passed out from the effort, but he turned his head to the right and couldn't believe his eyes.

The entire front of the café was gone, the window obliterated. Shards of glass covered the floor, tables were snapped in half, and people lay on the ground. There was no movement outside. He saw people sprawled and immobile on the street, too.

Claire! Where's Claire? An arm moved to his right, only a short distance away. The arm, dark, covered in charcoal, pushed a person up until he saw Claire's blackened face. He strained to slide toward her. He tried to say something but couldn't.

He looked at his own body. Was he injured? Did he still have his legs, his arms? *An odd question to be asking myself*, he thought. He flashed back to a grisly image of the aftermath of the Boston Marathon bombing — small, stunned children scattered among the explosively detached limbs of the people unlucky enough to have been standing within the blast radius of the two home-made bombs. But he was all right — well, at least he hadn't lost limbs. Adrenalin powered his body now. Only when its effect wore off would he know what damage had been done to him.

A sea of faint moans surrounded him. He heard a muffled scream from outside. Only low, bass frequencies at first, but soon he could hear the tinny whine of a woman in pain as some of his hearing returned. He felt something in his right ear, stuck in a finger to dig it out, and saw blood on his finger.

"Daniel. You okay?" Claire kneeled beside him, looking worried.

He sat and looked at his hand; bloody, covered with wood splinters and stained with black. "Don't know." He pushed himself up with both hands and, straining, heaved himself upright. His head throbbed. He fell back, faint. After a few seconds, he raised his head again, this time more confident. "Good enough."

"You're hurt."

She seemed in better shape than he was, but her hair was singed on one side, the side that faced the blast wave. Her face was blackened with soot and sparkly flecks, her eyes betraying concern.

"So are you," he said.

He waited until he felt his blood pressure had steadied,

and then he tried to stand. At first he wobbled, but Claire held his left arm, gashed and bloody but still intact.

"There must be others who are hurt over there." He extended his right hand toward the direction of a column of black smoke that now replaced the missing statue. "Over there."

"We have to help."

"Right."

"I'll see what I can do here. Can you go outside?"

Daniel nodded. He stepped over people who, like him, were now beginning to move and assess their own mortality. He started with the first person on the road directly in front of the café. A man in his early twenties. The young protester who had emerged from behind the tree. The man was still breathing. He groaned as he moved his arms. Daniel helped him, steadying him as he sat up. There was blood on his head, on his arms, and in a small pool near his feet. His right leg was twisted at an unnatural angle. He screamed at the effort to move. But he was conscious.

He stumbled awkwardly over the debris, heading toward Claire's voice. She hadn't gotten far. She was kneeling beside a woman who didn't move, a small puddle of blood beside her. Claire took a tablecloth, ripped it lengthwise into three strips, and wound it around the woman's head as a tourniquet.

"Can you hold the leg?" she said.

He held it gently but firmly, ensuring that it didn't move as she wound the strips around the leg. "You know first aid?" Daniel said.

"I'm a sailor, remember?" She tied another tourniquet in a tight knot. "What about you?" She flicked a glance his way before returning to the woman on the ground. "Is first aid part of every professor's training?"

"I had to protect myself in China."

"Like knowing how to use a gun and drive evasively."

"I also used to give tours to remote parts of the world. Sometimes the nearest hospital could be days away by foot. I had to learn the basics."

"Like one of Mao's barefoot doctors." She focused on the woman's leg.

Daniel turned to look at her with a new layer of respect. "How did you know that?"

"History major."

Daniel nodded then returned his focus to the leg Claire was bandaging.

She tugged on the knot to be sure it would hold. "You've used those skills before, haven't you?"

He nodded, but he didn't volunteer any details. He set the limb as straight as possible without seeing any signs of pain from the woman. He took a plastic cafeteria tray that lay nearby and snapped it lengthwise into two oblong pieces, which he placed on opposite sides of the leg. He secured the plastic to her leg using two of the tablecloth strips, forming a simple splint. The woman grunted either in delirium or appreciation, but otherwise she didn't move. There wasn't much more that could be done for her before the paramedics came.

As he fully concentrated on the wounded, he didn't hear the sirens or notice the blue and red flashes of emergency lights.

"Who's in charge here?" someone yelled from behind.

Daniel looked around to see an older woman, dressed in an EHS jacket and holding an bright red trauma bag.

"Don't know," Daniel said. "You a paramedic?"

"We were just leaving the Infirmary."

He knew that the Halifax Infirmary was a few blocks away. Lucky for the wounded. He pointed to his splint, and to the woman Claire had bandaged. "She's got a fractured leg, the other one has a head wound. We put pressure on the wounds, but you need to see them first. They've lost a lot of blood." The paramedic hopped over to the women and examined their injuries. She surveyed the depressing landscape and got to work.

Daniel and Claire stood a few feet apart, stunned, watching the medical professionals take over. Five ambulances appeared, and dozens of people in EHS outfits rummaged through the debris to locate and treat the wounded.

The paramedics bandaged Daniel's hand and treated his legs with antiseptic. They worried about his head, suspecting a concussion. They warned him that he needed to go to the hospital for tests.

Claire sat beside him. "It's a good idea, Daniel. You need to be checked out."

They walked the few blocks to the hospital since all ambulances were busy with victims in more desperate states. He stumbled often, Claire holding him up. What should have been a short stroll became a ten-minute effort.

The doors parted in front of them to reveal a scene from a war zone. Dozens of people lay on the floor along the right wall, some screaming, others unmoving, while nurses fixed saline drips, made assessments, and applied bandages.

As one of the nurses whizzed by, Claire flagged her and pointed to Daniel. "Concussion," she said.

The nurse barely slowed down. She pointed to the back of the main entrance hallway, saying, "See triage." There, a man in a white medical gown pointed and wrote something on a pad he cradled in his arm.

Daniel limped over to a young woman with a long ponytail. Her tag read *Jacqueline, RN*. Claire explained about the concussion worry.

The nurse scribbled down Daniel's name on her pad. "Put him down over there." She pointed to the wall where other patients were already lying down — some yelling in pain, others numb in silence. A spot had opened up. Meanwhile, a stream of gurneys rolled down to operating rooms, carrying the most seriously injured. Paramedics and hospital staff, shock and futility scarring their faces, wheeled one person by after another. Daniel caught sight of a man clearly missing a leg under sheets stained red and black.

He understood that he was low priority until the worst cases had been treated.

The entire room quieted for a few seconds. Daniel and Claire turned to see four soldiers, in full winter battle gear and holding C7 rifles, take positions in front of and immediately behind the sliding doors outside. A fifth soldier was instructing them where to stand.

Daniel turned to Claire. "What are they doing here?"

Claire whispered, "Must be a general mobilization."

"At a hospital?"

"Protect the critical public infrastructure and ensure that the government continues to function. Those are the first priorities when confronting a natural disaster." She stopped and looked at the soldiers with new eyes. "Or a terrorist attack."

SIXTY

TWO HOURS LATER, Daniel and Claire sat silently, sipping their coffees at the Tim Hortons that was crammed into one corner near the hospital's main entrance. The doctors told Daniel to wait a bit to see if he suffered any other symptoms of a concussion before leaving. In his mind, he replayed the last seconds before the explosion. He tried visualizing the explosive device. It was tucked into a small bag in a garbage can. Hidden from view. No one noticed it there. Probably a bag with some cute logo, people walking right beside it. Until someone opened the lid and glanced in before tossing their trash into the can. Claire had spotted it with only minutes to spare.

The other three customers at the café didn't talk. They watched the television over the lunch counter where a news presenter sat in Victoria Park, surrounded by an image of the carnage. A large CBC headline read "Terror Attack in Halifax." Daniel and Claire moved to a table close to the TV so they could hear.

He ordered a ham and cheese sandwich, two chocolate dip doughnuts, and another large coffee. The server at the cash noticed their rapt attention and turned up the volume on the television.

> … RCMP and Halifax Emergency Response Teams have isolated the scene that, around noon today, tragically turned from a protest march into mayhem and death. Police confirm four p eople were pronounced dead at the scene. The army has been asked to guard critical infrastructure. The Halifax Infirmary has treated thirty-three casualties. They warn that they have implemented their mass casualty protocol and will not accept any Emergency patients for the time being.

Daniel noticed in the video many more police in the background, including several holding automatic weapons. Some soldiers in battle gear milled about. It must have been taken not long after he and Claire had left for the hospital.

"We have political commentator Phil Robertson from Ottawa on the line. Mr. Robertson, how do you respond to today's event in Halifax?"

A bald, middle-aged man with a bushy moustache protruding from an otherwise unremarkable face stared into the camera. His eyebrows strained to show how serious he was. "It's a real tragedy. These were people assembled to march in support of the Alberta vote on Monday. We don't know how many were killed or injured."

"We just heard that there were four people killed. Are you saying they were deliberately targeted?"

"Clearly, yes. Only a few days earlier there was a counterdemonstration at the exact same place."

"Are you suggesting there was a connection between the two demonstrations besides one supporting and one against the vote?"

"It seems like the most likely conclusion."

"A deliberate attack from one group on the other?"

"It was murder. Worse, terrorism. This was a terrorist attack on Canada. They don't want the referendum to happen. They're scared about a Yes victory."

"But why attack Halifax? It's pretty much the farthest place from Alberta. The march was small, less than a hundred or so. Wouldn't it have made more sense to stage such an attack in Toronto or even Edmonton, where more people would notice?"

"The target seems obvious. Last night, as you know, the Yes side announced a series of speeches across the country to explain their message to Canadians. The first speech will be delivered tonight at the Scotiabank Centre. There is a lot of media attention. Whoever targeted them knew exactly when to strike. Everyone would be watching."

"What are you saying?"

"We have to ask ourselves who'd benefit most from a disrupted pro-independence rally?"

Daniel saw his meal waiting on the counter, and he suddenly felt the instinctive urge to eat. He focused on the food, leaving the interview to dissolve into a background of noise. Whatever happened next, he needed to be well fed. His instructor yelled in his memory: *How can you fight if you're too hungry? Eat when you can.* The sandwich was gone in four bites. He ordered another.

Claire got a sandwich and a doughnut, stirred her coffee with her good hand, and stared at the carnage on the screen.

Daniel thought that the reporter posed the right question: Who would benefit from bombing a pro-Yes rally? It was a cowardly act. All they had to do was to put a simple bomb in a bag, leave it at the statue in Victoria Park, and push a button. *Garth killed his father.* And he suspected that he would kill his own supporters just to discredit the No side. He shuddered in repulsion. *Can Garth be so cold and heartless?*

There was only one way to be sure. It was time to end this. He needed to talk to MacKinnon.

SIXTY-ONE

GARTH WAS MASTER OF the cameras that stood before him. The crowd numbered fifty or so Yes supporters, who dreamed of their own separate Acadia, either as a country or as a New England state. Not bad for a sympathetic audience so far from home.

The premier wanted him to clean the mess up. And he was doing it. Supporters had sent the word out. Many now openly accused the No campaign of using or at least tolerating terrorism to achieve their political goals. And with the last witness out of the picture, Larch had redeemed himself. The plan, his plan, was working. He felt good. He had persevered and won. Now it was time to close the deal, first here on the East Coast, then moving west to Quebec, Ontario, the Prairies, and finally British Columbia. He would speak to each part of the country in one final twenty-four-hour publicity blitz.

Of course, the police and the army had cancelled the rally due to the bombing at the park. So now he stood, proud, defiant, on a small elevated stage in the lobby of the Westin Hotel. He was surrounded by a charged phalanx of television cameras and reporters thrusting their microphones in his face, jostling for the best location to capture the important words he was about to say. Two soldiers stood outside the main entrance while two uniformed police officers milled about keeping an eye on a few dozen supporters and hotel guests.

He unfurled his notes onto the small podium and said nothing for a few seconds. He could still get his message out.

"Thank you, Halifax. Thank you for a warm and friendly East Coast welcome. I must first say that I was shocked to hear about the cowardly attack earlier today. Such evil has no place in our society."

He rustled his notes on the podium.

"Nova Scotia, I have come to you with a simple message." He raised his right hand. He did his best to look earnest. "Do not be afraid. Embrace your destiny, and help us as we make Canada what it should be. Tomorrow will be the start of something wonderful, and I want to tell you about it."

The reporters followed every word. He felt the cameras closing up on his face. He continued, "We want to make our own choices. Don't you want to make Nova Scotia the best place it can be? Control your fisheries? Natural resources? Economic policy? Control your borders to keep undesirables out? Well, so do we."

He took a gulp of water from the plastic bottle on the podium. "And who knows better than those closest to you, the citizens? You know what you want. You know what's important. You know better than a bureaucrat in Ottawa.

"Did you know that you're sitting on one of the world's true bounties? You know about your forests already. You've got fisheries. You've got oil and natural gas in the Gulf, and you're a world leader in tidal power, too.

"But who really benefits? It's not you. It's people in Toronto. People who have profited from the gravy train for a generation. Now they cry for your help. You've got it too good, they say. So Ottawa penalizes you.

"This is what we in Alberta have suffered for too long. We just want to be able to make our own decisions. We love our kids. We love our families. Just like you. We want a say in what kind of schools to send our kids to and which companies to help.

"You can do this, too.

"We can help you. Once Alberta controls its own destiny, we will be very happy to tell you all that we've learned."

Another gulp of water. "You've no doubt heard the cries of those on the No side."

Shouts of "Terrorists!" and boos emanated from people gathered in the hotel lobby behind the clutch of reporters.

He waved his hand to calm them. "They mean well, but they don't understand. They're not evil, just naive. And they're desperate. Desperate people do desperate things. I won't say that they were behind the bombing this morning. I have full confidence in the police to identify and prosecute those responsible. But clearly only desperate people would do this. Desperate to stop the will of a people when they couldn't otherwise win through the logic and passion of their arguments. When their tired pleas fail to convince the people, some turn to more extreme measures. They mean to hurt you. To kill your family, your friends, your children to get what they want. No matter what the cost.

"We're not like that. We're like you."

He looked directly into the nearest camera. "So, tomorrow night, when the referendum results are decided and we, the people, win, please join us."

The clapping from beyond the reporter group started even before he had finished his last line. He looked down and checked his cellphone. Larch had just sent a message: Need to talk.

Now came the hard part. He had to take a few questions from the reporters; most, if not all, were hostile to his party's goal. He had known what to do. Stretch out his planned speech as long as possible, squeeze the Q&A to a few minutes, and scoot out of the building before the crazies started ranting.

"I will now take a few questions." He pointed to the two microphones, where a short line had already formed. A woman in her thirties, professionally dressed in a dark jacket and skirt, and holding a notepad and her own microphone, approached first. Garth nodded.

"Sarah Glenn. Global News. Mr. Haynes. Can you comment on the bombing this morning? Are you saying it was the No side who did this?"

Garth smiled. She looked hot. Maybe after the speech … But no, he had things he needed to do.

"It was a cowardly act of cowardly people. I send our deepest condolences to those families affected. I have heard that at least ten people have been killed and dozens injured. This is the worst act of terrorism in this country since the Air India bombing. The worst in a generation. There are really no words that can express how I truly feel. It was just cowardly." He looked pointedly at one of the television cameras set up low and directly in front of him. "I say to all Albertans that voting Yes means voting for a renewed Confederation, a new Alberta, where terrorists and their sympathizers will never get power. They will be punished for their heinous crimes."

The supporters in the foyer clapped as loud as they could.

His phone vibrated. Another text message from Larch: I'm next.

What does that mean? He swung to face another hand held higher than the others. A man stood at the microphone, leaning heavily on his right foot.

"Mr. Haynes. You're a coward."

He tightened his focus on the man he didn't recognize. His right hand and head were bandaged, his hair dishevelled.

Garth squinted beyond the camera lights. "Am I?"

Daniel's world tilted a bit to the left. He heard ringing in his right ear and every sound was muffled. His whole body jittered, barely holding itself together. Two Advil and his head still throbbed. Standing sucked up most of his energy. *Symptoms of a concussion?* He kept going.

"Who do you think is responsible for the bombing?"

"Which news service do you represent?" Garth looked beyond the cameras.

"I'm a private citizen."

"Well, I don't know who is responsible, but I have faith in the police to find out."

"I'm surprised you don't know."

Garth pasted on his professional politician's smile, looking deeper into the crowd of reporters for another question to answer.

Daniel didn't stop. "You've managed two campaigns. One that everyone can see, but there is also a second one, one that has remained very much below everyone's radar."

"Thank you for your comment, but the gentleman in the back, you have a question —"

"I'm almost done. We've," he said, pointing to Claire, "been caught up in your second, secret campaign. By accident, of course."

Garth tried to encourage another question, but Daniel pressed on. "The bombing was just the final act of your second campaign."

Garth glared at him. "That's a serious charge. I had nothing to do with it. Nothing whatsoever."

The crowd in the foyer turned against Daniel. They didn't believe him. They lobbed shouts of "loser," "must be a sympathizer for the No side," and "wacko" at him. But he pressed on.

"Your bomb missed me, Garth. As you can see." Daniel held up his bandaged hand for the crowd to see. "You got very close, but you or your lackey set the timer too early."

"Probably a No sympathizer," said a voice from the crowd.

"You've left quite a trail of destruction trying to stop me. I think you've killed at least six people according to my count."

Garth began to panic. He looked left, looked right. He was under the glare of the media spotlight, broadcast live, and this was another ambush. *How does this person know so much?* Shadows moved at both edges of his vision.

The man stood closer to the microphone so every word, every breath, every gulp boomed throughout the room.

Garth ignored him and scanned for someone else to ask a question.

"You still don't know who I am? Here, let me help you." The man punched a few keys on a cellphone.

Garth read the text message. The police are waiting for you.

"How did you get that?" he barked.

The man held high the cellphone. "It belonged to your assassin. I believe you called him Larch."

Garth stared at it, his mouth open in disbelief. "I don't know what you're talking about."

"You hired a professional hit man to hunt me down like an animal. He got close. Tried twice. But then he got sloppy." Daniel stared directly into Garth's eyes. "Your man is no longer on the job."

Impossible. It can't be him. Larch confirmed that Ritter was dead. "You," Garth spit the word out like venom. "You're Ritter?"

"Full points." Daniel would have clapped if his right arm weren't wrapped in a bandage. "I'm sure Professor Fanshawe told you about me. He won't be joining you either."

Daniel was beginning to enjoy himself, even though his head throbbed with each word. "But these are only small parts of a much bigger plan. Your plan. At first, I didn't see it at all. I thought it was a murder of a famous businessman. Patrick Forrestal." The rising crowd murmur made him pause. "And I happened to be near when it happened. And I wasn't the only one. That's where your Mr. Larch came in. You hired him to kill Forrestal, and when you worried about being tied to the murder, you ordered him to kill me and the only other potential witness, the hotel manager."

Daniel looked around. A hush had descended on the crowd. Even the political cheerleaders, scattered throughout the hall, had quieted. All cameras pointed at him.

"Of course, there was much more going on. I didn't see it. But others did." He gestured to Claire, still propping him up by the arm. "Together, we busted your weapon smuggling ring. Biker gangs and members of your old right-wing group, the Alberta Independence Movement, doing your dirty work. Does the premier know about this?"

Garth said nothing.

Daniel pushed on. "And those weapons were military grade. What, for your personal army? Do Albertans know this?"

"We have heard of these perhaps overeager patriots. We do not condone these actions. An independent Alberta —"

"They reported to *you*. They took orders from *you*, just like Mr. Larch." Daniel held the cellphone high again. "It was *you* who coordinated all of this. From this phone." He waved his good arm toward the crowd and the cameras. "And you took revenge on the man who hurt you most. Your father."

Scattered gasps emerged from the crowd.

"Patrick Forrestal was your father. He abandoned you when you were a child, changed his name to hide his crimes. And you killed him for it." Daniel took a deep breath. "What kind of country would Alberta be under people like you? You murdered your father for revenge. Why go after me? I'm nobody to you."

"You were supposed to be easy to deal with."

"This is how you'd treat the little people in your little Albertan … Jonestown?"

Garth bolted to the left, followed by his two-man security detail.

No fucking way he's going to get away this time, thought Daniel. He turned to see the two police officers give chase. MacKinnon would be on the hunt, too. But with his bum leg and a chest burning with each breath, Daniel couldn't chase him. Claire shot him a quick look saying *I'll be right back* and then dashed off, too.

The podium stood empty, the reporters' energy unfocused. The same one who'd asked questions earlier thrust a microphone in Daniel's face. "Sarah Glenn. Global News. Those were serious accusations. Mr. Ritter, is it?"

"Daniel."

"And what is your relationship to Mr. Haynes?"

He didn't know how to respond. "Our paths crossed." He felt his grip tighten on the microphone stand. "I got caught up in Mr. Haynes's plans. With the help of the police, we were able to stop him." He looked for Claire at the far end of the lobby, without success.

A CBC reporter shoved a mike above the Global one. "What plans?"

Daniel gulped and stared into the nearest camera. He knew his words would capture for eternity every nuance, every hesitation. He had to make a clear message directly to the people of Alberta. They had to know the truth.

"Tomorrow, Albertans are about to decide on whether or not to become an independent country. They need to know some important facts before they vote. Until a few days ago, I was a regular person with a regular life. And then I got in the way of Mr. Haynes's plan. He wanted to build an army in secret. And he killed anyone who got in his way. Mr. Premier, did you know about this?"

In spite of the pain, Daniel felt himself stand straighter under the spotlights.

Someone in the foyer shouted, "Sounds like a lefty conspiracy to me."

Daniel pointed at where Claire had been standing. "She knows. She's the captain of the navy ship that intercepted the smugglers. She saw everything."

The crowd of reporters rustled, looking for her in the hallways behind Daniel in vain.

"Mr. Haynes ordered the murder of his own father. And he didn't want any witnesses. So he hired a professional assassin to hunt me down. He did manage to kill the only other witness, but he missed me at least twice. To finish the job, to scare you into supporting their cause, he either caused or ordered the bombing this morning. I'm certain. He missed me but not by much. Others, however, innocent bystanders, were not so lucky. We've been working with the Halifax Police all the way, and they can vouch for what we've said."

Daniel felt the cameras zoom in close. "So, people of Alberta, are you sure you want these people controlling your destiny?"

Then, pandemonium.

* ✳ *

Claire ran as fast as she could with her injuries. Garth disappeared down a corridor on the left, while his two security men, a few steps behind, stopped and turned to block her way. Their massive frames towered over hers. Their bulging muscles strained their tight-fitting suits. Their stance — one foot in front, weight evenly divided, bodies shifted slightly to reduce the exposed target in a fight — betrayed some police or military training. Any blow from such strong adversaries would probably knock her out, or worse. Their eyes betrayed overconfidence that they could easily take her down.

"That's close enough," said the goon on the right.

More over-testosteroned, underqualified men trying to tell me what to do, thought Claire.

Perhaps she should have warned them to step aside. She only wanted the man responsible for the weapon smugglers crippling her ship and wounding her crew. It was personal. The thought lasted only a fraction of a second before she surprised the one on the right. Showing no fear, she walked right up to him and shoved him, knocking him off balance, and punching him in the sternum with her good right arm before he had time to react. He fell over backward, his back slapping the floor with a loud smack. In a few seconds, he sprang back up to his original stance, this time with fists tight and arms half extended, telegraphing a look of concern. She approached again. He jabbed his right hand toward her face. She shifted to the left, grabbed his forearm with both hands, swung her hips around, leaned down, and pulled. His own momentum forced him to fall forward and land with a crunch on the hard, wooden floor. Her elbow smashed into his neck.

She pivoted to the second bodyguard. This one was better prepared. He pulled out a short metal rod and with a sharp flick, extended it into a metal truncheon.

It had only one use: to break bones.

Claire took a step back, assessing the new situation. She waited for him to make the first move. He swiped at her bandaged left arm, which she moved as she spun around, whipping her left leg out, sweeping a wide arc, and forcing his right leg to bend. He collapsed onto one knee. With his head now at a more reasonable height, she swung back around to the left, this time stopping to throw her body forward. She retracted, then snapped her right foot in his face. She moved faster than his ability to respond. The force hurled him backward, and his head slammed against the concrete pillar. He crumpled headfirst onto the floor. He wasn't getting back up anytime soon.

The first man struggled to stand up. She launched her body toward his head. Her elbow crushed his nose while her knee smashed into his chest. He collapsed again, holding his face, his nose gushing red. She grabbed the truncheon. The man screamed as she jammed it into his shoulder.

"Beaten by a woman? Maybe it's time to think about retirement." She smiled. The two men lay barely conscious, arms spread wide, one on his stomach, the other on his back. She couldn't tell if they agreed.

She didn't dwell on her victory. Ahead, Garth awaited.

As soon as he opened the rear door of the hotel, Garth knew his escape would be more complicated than planned. The door squeaked on tired hinges, revealing a parking lot half-filled with cars that glistened with frozen dampness from the sea air. Beyond the lot was a road and another lot with people milling about in front of a collection of glass and metal buildings. He squinted in the weak late-afternoon light. A large sign read "Seaport Market." Where his car was waiting. The one the AIM armourer, one of only a handful of loyalists in this province, had left for him. What was his name? Ted? Fred?

The problem was evident in the nearer parking lot. Police, lots of them, checking each car. Looking for him. He let out a deep sigh. The hotel was probably surrounded. He had to find another way out.

One of the officers looked his way. He tried to look innocent, but a raised hand and a shout from the uniform confirmed his failure. He released the door and scrambled along the narrow hallway that led back to the din of the lobby. There, scattered collections of people, dressed in business attire, professional looking, recognized him; a few media talked into their cameras, trying to get the news out.

Closer, on the floor, his two bodyguards lay motionless. And the woman, standing over them. *She did that to them?*

On his right, away from the crowd hovering around the now abandoned stage, one man stood out. One arm in a sling, head bandaged, scruffy, dark stains on his shirt, wrinkled pants, and hair in random directions. Ritter stood to the left of the wall that divided the hall from the lobby, took a few tentative steps, heavily favouring one leg, then stopped, and turned to look at Garth.

His plan had been exposed; he couldn't return home. He would be forever on the run.

Fucking pain in the ass. Larch was supposed to be good. I better get a discount from those bastards who sent him.

And Fanshawe. Winning the referendum will give me access to sovereign funds. Alberta as an independent country will raise billions. At least I don't need him anymore. Losing the professor, maybe that wasn't so bad.

Ritter stood alone at the end of the hallway. Garth whipped his gun out. Gripped tight. Aimed low. He held his destiny in his right hand.

I will take that bastard out right now.

He walked closer until he was staring straight at the man who had destroyed his dream.

Daniel stepped back until he was rammed against a wall. He felt for space behind. His right hand slid smoothly on the concrete wall. There was nowhere to go. Beyond Garth, Claire stood over Garth's two fallen bodyguards.

"It's over, Haynes." Claire took a few steps toward Garth, and he turned to face her, the gun now pointed at her.

"Back off. This is between him and me."

Claire froze. Garth returned his aim at Daniel.

Daniel paused the scene in his mind. *Is this it, then? Am I going to die on this floor, in this hotel? In front of random witnesses and the national press? In front of Claire?* It wasn't fear he felt. More embarrassment. And anger.

"Haynes?" He let the words die. "It's over. The media, the premier, everyone knows about your scheme. And about your private army. We know about your attempts to discredit the demonstrations. About your bomb. And about the murder of your own father."

Garth raised an eyebrow, then the gun, waving it as he spoke. "You ruined everything."

And then Daniel heard MacKinnon's serious tone from somewhere behind Garth: "Stop. Drop your weapon. Police."

MacKinnon and two other officers, guns held forward, appeared from the corner behind Garth. "Final warning. Drop your weapon."

But Garth's attention remained fixed on Daniel. Daniel watched Garth's eyes. He saw a twitch in Garth's right hand as his finger tightened around the trigger. Daniel knew that a bullet striking his heart or head would kill him instantly, while one elsewhere could permanently cripple him. *Will I ever see Emily again? What will she learn about my death? That I died trying to protect others? What will the news headline read? What will Vanessa tell her?*

He imagined Garth now realized that with his plan exposed, he had no future except behind bars. At least he would have the satisfaction of killing the person he blamed most for his troubles. One squeeze. And the shame would end, longer prison term be damned. It was personal, now.

Daniel saw Garth shift his right foot into a firing stance. *I hope MacKinnon is a good shot. I hope he has a faster reaction time than Garth.* It was at that precise moment that Daniel realized he was in the line of fire. Any bullet from MacKinnon's weapon could pass through Garth and continue toward him. He shuffled to the right, trying to get away from the trajectory of any round fired by MacKinnon toward Garth. He thought of his high-school trigonometry classes.

Daniel said nothing. There was nothing to say. He glanced at MacKinnon a few metres behind, holding his gun level at Garth.

Garth shifted again, arm outstretched. He levelled his arm and his gun —

A flash and a concussive boom split the silence. The echo tore at his ears.

SIXTY-TWO

FINALLY, THE BOARDING CALL. Air Canada 881 to London now boarding. He sprang from his chair, joined the short line forming in front of the business-class access. The race had begun. Garth's public demise was splashed across all the news sites. The guy always hogged the headlines, even in death. He had to assume that Garth would have explained his link to the weapon smuggling, and the police would be looking for him. He just needed to keep a low profile and to get out of the country fast. He checked with the Foreign Affairs Department website and selected the palm tree–laden Netherlands Antilles as the perfect spot. Because they had no extradition, he could relax there, and his money in the Caymans would be accessible. Yes, he would miss a few of his friends. But, with his financial bounty, he could fly his family down anytime they wanted. His first purchase was a fake passport.

His thoughts were interrupted by an announcement over the public address system. "Passenger Harrington. Please present yourself to the agent at gate twenty-six."

He'd asked earlier for an upgrade to business class. It was a good start for the trip and a good omen. He wasn't going to take the fall for the premier's catastrophic choice of campaign manager. He had done his duty to help start the country he longed for, that he had dreamed of since he was a young man on the Prairies. That little weasel of a manager had lied to him, and now he had to abandon his noble military career and flee the country.

He stepped out of the line and walked to the ticket agent at the gate immediately ahead. He could see the plane outside being loaded with baggage. On his way to his new home. And with an upgrade to boot.

He forced a smile and handed his boarding pass to the agent. She took the pass, nodded, and looked behind him.

"Going somewhere, Commodore?" said a familiar voice.

He spun around to face Captain Hall, Lieutenant Commander Marcoux, two military police, and three armed and uniformed RCMP officers.

"Commodore Miller, we have a warrant for your arrest," said one of the MPs, hand ready on his sidearm.

Miller scoffed.

"The charge is criminal conspiracy to commit treason."

Before he could respond, one RCMP officer took a step closer, spun him around, leaned him against the ticket counter, and slapped on the cuff. Another read him his rights, while the third picked up his carry-on bag. The other passengers shared shocked looks. Two whipped out their cellphones to capture the arrest, no doubt so they could share it on Facebook. Claire stood, arms crossed, her satisfaction evident. She noticed that Hall was grinning, too.

Earlier, in the cruiser speeding on Highway 102 to the airport, Hall had explained how the commodore worked for the Yes campaign. His job had been to ensure that the heavy weapons moved undetected along the Atlantic coast. When the *Kingston* intercepted the first shipment, he tried to divert any navy vessel away from the coast under the guise of a surprise readiness exercise. But Hall was suspicious and had sent the *Kingston* on a low-profile mission, just in case a second shipment was attempted. The commodore had exploded in fury at the insubordination, threatening a court martial, only deepening Hall's suspicion. Hall called Claire to ask if she wanted to participate in the arrest. She showed up in a flash.

Claire smiled. She knew there would be more celebrating later.

SIXTY-THREE

AT NINE SHARP the following evening, Daniel met Claire at the Carleton on Argyle Street. He had spent the day dealing with the repercussions of the demise of Larch and Garth. Deep in HRM Police headquarters, he reviewed the events with MacKinnon, signed countless forms and, more importantly, learned what lay in store for Lloyd. MacKinnon said the professor wouldn't be teaching anytime soon: He was still in custody, faced serious prison time, and Canada Revenue had expressed a keen interest in knowing where he had stashed all of his money. Best of all, Touesnard was out of surgery and his prognosis was good.

After explaining to MacKinnon how she floored the two bodyguards and describing what she saw of Garth's final confrontation, Claire had returned to her ship. It sat alongside a dock at CFB Halifax, illuminated against the night by a bank of lights and occasional flashes from welding arcs. Everyone she passed gave her a knowing nod at the sight of her bandaged arm, a sign of respect to a fellow sailor injured in battle. As she reviewed the damage with the chief engineer and the XO, she began to formulate her plan to overhaul the ship. The engineer's initial assessment had been detailed, complete but optimistic. The repair list quickly grew through the night and into the morning. She saw how cleverly the engineering team had improvised the engines to get them back to port after the attack in the bay. Wiseman showed her the charred remnants of the RHIB launcher. Sullivan described the characteristics of the antenna array on the missing tower. Barry described the repairs necessary for the navigation system. New engines, a new RHIB launcher, new tech, and a large percentage of the ship would have to be rebuilt. By noon, she concluded that the *Kingston* would not return to sea for at least a year.

Her impression of Wiseman improved, too. He started the repair work, as instructed, while she and Captain Hall had participated in the arrest of the commodore at the airport. He hadn't waited. He hadn't questioned her orders. She wondered if the combat in the bay had shown him what kind of captain she was under fire. She could see that he genuinely wanted to show her how he could take command of the repair work. Maybe she *could* help him become a CO one day. She didn't care about the mole anymore, as she sensed the crew's confidence in having her as captain. As the sun set at the end of a busy day, she told Wiseman that she would return after sunrise to review the progress.

Now, at the Carleton, Daniel and Claire buzzed with the adrenalin high of what they had done. He had evaded a professional assassin, rescued Claire, and exposed Garth's plan to the nation. She had saved Daniel at the demonstration and stopped the weapon supply. Her boss's boss was now in custody. And she had confidence in her crew and second-in-command to make things right.

They both smiled at the past few wild days but they didn't know what to do next. Neither wanted to make the first move. So they talked in between sets of local bands and the hours flew by. He gave her an abbreviated version of his life, filling in a few gaps that their exploits had exposed. The more traumatic details could wait. He didn't want to scare her off. She told him of growing up in Montreal, her perpetually disappointed parents, her deadbeat brother, and her ambition to become captain.

Even in jeans and a grey navy T-shirt, she looked incredibly attractive to him. She also looked re-energized. Her smile melted his will to be anywhere else. He felt he could talk about everything, well, almost everything, with her. The rest of everything might come later. What mattered now was that they shared this moment of having done something good.

Distracting them, though, was the referendum. As they talked and sipped glasses of red wine and made their way through a fine meal, they felt compelled to give some of their attention to the coverage of the referendum on a small television screen behind the bar. Daniel wondered if his impending sense of doom was due to his recent experiences with Haynes, Forrestal, and Larch, or more from the news station's attempt to generate suspense, lock in viewers, and raise ratings.

Around midnight, during a lull between sets, Claire's phone chirped at the arrival of a new message. Whatever was on the screen transfixed her. Eyes wide, she whispered something Daniel couldn't quite make out.

"What's it say?" he said.

"It's from Captain Hall," she said. "He says he's been talking to the head of the Pacific Fleet."

"Sounds like good news then."

"Better than that. I have my next posting." She stood up, hugged the phone close against her chest, spun around, and looked at Daniel with probing eyes. "It's a wish come true, Daniel. I could be a commander in a few years. Captain of a frigate. It's everything I could wish for." She beamed when she said it.

"Wonderful. What do you have to do?"

"Transfer to Esquimalt."

Daniel didn't know how to react. He wasn't moving to another coast.

By two in the morning Halifax time, as the final band packed up, the verdict was clear. CTV, Global, and CBC announced that the referendum was officially defeated, with the No side winning by a narrow margin of 2.7 percent. Premier Brewster resigned thirty minutes later, holding his distraught-looking wife, their two photogenic blond kids, but not holding back his tears.

Claire grabbed Daniel's hand. "Even with their dirty tricks, the bombing, and the disinformation, they were so close to winning."

"Scary, isn't it?"

"We stopped them, though, didn't we?"

"You more than me. You blew stuff up. I just talked."

She used her good arm to thwack him.

On the sidewalk outside the bar, he stopped, turned around to face her, and took her hands. And then surprised himself with a first kiss. It was unexpected, but they had both been waiting, wondering what it would be like. For Daniel, it was full of light and softness.

Claire pulled back, held him at arm's length, smiled, and looked into his eyes. "You need to know that I'm not home a lot. I hope that's okay."

Daniel nodded. He relished the last fading seconds of intimacy before responding. "Of course it is. I have to pick up my life where I left it, too."

He squeezed her hands. "So what's next?"

"Time for a vacation. A quiet one."

"Can you get some time off? The dean owes me a few favours. He'll cover my courses for the next term."

"Are you kidding? I've been ordered to take two months off. The *Kingston*'s in dry dock and needs extensive repairs. I have to go back soon to check up on them. Any ideas?"

Daniel paused a moment before saying, "Ever been to New Zealand?"

ACKNOWLEDGEMENTS

THIS BOOK WOULD never have appeared in your hands without the help of many friends and supporters.

The Banff Centre gave me my first taste of what being a writer is about. The Quebec Writers' Federation opened the door into the world of writing, and their workshops were critical in developing my writing ability. The Writers' Federation of Nova Scotia introduced me to the Sunday Seaport Writers' Group. (Thanks to Rosemary Drisdelle, Sheila Morrison, Judith Scrimger, Jodi Reid, Bretton Loney, Susan Drain, Dave Johnson, and Valerie Spencer for guidance and encouragement.) Howard Shrier in Toronto showed me a more technical understanding of thriller writing.

I am also indebted for the support and inspiration from James O'Brien, Camilla Holmvall, David Westwood, Natalia Boroczow, Doreen Redmond, Barry Morshead, Cyrus John, Anna Kim, Alex Bitektine, Melanie Robinson, Andrew Papadopoulos, Peter

Patomella, Rubina Qureshi, Mike Sullivan, Russell Smith, Claudia Hubbes, and Oliver Slupecki.

Mike Mandryk, Anouk Zabal, Tom Kozlowski, and Haidi Albertsson were friendly readers brave enough to read early drafts.

My wife, Teresa, daughter, Catherine, brother-in-law, David, and my family in Guelph provided never-ending support.

Valerie Compton, Alex Schofield delivered awesome editing. Licia Canton has been a wonderful editor and mentor. And the dynamic Dundurn team — Kathryn, Rachel, Dominic, Laura, Stephanie, Jenny, and Elham — was always enthusiastic and supportive. I want to thank them all for taking a chance with me. It has been a wonderful experience. Any errors are mine alone.